Praise for
Love the World or Get Killed Trying

'An ode to the complexity, pain, and beauty of trans life (...) recasting tired, old literary tropes about the so-called "limits" of autofiction.'
EMMA SPECTER
Vogue

'Alvina Chamberland writes with every part of herself. Hers is an honesty in perfect balance with generosity, and reading this book is like receiving an ongoing gift.'
TORREY PETERS
author of *Detransition, Baby*

'Like a transgender collision of Valerie Solanas and Michel Houellebecq, Alvina Chamberland writes with a passion, rage and longing that blaze on the page. The urgency of her writing – her demand for connection, recognition, dignity – is sweetened by a playful sense of humour, a disarming candour and an unfettered, eccentric charm. Hers is a voice to fall for.'
ROB DOYLE
author of *Here Are the Young Men and Threshold*

'A work that literally begins with repeated refusals – NO! NO! NO! NO! NO! – ultimately mouths, against the odds, a throaty carnal YES to life in all its broken, impermanent glory. A beautiful book about being here, for now.'

SUSAN STRYKER
author of *Transgender History: The Roots of Today's Revolution*

'Reading Love the World or Get Killed Trying *is like entering a universe in which the very best parts of Louis-Ferdinand Céline's writing – the narrative drive, the tonality, the immediacy – are fused to an unparalleled interrogation of raw human need. Every epoch creates its own people. With action spanning from Reykjavik to Berlin to Paris, Alvina Chamberland has given us a unique gift: a first person account from a child of the new dawn. A book of huge value.'

JARETT KOBEK
author of the international bestseller *I Hate the Internet*

'Chamberland shows us, in immersive, stream of consciousness genius, that to be a transsexual is to love the world at all gnarly costs. A generous and staggering novel. Raw, intimate, necessary and poetic, Love the World or Get Killed Trying is an affirmation, a shimmering catalogue of a brilliant, particular mind that binds her experience to a universal swell. Lispector and Woolf's virtuosic daughter. A must-read.'

ELIOT DUNCAN
author of the 2023 National Book Award nominated novel *Ponyboy*

Love the World or Get Killed Trying

LOVE THE WORLD
or
GET KILLED TRYING

a novel by
Alvina Chamberland

To those who exhale so others can breathe. To the existence of
the practice of mouth-to-mouth resuscitation –

13
A meaningless procedure
– Ljubljana, Berlin, Amsterdam,
New York City, Malmö, New Delhi,
Stockholm, 2005 –

21
Iceland, late July 2018

135
HomeSick – Berlin

165
Paris, late August 2018

Transgender porn has presumably become the largest, most popular genre of porn among heterosexual men. A spokesperson for Evil Angel, a US porn production company, cited transsexual porn as the company's most profitable category, commanding premiums of about 20% more than other genres or scenes. In July 2019 Gamelink.com, the 'Amazon of Porn', featured 5 trans-porn titles in their top 20 bestseller list, with 'Jay Sin's TS Playground #28' placed at no. 1.[*]

---

[*] Sources:
Gamelink.com
International Business Times: https://web.archive.org/web/20200404014718/https://www.ibtimes.com/transgender-porn-best-seller-it-good-trans-people-2028219
Wikipedia: https://en.wikipedia.org/wiki/Transgender_pornography

'These streams don't flow into one definitive sea, these rivers have no permanent banks; this body no fixed borders. This mobility, this life. Which they might describe as our restlessness, whims, pretences, or lies. For all this seems so strange for those who claim "solidity" as their foundation.'

LUCE IRIGARAY

A MEANINGLESS PROCEDURE

– Ljubljana, Berlin, Amsterdam, New York City, Malmö, New Delhi, Stockholm, 2005 –

NO! NO! NO! NO! NO! NO! NO! NO! NO! NO! NO! NO! NO! NO! NO! NO! NO! NO! NO! NO! NO! NO! NO! NO! NO! NO! NO! NO! NO! NO! NO! NO! NO! NO! NO! NO! NO! NO! NO! NO! NO! NO! NO! NO! NO! NO! NO! NO! NO! NO! NO! NO! NO! NO! NO! NO! NO! NO! NO! NO! NO! NO! NO! NO! NO!

I've lost count of how many times I've repeated that word. No. The last time I was *here* I didn't even say that word, because what difference would it make? And besides, what exactly do I mean by *here*? It started with a relatively handsome young man seeing me pass by on the sidewalk. It continued with his face undergoing an extreme makeover, from expressionless to Punch or Fuck or What'sThatFreak? I've seen millions of stares in my lifetime; still I can only decipher their message in blatantly obvious cases. Follow me, reader, and we will find out what this one means, as he follows me to provide an answer. *Lust?* Lust. He tells me: 'I got so fucking hard just watching you walk by.' *Love?* Love. He affirms: 'I LOVE shemales, skinny blonde ones with big lips especially!' *Hate?* Hate. He ignores all my attempts to ignore him. He shadows me for three blocks. Then he pulls me out of the spotlight and into an alley.
Then.
Then he says: 'Don't worry, sexy girl, I just wanna talk. How old are you? Let me guess: 22.'
Then I say: 'No.'
Then I try to walk away.
Then he yanks me back.
Then.
Then he says: 'Why don't you want me, do you think I'm ugly?'
Then I say: 'No.'

Then he uses his weight to force me to the ground.
Then I say: 'No.'
Then he says: 'Oh, you drive me completely CRAZY.'

The temperature outside: cold – October. A wasp can crawl but not fly. My temperature inside: colder – December; darkest – the 21st. The wasp is hibernating to evade death. Am I saving my feelings for later? I don't know. No whimpers. No pleas. How can I stay so calm in such a predicament? I am like a stick, a stick that thinks: *How can I get stiffer?* I am trying to talk him out of it. How many times have I been *here*? I have lost count. I think to myself: *Not again.* In a bed, on a sofa, on the subway, in my doorway, on an avenue sidewalk; never in a city park, but once in the backroom of a shop. *Again.* My dear reader, you sense that I am in danger, but since I'm not screaming you don't know where to run to help. *Again.* I am strapped underneath a car that is driving sideways. What do I see on the ground? A dog's faeces next to a rabbit's faeces? I think so. I do not specialize in identifying the excrement of different species. Candy wrappers (RUSTLE-RUSTLE). Cigarette butts. Yes. No, I was not smoking them. I was doing nothing wrong. I was not using their embers to burn my skin. I swear to god they were already littering the ground when I was brought here. The labels? *Prince, Marlboro, Gauloises, American Spirits.* Most probably more. They wish I would shut my trap. They have no interest in making an advertisement out of this situation. Rape does not provide good publicity for their brands.

Dear Prince, Marlboro, Gauloises, American Spirits, please do not sue me. I am telling the truth. Your stubs were there. I am not making up their presence. It is not my fault they were getting stuck in my hair. *Leaves?* Yes, leaves are on the pavement as well. Very many of them. It is autumn, no, *fall*. Any budding flowers hidden underneath? Not till late February. The fatigued wasp buzzes with annoyance at having her perfect hibernation spot disturbed. The leaves make crunching noises (CRUNCH-CRUNCH) to interrupt the young man's heavy breathing (PANT-PANT) and awkward movements (WAGGLE-WOBBLE). And me? I am here as well. Although I might as well not be. I murmur tiny *egh-nehjk*s of discomfort. A red brick juts into my left shoulder, scraping it coarsely each time he gyrates against me. A road made of rough concrete threatens to impair my clothes, reaching for the blood beneath my skin. A muddy puddle wets my right thigh, not frozen yet – that's my own body we're talking about. The young man's attempts at kissing feel as appealing as eating a sticky piece of food – cream cheese or moussaka – which has spent a full day exposed to the elements on a beach. His stubble grates like coarse grains of wet sand, the wind stings with no need for a metaphor, and the saltwater is replaced by plenty of sweat mixed with the scent of Axe instead of ocean. *Axe*. Another brand which won't wish its name mentioned in connection with rape. Yes. Commercials display Axe making the girls go craaaazy for you out of their own free will! *It's a lie, it's a lie,* they're lying to you. Sue me, fine me, send me to prison, stoning threats, yesyes, modern people do it on the internet! RapeaXe – too exhausting to constantly carry one inside of me. But straight from the sweatshop to the rape scene: The man is wearing a pair of Nikes. My entire body is behaving like a scrunchie. He tries to stretch it out. He fails miserably. He is realizing that it's hard to take off the clothes of a person who's not cooperating – especially since he's a fumbling bundle of nerves, huffing&puffing he is groping&gasping, lacking all skill. I am no longer a stick. I start squirming like a trapped salamander. A trapped salamander out of water. Dry. And in hell. *This. Is. Just. So. Meaningless.* Could he even manage to penetrate holes that are this closed? If he succeeds at forcing one open he will use it as his own private toilet bowl. Flushing down god knows what and hoping he'll never see it again.

I look towards the street. I hope someone will pass by. I hope this someone will be kind and rush to my assistance. I hope this someone will not be mean and steal my pink backpack and scram. Three of my favourite books by Lispector, Leduc and Roy are lying there with their quests for truths. My laptop-lapdog with the script of my own book too. I see a raven circling overhead as she *kraa-kraa*s. Where is my black cat? And why hasn't she fetched a growling, barking stray bitch to bite him in the ass? I have gotten myself out of this situation before. How many times? I've lost count. How many fingernails do I have? 10. Are they all sharpened like claws? No, 2 recently broke. That leaves 8. Enough to dig into his cheeks while scrunching up the skin on his face and yelling: *STOP IT! RIGHT NOW!*

(I dig my nails into his cheeks, scrunch up the skin on his face, and yell: 'STOP IT! RIGHT NOW!')

Statistics, reader, statistics: 8 out of 10 = good odds. 5 in 10 – a scene from a panel at the trans film festival: all the directors keep repeating: 'I made this film so people would know trans girls exist.' The only trans woman director interrupts: 'Shut the fuck up, half of all men have slept with us!' Five in ten. These odds would be fine if they weren't secrets kept at the bottom of the back of the closets for exactly 97.3 percent of these men. *Again.* What is a dream about you that does not include *you*? *Again.* Why am I here? *Again.* When secrets remain unspoken they do not seep out. They explode in your face. *Again.* Back to the eight sharp nails. Somehow, someway, something changed inside this particular man. Perhaps it was the pain inflicted on his face, perhaps it was the raised decibels of my *STOP IT*s, perhaps his knee brushed up against the fatigued wasp one time too many, perhaps it was a eureka moment where I became human, perhaps it was something entirely different; I cannot read his mind. I can just breathe a sigh of relief at his reconsideration, his scurrying off into the night, his aborting the mission without a mission accomplished.

Alone again at last. My heartbeat pounds irregularly, heard by some soaring birds, burrowing insects and blind mammals. The icy wind blows itself into my fresh bruises to enunciate their pain. I hover somewhere between empty and invincible. The emotional landscape of this body quivers just short of an earthquake.

And so it was and so it is that as I left the alleyway dishevelled, dusting off the Fall's mud and leaves from my thighs and knees, I thought of Clarice Lispector tousled with her dress torn after winning a prestigious literary prize and being molested by a top-ranked official backstage. A man trying to rape me is nothing unusual. A few have succeeded. Many have failed. It is sick that I state it so matter-of-factly. It is sick that it is a matter of fact. I'd rather be raped than dead, yes, but I'd prefer other alternatives. A unicorn packs a strong back kick. Dear rapist, please refrain from arriving like the next tram. I'm not the one who can ensure that. Little scars on the canvas of life. Little scars that I refuse to hide lest they upset – *whom*? And how many scars? *Again.* I've lost count. *7, 9, 8*? They have their minds made up, and I am uncertain. How can I focus amongst all this noise? The canvas was never blank. I was born into a history that shakes its dreadful head at a better tomorrow. I hold one paintbrush, the others hold eight. I work, I work, I work on the thickness of my own brushstroke – I was taught that life is in our own hands. I work, I work, I work on my own technique. I paint a pretty picture, a picture perfect. Several brushes cross over it. More and more colours (Pink! Purple! Green! Glittery Grey! Black! Blue! Ultramarine! Red! Violet! Red!). I settle for something very messy/deeply intricate. And the damage the others can do is severely diminished. Certainly, they can still hurt me. The price of the opposite is much too high. I refuse to pay with that currency. More detailed information? Wait. Wait... And find out. Later. And Louder.

Later that night, shaken drunk by one single drink, another man tries to trip me as I'm leaving a bar.
He: 'I will go home with you!'
Me: 'Did I say you could come with me?'
He: 'BUT I AM THE GREATEST!!!'

ICELAND
late July 2018

1

Dear reader, I know one isn't supposed to expose one's own weaknesses and insecurities. In the animal kingdom it often results in death, and I'm not sure if human beings have evolved past that yet. Still, I feel I must begin by confessing something mortifying to you as I pray it will open doors to an us: *I don't know if I have any kind of creative talent.* Sometimes I believe I should just go for a five-mile jog each time I get these urges (write!), these drives (write!), these needs (write!). Run-Bitch-Run! Then the entire planet would be saved from my tatty magnifying glass! Since I am lazy and the keyboard is much closer than the jogging trail, the world cannot consider itself quite so lucky. But... these words really only managed to explain my own record-low self-esteem. Truly, reader, I write to give back to the imagination I've resided within for over half my life. It is like a thank you-card to that which has saved me from an early grave, buried underneath the ruins of numberless defects and loveless brass beds. I return to these crashing sentences every day to expand the death threats of my reality into a domain far mightier than my own final breath. Now, my keyboard is breaking dowwwn, allergiiic to the chill of Icelandic summer, and I have no one to share my anger with or blame my shortcomings on. No, my frustration can only be directed inwards, canalized into a firm slap on the cheek. *Water damage.* Keyboard, I know you are punishing me for all the times my eyes have skewered you with their monsoons. But I promise, I've never wanted my tears to hurt anyone; for so many years I have protected you from the blood, the vomit that would have caused such massive harm you'd be beyond repair...

Reader, I need a present from you: I need you to stay with me in the now-instant and trust in my brief memories of the past. My thoughts have forgotten what happened. I recall only how I felt. You&I, we're embarking on a journey together that shall force us between the extremes of weeping and laughter. And silence. Silence too. However, I cannot tell the story before it has been told. Please, let us begin with some basic facts & particulars. I'm in a hurry to sweep them out of our way so we can hike to stratospheres with ephemerally everlasting views beyond vision. *Age: turning 30 next month. Height: 180. Blonde hair, blue eyes, Swedish and US passports. Living in Berlin. Indifferent to two things: trends and podcasts.* Hi, my name is Alvina and I'm always late, so I nearly missed my flight here. I'm afraid of flying, so I needed to swallow the last Valium in my stash just to not get a panic attack. And at the security check I created quite a stir between Henry and Renate, who didn't know who should search me or if I was a sir or madam. Luckily, like bonobos, black swans, seahorses and children under the age of four, the X-ray machine didn't give a shit.

Reader, this dead-serious and gallows-silly mission we're on together takes the form of a non-guided travelogue. Just that? No. I must dig much deeper, into rigorous investigations and vast emotional terrains that always expand past two wrongs and one right. I'm trying to find out if the sun can shine on the us's who live on the darkest side of patriarchy. Will a soul inside a deep stab expand or shatter? I'm scared of losing thin skin, not bleeding, but... reader, may I reach for your hand to rescue me from the rough hooves of a stampede?

Yesterday my plane landed in a bed of magniloquent scenery that demands to be placed centre stage. Iceland – my fourteenth international trip alone. I fled here from the trampling city to come to terms with my longing and be left in peace so loneliness won't rip me to pieces. Certainly I'll make many mistakes along the way. Will I forgive myself for them? Will you? There are humans who never travel solo; I am neither better nor worse than them. They are supposed to look down on me with sympathy, and I am supposed to look up to them in envy. I don't. I am used to this lifestyle and it suits me fine. I'm not afraid of being followed by my own shadow, and I quite enjoy the company of my thoughts and feelings and temperamental carnival rides. But... Some days the ripe shows signs of rot: eager worms, chunks turning to mush, losing their hold, plunging to the forest floor with no Sir Isaac Newton to catch them with a groundbreaking theorem. Yes, there are risks. Yes, risks...

 Earlier this afternoon I hopped on a bike for the first time in two years. I wished to cycle along the scenic coastline outside of Reykjavik. I ended up zigzagging between hideous grey factory buildings and rusty ship wharfs for kilometre after monotonous kilometre before finally finding something that remotely resembled 'scenic coastline'. I crossed the threshold into nature and sensed the contrast in acoustic scope and light absorption. A steep climb arrived. It became clear that although I remembered how to ride a bike, I'd completely forgotten how strenuous it can be. Sweat exited my pores... dripped...

then poured. My breath grew heavy. My muscles, they ached. I gave up and hopped off the saddle. I walked my bike to the top of the hill. I parked it near the roadside and wandered into a grassy-mossy wilderness, stumbling upon something that looked like blueberries. I wished to eat them. I hesitated. I decided to leave them be. They could be another berry altogether. They could be very poisonous! If I had a boyfriend, he could be a botanist and a botanist would know this. If I had a boyfriend, he could also be a well-planned person, a person who reads maps, a person who finds the perfect cycling route that only lays out beautiful scenery before us. We would complement each other. Most people spend more time touching their smartphones than their partners. Reader, I guess you're thinking: *You've got no partner, so look it up on your phone.* But I own no smartphone, no GPS, no data, no way to check where I'm going or which berries are edible, just my self, alone in nature, internet-free, with one less problem running up that hill in mad pursuit of my attention span. I name this: Providing Space for the Surfacing of Deeper Emotions. A purple lily rises up three feet from the berries, and I listen to her as she hums the melody of an inaudible lullaby. An exhausted ocean-crossing butterfly slumbers inside the delicate swaddle of her silken petals. This symbiosis between butterfly and lily reminds me of how I long to love... Freed from my death wish spawned by amassed past seasons of bloom, buzzing with men springing from every street corner whispering, *Pssst, assfuck now,* while the boy who whispers sweet nothings and secret-secrets in my ear, who makes breakfast, kisses me goodbye and thinks of me when I'm away has spent his entire life as my imaginary friend.

I reach the edge of a cliff towering fifty feet above the bursting Atlantic waves. I never got to travel to this kind of place with the Kays or Shawns or Johns of my past. At present, no human beings are in sight. I'm free to throw myself into a multitude of imaginations and fantasies as I put on a solo sex show for the seagulls and the spraying H_2O. Warm cum pours over my stomach. My only facials shall come from cold winds, salty ocean water and aspirin-tablet face masks. They're vegan. They provide more sufficient nourishment than anybody's ejaculated fluids. In my masturbatory make-believe, I was taking Cristiano Ronaldo's dick into my mouth, tasting its texture, sucking it soothingly, deeply, rhythmically to a velvety climax that sees us now crying in each other's arms. CRYstiano RoRo. Yes, that's what I call him, after his many tears and over-the-top emotions during Portugal's dramatic win in the European Football Championships in Paris two years ago. I don't know RoRo, he's probably a chauvinist&sexist&misogynist. But I do know that on the morning of the finals, I let a gamma moth fly out the window of my room in Berlin. Attracted by RoRo's scent of nectar, she flapped her Bible-paper-thin wings straight towards the Stade de France to comfort him, landing on his eyelid right as he collapsed from injury, as if to say, *RoRo, no worries, everything's gonna be alright.* Somebody should inform him that the sender of this carrier pigeon, his good luck charm, was *ME*! As I lose myself inside the majestic cinema where lofty miracles play on a loop, a prankish seagull splats its poop right onto my forehead. *WAKE UP AND SMELL THE COFFEE*, she screeches in her gull language before soaring off. I do not give her the bird. I understand. I too get the runs from too much coffee. This was an alarm, urging me to bike back into Reykjavik to wash myself off at one of its geothermal swimming pools, contaminating the water with bird shit and human cum.

Reader, if I listened to everything a seagull tells me, I wouldn't get very far in life. I still haven't gotten very far in life... I only feel fine with disgusting myself, never others, so I cycle home instead, where in the shower the soap won't lather properly, irritating me into an expanding hesitation: Alright, Ms. Alvina Alone, you can postpone receiving all the confused stares of *who's that girl intruder in the men's locker room* until tomorrow, the day after, or the day after that... Perhaps then I will show off my masterly synchronized swimming skills, making a beautiful boy consider leaving his girlfriend and adopting a feral cat! It's definitely a better method of seduction than my written words, which make every man in his right mind run, run far away. Is this the price we pay for sharing our deepest secrets in unshielded soliloquies? Helping others feel less alone while remaining so ourselves? Always: *No*, mainly: *Yes*. Reader, though most men have fled, some have grown infatuated. But they've looked up to me like a mountain... and that devastates my eternity unless he has a mountain or ocean of his own. Oh, there could be 6 or 7 men in the whole world with veins pumping molten lava and crashing waves who could shock me as though I've been cast into a flooding meltwater cascade, 6 or 7 men with whom I could lie completely still for one full day: never quite housebroken, but no longer stray. I hope for too much, but could *he* be reading me right now?

Teardrops, living water, trickling down my face, to flow endlessly and never hold back, the thought of him, the thought of him, the thought of *you*, reader, may I tell you a bit about my Now & Then through the language of feelings? Exit your home for the next few pages. Leave your furniture alone! We all know that the wildest house party is a completely empty space where all the possessions you could never own are left unchaperoned. Are you outside now?

Love Remains

I know: The light is blinding without the penumbra.
I know: A herd of humans is worse than a pack of wolves.
A substitution for an end
Within the limits of always and nevers
The inevitable
To die strangled by scarves
My wiggle room is sparse
The present simply cannot see where to tread its feet
To gaze over the tombstones

Surrounded by a budding spring
A boy is lying on the train tracks
He is my first love
(Nijinsky stealing men's wedding rings at Kreuzlingen)
A train passes by on the opposite track
The boy is preserved inside his blooming cactus
Best before October 24 2014
While love remains
Stillborn

Death shreds our passports
Granting entrance to more than heaven
A witch burns a flag

A hypochondriac hears a running nose
There is no waterfall
In sight
To provide a rest stop of relief
From the carsick drive to eternal sleep (???)
Meanwhile
At the mausoleum of lovemaking skeletons
A sonorous miracle
Vibrates inside reverb
Holding a 19-second lifespan
Named infinity

Ordinary life is letting us down
Killing the insect
Drowning in a teacup
That tears could not spare.
An outlet
Never a solution
The beginning
Water and salt
Resuscitated equilibrium
Drunk on caffeine-coated power
The sheer force
Of my left hand
Shatters a crystal glass
Pink bloodied champagne
Runs down the drain
A recluse moon
Turns her back to the earth
She's seen enough

Without giving up
An invitation
You must be silent to hear
Listen.
And love all of us
To death

(Virgo sun, Gemini moon, Gemini rising. Is it nonsense or not, to not know is fine, ambivalence, two strong emotions in opposing directions – my life, unsolid embrace of earth, of fire, of air, of water. I am terrified by all the feelings I can experience at once! And I remember now! That time! Age five. I gave all 29 tiles in my hallway first & last names; and one Arthur Russell, my lover. On April 4, 1993, my dad hammered him dead in a renovation of rugs. It was the first time I recall having to attack my memory and restart my heart just to sustain my breaths of life.)

2

Reader, immediately after arriving in Iceland, I took a walk by the seaside into town. I stumbled upon Reykjavik's only queer bar. I walked in. I walked out. I went straight home, warmed by the company of my intact peace of mind. I said to myself: *I'm not here to meet people. I came here to engage in existential ventilations with the Earth, to put miles of ocean between me and my 7 heartbreaks, the 9000 times I declined a sex invite, the few 'ok, fines' that only increased my lonely, the 8 no's that didn't stop him...*

Now I'm on day three on this island, and it is getting harder to stick to my isolation. Apparently it's Pride Week. I lacked prior knowledge of this, and I'm not strong enough to resist the compulsion to participate. I have made the incorrect decision to go out clubbing tonight, hyperventilating in the wrong direction.

Reykjavik's main street is named Laugavegur. It's filled with rainbow flags *everywhere* save for the many spaces where fresh roses are placed, dyed in the colours of the rainbow. I wish to start a petition to rescue these poor unfortunate flower souls, devoid of soil, deprived of water. I'm sure they support LGBTQ rights, but that doesn't mean they wish to be sacrificed as décor! The street is not so busy this evening. There are some tourists for me to ignore, and four cats scampering about for me to pay attention to. Wherever cats roam I am sure to obtain a certain degree of comfort and well-being. They are most often in their own mysterious worlds where humans play secondary roles or are just in the way. This apartness has frequently been my cradle for togetherness. I enter a restaurant. I eat raw vegan enchiladas with three small side salads and ten added kilos of chili pepper. I curse the cigarette I smoked earlier as it ruins my illusion of perfect health. I walk over to Reykjavik's Old Harbor expecting the sunset to stir my heart and induce goosebumps. It doesn't let me down. I wonder: *Why did I ever let myself think I needed more than this?* It gets dark. I grow cold. My goosebumps are no longer happy goosebumps. I cry to myself because I never figure in anyone's future plans. I convince myself that I should be on the lookout for *A. Someone-Else*. That was fast... Rapid mood swings are the gift that never stops taking.

I walk back to Laugavegur to attend the Pride opening party at the queer bar, passing by a building site, adoring the fact that the construction sites here aren't properly fenced in. They are allowing me to pass right through. They are telling me I don't have to walk around a whole other street. What other story does this scenery propel upon my eyes? Something abhorrent. Reykjavik, are you another city where another old building is being torn down to make room for a monstrous generic abomination? I am not an architect, but I can already place my bets on the construction of a sterile, beige and metallic Scandinavian Design temple, dedicated to the fear of inflicting stains and the feeling of being dead inside! However, 80 or 90 times in my life I've been dead wrong, and I hope and pray now is the time for number 81 or 91. The world rarely provides reason to hope for the best; still we cling to hope when we deem stitching together the present-trouble too complex... I step in a hole of wet concrete and my new shoes are horribly stained forever. This isn't a life-altering situation, so I trek onwards and forwards. I reach the bar. I take one big gulp of air before entering and remember what my singing teacher told me: *Flex your stomach muscles while exhaling for maximum breath control and vocal power.* It serves two purposes, as it also eases anxiety. *A party.* Am I really so unhappy that I need to go out searching for Life? To be a Not Enough: downhearted, and double the tragedy, with the music, the chatter, the dance steps all sounding like the crunching of fallen, dry November leaves underneath a dying black swan's stumbling feet.

The bar is half empty. It's still early, not even 11 p.m. I order a beer. It's happy hour. Good. Everything's super expensive in this country, and I'm not about to violently shake my piggy bank for the sake of alcoholic beverages. I seat myself in the corner. I could stay here all night, just relaxing and observing, but my nerves are too high-strung for relaxation in the midst of swarms. I quickly grow uncomfortable, afraid of being looked down upon with patronizing sympathy and scapegoated as the pariah freak of the evening. I am wary of the Scandinavian brand of reserve that has my brain traveling straight to the thought that *everyone* hates me, that I am dirty, that I should be swept aside even when I am not in the way. What to do about this problem? Talk it off. Yes, my dear, at times one could almost believe I was a social butterfly! I certainly act the part, before swiftly tiring and cursing myself for being so goddamn social, getting myself stuck in a situation where people don't want me to leave since they've now grown ever so fond of me. And as for my own perspective? I've lost sight of who I am. I have become very curious about this party. I have forgotten that curiosity killed the cat so many times that nine lives simply aren't enough. I strike up a conversation with a straight man and his girlfriend who seems to find me exotic, or at least that's why I think she's so keen on taking selfies (wefies? wifis? whyohwhys?) with her face smeared against mine. I smile obediently because I don't feel like ruining the mood. I was the one who started this, so I have only myself to blame. I listen to their funny anecdotes, missing all the points and laughing only in the wrong places.

The man turns to a more serious topic. He tells me only 1 in 1000 people in Iceland are homophobic. He himself has very many gay friends and relatives. I find this conversation relatively tedious, but I'm also a bit fascinated. After all, tight-knit island communities tend to hate queers more rather than less; just look at the nearby Faroe Islands. This could be an interesting comparative study for somebody's future PhD in anthropology, sociology, or gender studies. The conversation moves on, I tell him I'm transgender. He's never met one before. He is shocked: 'Fuck! And I thought you were hot!'

I roll my eyes high to the sky and decide to swallow my standard speech of *imagine handling guys' identity crises nearly every time they fancy you. Straight men will inevitably be attracted to some trans women, and the faster we all realize that the better...* Ms. Alvina Aurora has taken a one-day break from her teaching job.

Student's query: 'But wait, you've had your cock chopped off?'

Response: 'No. I have not.'

'What?' he sighs with grief, and continues: 'I thought being trans meant that if you were a man you got someone's vagina, and if you were a woman you got someone's penis.'

Yes, dear, this is what we call the transgender genital trade. Each trans girl must find a trans boy. Subsequently we enter the hospital together hand-in-hand and request an exchange of genitals. The surgery is conducted overnight. And then everybody lives happily ever after.

We have a long way to go, but I just don't know what more to say about this issue. I'm not the only one, so I won't sound out the battle cry of raw self-pity, self-absorbed existentialism and Nancy Kerrigan: *Why me?* The night continues, it goes on; human beings begin to cram the bar. Thankfully Iceland has a much wilder and more rebellious soul than Sweden – the dance floor would never have been this rowdy at a quarter to midnight in Stockholm. Swedes either dance in friends-only circles or not at all. Here things are a bit more in-yer-face-all-over-the-place. There are many people from the United States out tonight as well. I talk to them, they talk to me, the DJ plays Christina Aguilera's 'Dirrty'. During my brief 2011 stint at a gay strip joint in San Francisco, I used to dance to this song. I was far too feminine to last there for long, my audience never larger than three wise men. But at this establishment in Reykjavik, a big circle forms around me as I parade my moves. '*Gurl*, you're on *fire!*' yells a someone from Los Angeles. LA: a city of 10.2 million people, depending on how you count, and 10.1 million broken dreams, depending on how you count. LA: 10 hours by car from the constricting Petaluma, California of my childhood, 10 hours by plane from the constricting Torslanda, Sweden of my teenage years. A geographical fact, a biographical particular...

The song ends, a new, less memorable one (I don't remember, maybe Ed Sheeran?) begins. '*Gurl*, you're on *fire*,' the someone from LA repeats... Yes. Yes, I am on fire. Another biographical particular: I am made up of flames that are in constant need of being put out! The someone from LA tells me she's RuPaul's assistant. I instantly start searching for ways to impress her. I don't even know why. This type of behaviour is understandable if you come across someone whose work you've actually connected with; to share your deepest self or express honest admiration is not a sin. However, in the case of RuPaul – he's ok and all, but hardly a person I've felt drawn towards. So, one of the top 10 reasons for me to hate myself is the rush of adrenaline that flows through my body when I'm in the vicinity of *status*! DING-DING-DING rings the bell for Pavlov's dog! First: salivation. Then: begin to show off my tricks. Sometimes I succeed and they like me. Most of the time I overdo it and they do their best to ignore me while I bark and bark in mad protest. This time I seem to be coming across as 'likeable'. RuPaul's assistant buys me a drink and we dance together until I get up on a tabletop to seek more attention and be a worse person... But that isn't the main reason why I'm transforming the furniture into a stage... Really, I feel the need for a panther's perch – solitary, safely distanced from the social games of the intimidating Homo sapiens. It improves my emotional state, though I'd still rather be at home reading a book, yes, even a boring one.

For now this is a secret I keep from the rest of the party. A man in his mid-thirties notices my table dancing. He winks at me. He might be flirting, or maybe he just finds me Absolutely Fabulous. He yells: 'You're the Madonna of the night!' Since he's wearing an 'It's Madonna Bitch' T-shirt it must be meant as a compliment. I respond that I'm not a big Madonna fan. He reveals his country of origin: *Switzerland*. I tell him I'm very wary of Switzerland because my most beloved authoress, the goddess of thoughtfeelings, Clarice Lispector, became deeply depressed there, and Vaslav Nijinsky and Friedrich Nietzsche went mad there. There's a great big question mark between us. He doesn't seem to have understood any of the words I said. I don't think I'm interested in him, but as usual I'm uncertain and overwhelmed: too much is going on in this room. I can't think of a sentence that will bring our conversation back to an even playing field. He viciously shakes my waist at an arm's-length distance and screams: 'Anyways, you're *fab*, gurl!' before turning away to dance with his friends. *Fab*. Yes. I knew it from the start. *Fab*.

I see a man I find attractive. He starts kissing someone who must be his boyfriend, as the kiss looks far too familiar and romantic to be the prelude to a casual one-night stand. I rush to plug my inner tub and save my few positive emotions from whirlpooling down the drain. I don't stand a chance with this man, but I will still make an attempt as soon as the smooching session is over. After all, perhaps he's bi and in an open relationship, and I can be the guest star, while actually feeling more like the third wheel... I jump down from the table and gather up the courage to talk to him. After all, I have nothing to win. I don't wait until his boyfriend leaves the room. Why hide when you're the type that's always in plain sight? I stand beside the man I wish to embrace, remaining totally ignored before tapping him on the shoulder. He acknowledges my presence. Barely. I will never tire of being the peculiar schoolgirl who brings handcrafted gifts to those uninterested in receiving. I ask him questions about his life. Boring basic stupid insipid ones: 'Are you from Iceland? ... No, okay, then where are you from? ... Oh, Latvia! ... Are you here on vacation? ... No? Living here? ... Okay. So, what do you do? ... Aha, you work at the National Theatre? Interesting!' He asks me zero questions about my life. And before I have the opportunity to ask him exactly what he does at the National Theatre (*acting? dancing? directing? lighting? costuming?*), one of his friends swoops down and pushes me out of the way in order to dance with him. She has knocked the wind out of me. I was like an ant to him, and she was the one to come and trample over that ant. Now they are laughing and dancing without me. I am a downhearted ant. Once again: Stifled & Baffled. Reader, if I were to tally up the amount of time I've spent sexually and romantically invisible to men at queer events, the sum might be one full year. Meanwhile, the innumerable straight dudes who are especially into trans femmes drench my body in their saliva, yet though I've only taken oestrogen in irregular doses, my feminine charms are useless to gay men. And as for me, if my opinion even counts on the matter: I never thought my body was that interesting to begin with! In order to not go way over the heads of tranny chasers (I HATE THAT WORD!) I am supposed to dumb myself down 100 notches. So, no Nietzsche, Nijinsky, or Clarice. Too bad I'm the kind of girl who could never play stupid for even a second and has suffered countless losses for it. They want dirty talk, with me being extremely submissive or dominant, depending on which fetish I'm expected to cater to. You do understand how boring this gets, right? I flee to gay men in an attempt to be treated as a full human being and escape my place in the lowest rank of the female class. The effort never bears fruit. You wonder: *Don't you want to be treated like a woman?* I wonder: *What's that even supposed to mean?* I am certain it needn't be equated with getting down on my knees and begging to be mouthfucked by a large penis or a small penis that must be called large in order to cater to the mammoth ego of its owner. As I consistently refuse to comply, they go from calling me a beautiful woman to saying 'You look like a man.' I feel stuck. Retreating into myself appears to be the most legitimate alternative. It is of utmost importance that this does not become a horrible place of residence.

It is getting harder and harder to pretend like I'm having fun at this party. The music is the worst hits of the '90s. The rejection is smarting. I look around and grow jealous of the gay men and lesbian women making out on a level playing field. Some straight couples are cis-kissing as well. They act as if they own the place. This is a common behaviour to carry with you everywhere you go when you own the world. A pale, thin-bearded man screams: 'YOU'RE GORGEOUS!' He starts dancing close to me while exchanging broad smiles and tee-hee-hees with his friends. Is he flirting with me? There's something about his exaggerated manner that feels like it's meant as comedy. It wouldn't be the first time. The man pulls my arms and tries to make me do little twirls. I half-heartedly cooperate, flailing about, all the while feeling like his Raggedy Ann doll. He looks into my eyes. Again with that stupid grin on his face. *Ha-ha-ha. Very funny. Everything is just so funny! Dimwit, laughter is not always the best medicine!* Oh, Alvina, what if you're just being overly suspicious? It wouldn't be the first time either. What if he is in fact interested in you? It would do me no good. Sure, many gay men, and straight men *who aren't alone,* find it a funny joke to flirt with trans girls, but regardless of sexual orientation, I consider this particular man's personality as attractive as a piece of Scandinavian Design furniture – odious beyond belief, I explained that already.

Shit! Where's my backpack? I left it in the corner several hours ago. And now it isn't there anymore. Face it: it's gone! Stolen. Iceland, how dare you pretend to be so tiny and innocent when you're teeming with thieves just like all the rest! A travesty: The world is forever against me. The man pinches my waist, craving my regained attention. I push him away. He laughs and shouts, 'What's the matter, hon?' before turning back to his buddies. Then the whole room becomes a blur. The sound of the horrible music starts grating against my intestines. My heartbeat increases, I pace around back and forth in a panic, looking for something or someone stable to grasp onto. I find no one. The closest person I can think of is RuPaul's assistant, but she seems to have gone home. We didn't even get each other's contacts. All my efforts in the art of 'Making An Impression' have gone down the drain where they belong. I ask the bartender if he's received a backpack. He has not. *Lapdog, journal, credit card, 20 euros, keys, passport, wallet.* All lost! I wish to cry in the bartender's arms. He is adorable, but I refuse to embarrass myself any further tonight. The manuscript of my novel is saved in an email. A sigh of relief: The most important thing is safe and sound. Then I remember: I never even found a legible form for that pile of unreadable scribbles! My grand ideas were those of a WORTHLESS DILETTANTE! They won't even suffice to make me the 20 euros I lost in my wallet!

I head for the toilets. There's a long line for the women's bathroom. I must run to the empty men's room to lock myself in for a good cry-a-thon. I have only been to male toilets a couple of times in the past few years, and I am shocked at how awful it smells. I wash my hands thoroughly. I dry my hands with a paper towel: *Don't use two, you'd waste one, don't miss the trash can, someone else has to pick it up from the floor, and that someone will get chronic back pain for life ALL because of YOU!* I'm ready to leave. I suppose I can always sleep on the streets. The temperature dropped from 13 to 6 degrees Celsius as soon as the sun set. Iceland, I commend you for your seasonal light, but your frostiness in July might end up killing me like Jack in *Titanic*! At least your thieves left my scarves&sweatshirts alone in the corner. The bloody bastards are already bathing in scarves&sweatshirts, that's why!! I drape myself in all of them and prepare for hell to freeze over.

At the door a security guard stands with a pink backpack at his feet. A stranger has turned it in! I am elated. I look inside. Everything's in its right place: *lapdog, journal, credit card, 20 euros, keys, passport, wallet.* Why am I so negative and distrusting all the time? Do I really hate people? No. I love very many people, but I cannot rid myself of all the animosity residing inside my body, it regularly seeps out, often onto people who deserve it, sometimes onto people who don't. *You* deserve my sincerest apologies. I rush back into the club to have a victory dance, but my black mood prevails, and I am screaming and thrashing about in order to experience a form of catharsis, transforming darkness into freedom. This process reminds me of the singing-shouting-dancing-crying ritual I had to repeat every day when I was between 18 and 21 in order to not suicide.

The club closes. On the way out I meet a broody-eyed, skinny, blonde boy from Arizona who's spent most of the evening alone in a corner staring at the ceiling. We speak to each other. He seems friendly, his spirit immersed in shyness and timidity. He tells me he's got a lot of social anxiety. Our misfortunes are a spiderweb binding us together yet trapping us inches apart. He's in the near vicinity of my soul's stout introversion, but he seemingly lacks my bouts of explosions and cravings to extrovert *all* the energy. He is better off without. My mixes that don't blend make life harder to live. Somehow, his aura calms me down. We have a brief talk. It is sincere. 'Well, I should be heading home,' the boy announces. We do not exchange any contact details. He says he'll be leaving Iceland in 36 hours. I notice him struggling to put on his jacket. He isn't drunk. He is clumsy. Clumsy people are almost always kind-hearted ♥. I want to ask him if this year has been tough for him too. I am beginning to make up his history and plan our future together. He says: 'Goodbye, have a nice night.' I glue my eyes to the horizon. I tell him I will sing Amy Winehouse songs all the way home. I do as I say. On the 45-minute walk back to my bed & breakfast den, I manage to sing eleven of Amy's songs as well as Björk's 'Bachelorette' and 'Hyperballad'. I baptize my face and arms in seawater. Like Lorelei's siren, I wail at the tranquil ocean: *Your surface, no, all surfaces block the view of 98 percent of life!* I wonder if anybody can hear my cries of love, of fervour, of dejection in Greenland, in Scotland, in Antarctica, in Madeira, or whichever other island is nearest in the direction I am facing. It does not matter. I can make do with this audience of jellyfish, whales, eagles, seagulls, seahorses and kelp. Their perception of sound is very different from humans', and I hope they are satisfied with my impromptu concert, counter-vaults of broken octaves. Applause is not necessary.

(Reader, I'm foraging this forest floor of my 64,000 words to you, searching for a million meaningful things, one of which is the home as basic for some as it is elusive to others... like me-you-us? I can't quite seem to find it, I only know it's not where I grew up. I'm still fully unable to speak of Petaluma or Torslanda without registering a shudder and a significant change in blood pressure and pulse rate. Some may run away from home and find it in some other place or person. Others can't define what is neither empty nor overflowing, full nor hungry, much less point it out on a map or a first date. For us, home remains a place somewhere over the rainbow, regardless of whether we're friends of Dorothy or not. The following is a description of my life at age 6 in Petaluma, California: all my friends are cows grazing on the golden-brown grassfire-begging hills surrounding my walkway from school. Once a week I stop for 30 minutes to show them a freshly choreographed dance before a tomorrow rolls in when all their tomorrows dissolve into slaughter and I gobble only carrots and greens and ruminate in memoriam. My Family: A Mother with big hair, A Father with untrendy glasses, A Sister with lots of friends – sounds normal. Well, normal is neutral at best. It says nothing of good or bad. In '94 I flee out the door to indulge in a dream, Olympic ice skating with Tonya Harding and Oksana Baiul on the living room floor, till I'm alerted that the backyard offers a better buffer against endless nameless heaviness as well as an activity that won't bother a father who'll vote no to gay marriage in '08. I am Stefan Edberg, Steffi Graf, Goran Ivanisevic in the Wimbledon final, banging a tennis ball against a garage door named Pete Sampras or Monica Seles, and I will linger, HÅÅÄÄ, grunting louder than any married couple can shout 'Divorce!' till it's too dark to see my hand waving in front of me and all the crickets cheer 'Stefan!' (clap-clap-clap) 'Steffi!' (clap-clap-clap) 'Goran!' (clap-clap-clap),

and I shall choose between Sylvia Plath and Anne Sexton for my bedtime rhymes, and they will tear me into nightmares more bearable than daytime realitymares where home is endless fights, and school is ceaseless bullying, so childhood bears the name 'In Hell with Nowhere to Run'. The horrifying advice to the bullied: 'Don't show that it hurts you, it'll only ENCOURAGE(!) them.' Tomorrow a classmate will smack me till I cry to forget his name, repeating nicknames I'll never unlearn mixed with '94's top 10 tennis players & figure skaters: Baiul, Ladyboy, Bonaly, Gayrod, Goran, Sissy, Agassi and so on, etc. Reader, the rankings have changed more than my situation, so please stay with me in the present, and... don't cry for me too much. Remember, to be raised inside a pony stable can profoundly decapitate one's empathic capabilities... which raises the question: Must every you ache like every I in order to inflict less pain?)

3 —

I wake up feeling depleted as the *bang-put-put-put* of a 30-year-old car. My first ever Icelandic party left my body rusty, my hair a bird's nest, and my mind a neurotic mess. It is 11:35 a.m. and I make a massive effort to rise from bed. Now, I must eat breakfast, drink strong black tea, then read some pages in *The Wall* by Marlen Haushofer, engulfing myself in the story of a woman residing in complete isolation. Afterwards I will take public transportation to a black-sand beach a few miles from Reykjavik. Hopefully this will be enough for me to regain my stability and sense of purpose in life. I'll make two new friends: the wind whipping against my face and the tiny little raindrops. I'll wear a sufficient amount of clothing, four layers, so the cold can't convince me to be a miserable person. I'm not here to meet people. There's no one I need to entertain and nothing for me to prove.

When I think about epic accounts of traveling alone, they all have one thing in common: they are written by men. Reader, you are probably making a list of women I am forgetting, and you are correct, you have found a gap in my knowledge of literary history. And as for this little book you're holding in your hands? If you thought it would provide an antidote, you'd best get that idea out of your head quickly, and once & for all. My adventures are not epic. And my anecdotes? Monotonous, the opposite of entertaining, nothing worth telling at a cocktail party. Still, I will not quite let go of my point, for yes, I do have one to make. Yes, those of us who are not men are tired of constantly being disturbed in our deliberations. We sit by the beach contemplating and writing in our notebooks, only to be interrupted by men wondering what such a pretty little lady is doing there all alone. We are flaneuses strolling, idling, pondering through the streets, not passing by undetected, never passing by undetected, showing up on the radar, becoming moving targets, and receiving uninvited hands on our inner thighs. We are on the road hitchhiking to taste freedom and end up raped with bruises and ripped clothing. And those who are like me? We may also have stones and glass bottles thrown at us or get chased through town while the throngs cheer rather than rushing to our assistance. And... if we are very unlucky, we will get badly beaten up and wake up in the hospital with broken bones that can no longer write a single line.

Our trauma stubbornly refuses to fit into singular incidents with simple storylines that make it easy for everyone to sympathize. It's like Tonya said of Kerrigan: 'Nancy gets hit *one time*, and the whole world *shits*; for me it's an all-the-time occurrence.' Perhaps this is one reason why these words of mine are being crafted in a country with six times more sheep than people. The sheep may *baaaa* in hopes of some fresh grass, but they certainly won't do what over 200 men have done (grope my ass). Of course, even in the most remote of areas people keep popping up. After all, they are more or less everywhere. But the people here are not like most people. They are very friendly. Perhaps too friendly. I don't really know if it's possible to be *too* friendly, but if it means you lack the experience to see dark or deep, then maybe... As I stated before, I have noticed that Iceland has a more anarchic spirit than Sweden, the country I lived in for 14 years without ever feeling at home, where rights might be given to certain approved minorities, but not without dumping a pariah stigma on all forms of 'excessive' or 'intense' behaviour. Yes, even the homos average 2.3 children per twosome and prefer to invite you home only for double-couple dinners at 6 p.m. sharp! Sweden is a pretty conservative country. Perhaps not in traditional terms. In my terms: It is one of the easiest countries for me to live in, and one of the hardest countries for me to have a life worth living in. But now I am straying from the subject, Iceland. In four days on this island I have only been harassed twice, and the nature of these harassments was only mildly disturbing – no screaming, no stalking, no spitting, no throwing shit, no feeling for tits. I have nothing to complain about; Reykjavik Pride is filled with cis straight families, and the only city space lacking a rainbow is the sky. Nevertheless, I insist on filing a complaint: Many of the children partaking in the Pride festivities still stare at me as if they're having an existential crisis, at times even pointing and laughing like I'm a circus animal. And the parents, they smile a smile that says Please Do Not Disturb – Busy Being Blissfully Broad-Minded, completely oblivious to the fact that their perfect kid with rainbow-painted cheeks could ever do such a thing. This does not give me an incandescent love for life. It's high time for me to leave the city. At 13.35, pretty early by my standards, I am taking a bus that will help me do just that. The bus driver is very friendly. He tells me it takes roughly 45 minutes to drive over the hills to the black-sand beach. He adds that he'll alert me when we're near. I thank him for his kindness. As I walk to my seat, three elderly women and two young men glare and assess me for a brief moment, but largely I am left alone. The bus passes by several adorable Icelandic horses and pine trees that seem unable to grow taller than six feet. There are very few trees in Iceland. I remember the time I heard the expression: 'In Iceland we say "Look, a forest!" each time we see more than two trees growing next to each other.' I smile to myself. I am experiencing happiness.

I walk along the beach hand in hand with no one. It is for the better as I now have both hands free to save jellyfish. If reincarnation turns out to exist, I wish to become one. Jellyfish are the potentially immortal life form of living, breathing water – Água Viva. Adults are called medusas, and some species can return to the ocean floor to be reborn as infants once more. There are at least one hundred of them stranded along this beach. They shall not die today. Not on my watch. They shall continue their delicate existence of peaceful earless eyeless directionlessness, which I shall join when death arrives. Why? Because I wrote it down here, and at least something I wrote *must* come true.

It is possible to focus more on your surroundings when you're not preoccupied with a boyfriend or any other kind of friend. I'm not saying this is always a good thing, but I certainly won't let it cause me a nervous breakdown today. I count the number of buildings on the horizon: 27. Mountain peaks: 14. Sheep in a field: 9. People? 0. The number of jellyfish saved: 38 + ca. 60 before tallying commenced = 98 or 100, give or take. I count the number of flies in a swarm: 23. Or more. Or less. The pesky prima donnas are refusing to hold still. Perhaps several were counted twice or not at all. I count the number of grains of sand: 1700-impossible, but *not* infinity.

My motionless feet are sinking into said sand, which by the way is more bland and grey than black. My muscles are aching. I have spent the last few days biking and hiking very long distances. I am not used to this amount of physical exertion. Is this sand or quicksand? I do not know. Probably the former, or else I'd be dead already. I must trudge through this grey strand to the nearest meadow, where I can finally rest my exhausted body. I make it to my destination in one piece. I plan to read. I fall asleep instead. I don't know why I wake up one hour later. Manners, I suppose. It is neither polite nor safe to sleep in public for long periods of time. But there are no humans here to have-a-laugh or feel-me-up, so why bother with such etiquette? And as for the 9 sheep? I told you, they say *baa*, not *boo*. SCHEISSE, SKIT, SHIT, GOODNESS-GRACIOUS-WHAT-IS-THIS???!!! 15 worms are creeping over my cheeks, hands, and neck. OFFOFF!!! Worms, how dare you?! Pick on someone your own size! Worms, do not be so eager! It is not polite! I am not dead yet! I am just very tired. I am holding my breath. I am leaving myself breathless. I am picking the sticky worms off me, flinging them back into the grass and wishing them good luck finding a real carcass, 'cause this girl is alive and kicking with boots that are made for walking!!! *Oops, I'm terribly sorry dear-darling wormies, I hope I didn't hurt you!* They wriggle about, ready to move on with their lives. I suppose I ought to do the same. I glance across the bay in the direction of downtown Reykjavik like Cinderella looking towards the ball to be held at the castle. It is Friday. There are two large parties tonight – one straight, one gay. Endless opportunities are calling my name. And the wind blows me in their direction like a hollow ghost with business left to attend to.

5 hours later: the sun sets over my bed & breakfast den, and the contours of a couch comforting a fatigued body have won. They have pieced together a puzzle. A cup of lemon tea has served its purpose. I place my nose inside the centre of a book and it smells like a new place to call home. I read a few pages before reclining into the placid repose that precedes deep sleep. My soul is not weightless. There is a victory being won tonight. It is not visible to the untrained eye. Here lies a mind that is neither ecstatic nor despairing. And an exterior that neither smells heavenly of perfume or sweet conditioner, nor stinks like days of sweat piled layer upon layer until you are granted a migraine from your own stench. I am at rest in a cradle between the Eurasian and North American tectonic plates, inside the Atlantic Ridge of an ocean my life has constantly straddled. *A home has at last been found?* It is growing apart by the minute. I cry out! I cry out because I have felt a constant pull in two opposing directions for as long as I can remember! My forgotten sleeping pills are dancing on a nightstand 1,200 miles from this couch. I am in no need of them tonight. I am winning victories. Small ones, for sure, yes, the very ones that must never be taken for granted. I realize: I can manage life. I may never become good at it, my showers take forever, I leave the house to begin working two hours later than planned, and each day I think it will be different tomorrow, but it never is. A repetition: waking up feeling so depressed, worthless, and sensitive that half a day goes by before I can take in the outside world without crying at every little detail. I'm too volatile to drive a car, I can't fix anything around the house nor do I dare ask for help, I eat breakfast at 2 p.m. and dinner at 1 a.m., and in a matter of minutes I can go from the life of the party to wanting only to go home alone

and never ever meet a human being again. But we mustn't focus on my quirks and shortcomings in the tranquillity-of-mind department. Not tonight, when I'm managing to stick with contentedness without asking *What's next?* Dear restlessness, I am caressing your cheeks and sucking gently on your earlobe. I know you'll always be by my side. Like so many of my problems, you're not going anywhere, therefore I will learn to love you in the only way that will not kill my spirit. The lesson to be absorbed is the following: Just because something provides 'a chance' does not mean it must be a Grab It While You Can. Dear restlessness, tonight I am tucking you into bed. Kissing your forehead. And as you fall asleep I am allowed to do the same, without sleeping pills, on my own account, in a life that is slowly learning how to live with itself.

(The logic side of mind states its agreement: *Get over your neurotic fear of missing something 'important' that never happens. You have attended exactly 198 parties in your lifetime, and I can't recall more than 6 where you actually enjoyed an experience remotely near a milestone. It's not 'cause you're getting older, it's 'cause you never liked it to begin with.* HOWEVER, the logic side of mind also worries: *There's a risk that this girl resorts to doing nothing but studying blades of grass, meeting no one but the occasional caterpillar. It seems to be a deeply ingrained part of her nature and it can be very dangerous if played out to its full extent...*)

4 —

Dearest reader,
I am going to be completely honest with you. In the creation of this body of work, I have not always been disciplined enough to write the proper sentences in real time. Sometimes life happens and all I am able to jot down is the half-gibberish of fragmentary morning thoughts. Yes, it's true, they colour outside the box, and their lack of legibility may not disturb you. Personally, I discover an exploration of marvelocity and cannot even be bothered by my uncertainty regarding whether or not that's a 'real word'. Therefore, it is not my own embarrassment that blocks the road. No. It is the gatekeeping publishers who hinder our freedom. They do not wish to put you through the chaos that lives within without a sense of solidness. They crave spacings and paragraph indentations.
(space)
Two deaths have occurred in my near vicinity since I left Iceland. I am not even including the ossifying cadaver of the bird I almost stepped on, though it too left me short of breath. My perspective has changed. I find myself lunging between cursing and celebrating the many trivialities that make up the majority of a life. Dreams envelop my reality; there is an 18th-century house placed between a cemetery and a church. I did not require further reminders, but life is a soothing irritation that I cannot control. And death? The word can be pronounced in

several different ways. It does little to alter its definition or make it confess its secrets.

Reader, it is 15 degrees outside. The air quality is crisp and clear, like the Icelandic weather in late July. I am now ready to return you to that time and place where 14 hours have passed since I fell asleep without sleeping pills. It is midday. I am already out and about, dressed like a slut in my pink short-shorts. No one on this entire island seems to care. I am torturing myself in the freezing cold, receiving neither praise nor blame. Day in and day out, I am a hypervisible object longing to be invisible, but I've grown so used to abuse, and its method of war fights all peace of mind. Yes. If you're used to abuse, you no longer recognize the face of respect: *Just a minimum* – of course, at times respect is just a mask worn by people who are afraid of being politically incorrect. I did not ask to be in the middle of all this. But what can I do about it? Start jogging in order to raise my body temperature? Go to the botanical garden so I can be A Blissful Woman With Her Flowers? The entrance costs 12 euros, and I'm too cold for any floral scents to enter my nasal canals. *Brrr-brrr.* Nothing's fun when you're freezing. Solution: *finally visit the geothermal hot swimming pool...* I dupe my way around the gendered locker-room talk by changing in the disabled toilet. 30 seconds later, I jump straight into a 44-degree jacuzzi. My mood vastly improves, save for one detail: When you're shivering you forget about all your other Needs & Wants. When you're heated up, they slowly return. I am gravitating back to my desire towards men. Look, look, stupid girl with standard taste: a man with beady green eyes, high cheekbones and toned muscles is grabbing his crotch and rearranging the position of his cock just 10 feet away! Who cares! Hot tub, would you please quit vibrating, you're making matters worse! Everything was simpler during the years when multiple rapes made me feel entirely asexual. Now look at me: a glutton with no idea how to indulge. *Radical feminist reverse objectification!* Ha, more like Hysterical & Barren & Worthless! Furthermore, it isn't radical to become what you abhor and run a race in a hamster wheel. I'm better off sticking to my neuroses. What's with me at this moment? A 30-year crisis? How pathetic! It is alright. I'm used to being pathetic. Once this phase passes I can go back to being thrilled about getting older… I wonder what I'd do if the entire national football team showed up here. My ex-lover in California once told me that everybody has fantasized about getting fucked by 15 men all at once. I've never had this fantasy; I wasn't included in his definition of 'everybody'. I suppose that's one reason we're no longer together. Yes, if the Icelandic football team arrived, I would simply have to apologize to them and choose only one, or perhaps two just for good measure.

I halt my birdbrained acrobatics and jump in the big pool to swim laps. After four, I sit down in the shallows and allow myself to rest in thoughtfeelings. When I was 22, I read Erica Jong's musings on liberation and zipless fucks. My sex life has forever been a string of zipless fucks with no strings attached in beds, baths & beyonds. They've always given me near nothing. I hardly even enjoyed them in the moment. The few times they culminated in cumming, the orgasm could only be described as lacklustre, scarcely better than masturbation in the shower. I buoy my body up through the water and complete a few short synchronized swimming moves – sailboat, flamingo, ballet kick – before somersaulting underneath the surface, shocking my upper respiratory tract with a flood of liquid azure. Yes. There is sex between body parts and there is sex between people and, yes, there is also sex without touching. I am yearning for the mindbody fucks that always seem to elude me. Yes, men constantly see me as either a hot piece of meat – doggy style, 69 – or a brilliant brain – IQ score 169. Since men have trouble multitasking, they never see me as both. *Their* lack becomes *my* problem. Stated simply: *The straight men who 'respect' trans women rarely want to fuck us, and the straight men who want to fuck us rarely respect us.* And as for the avant-garde? Gone are the days of Candy Darling and Lou Reed... Indeed, the avant-garde has perhaps never been as rigid, gentrified, boring and bourgeois as it is today. If I go to the theatre, the reading, the vernissage, zero men will flirt with the only trans girl in the room. However, on my way home four men will wolf-whistle or holler. Hypersexualisation/desexualisation paradox: two sides of one coin: a trapped existence leaving room for only microbreaths. At the end of the day, most people would rather be sex objects than left untouched, though let's not pretend it's a real choice.

Underneath each layer of sorrow lies a sweltering anxiety fire that tears try and only occasionally manage to extinguish. I am now in the bathroom of my rented den applying makeup: foundation, eyeliner, mascara, neon-pink lipstick. Vast amounts of blush shall make the men I desire either believe I'm blushing All The Time or Not At All. Reader, I know what I said about parties, but earlier this evening the devil on my shoulder shouted: *You can't stay at home wasting every single night away during your holiday and Pride!* So my mind decided to force my body to go out again. Now, my face is on fleek, and my mane is voluminous. I spray a perfume called Good Life, which shall ready me for life's pleasant surprises. I rub my fingers against my crotch, smearing them across my neck, since I once read in a book that this scent attracts males. I worry: the mixture of these two smells might repel my soulmate. They're both meant to be used alone. Together they'll surely ensure that *I* end up alone! I shrug. I am wearing a Frida Kahlo sweatshirt to remind myself that I possess a certain strength. I hit the streets. It is 9:30 p.m. and I am disturbed by the sheer number of Loud-Annoying-Amazed Americans, Tacky-Drunken-Bewildered Brits, Thrill-Seeking Scandinavians and Quadratisch-Praktisch-Gut Germans who dress like they're perpetually ready for an excursion deep into the wild. Reykjavik is not big enough to have a specific tourist area, as all the city's cafés and shops are located on three or four avenues. Right now, vacationers like me are completely dominating these streets, as we're the only ones dumb enough to look for a pub this early. Alcohol costs a fortune at the bars, so most Icelanders are drinking at home in preparation for The Big Night Out. It is summer. It is Saturday. It is Pride. Gay, bi, straight – everyone must celebrate!

  I find a bar with happy-hour deals: a glass of white wine for 8 euros. If that's a steal, the unhappy hours must leave you penniless and in tears. I take one little sip of wine every 3 minutes. I force myself to do most outer activities in moderation as my inner world is so far from moderation it derails and crashes fastfast with pieces of brain oozing out of my cracked skull. Plus, my budget can only afford one more drink tonight. Between each sip, a new group of people arrives. As my glass goes from full to empty, the bar does the contrary, and I'm forced to squeeze through a crowd to find my way out. I cross the street, passing the queer bar in favour of a Pride-night at the city's largest straight club. I choose my choice consciously: at these kinds of parties you'll generally find a mixture of the regular heterosexual clientele with an added shot of heterogenous queers. This cocktail brings me higher hopes; straightness is supposedly my new home, or home away from home, or just... doormat for straight men to wipe their dicks off on before arriving home to wives and kids... I worry the club will play terrible music too. Still, I'm thrilled it's not hip, that Reykjavik's level of hipness is about 1/12 of Berlin's. A group of straight men stand in front of me in line. They ask me about Berlin's nightlife. I tell them most Berlin clubs resemble 'the club scene' in bad movies – you've seen hundreds of them, with techno music pounding as a group of trendy 20-somethings discuss ketamine. I sound savvy, urbane, cosmopolitan. They're very impressed that I'm able to get into Berghain. I find it irrelevant. Just as I find it irrelevant that my beloved authoress Violette Leduc knew Camus, de Beauvoir, Genet, Sartre and Cocteau. They recognized her writing talent while keeping her demand for a hand to *always hold* at an arm's length. After I perused one page she jumped out of her book and embraced me without restraint. Now, together, we crave miraculous impossibilities which are easily achieved in our divine worlds. Yes, Violette & I are nothings clinging to everything! So these straight men had better watch out! Oh, they've got no reason to worry. I won't fall in love with them. They ask such stupid questions. They wonder if it's true that it's rude to announce that you're straight when attending a queer party. I wonder if anyone asked them about their sexual orientation? *No?* Then why bother presenting it. Your sexuality is not a beauty pageant for toddlers in tiaras!

I look out towards the open road. I am giving myself a moment alone. I am getting ready for a night full of endless chatter, of alternating between dancing and standing amongst throngs of people. I should only put myself through this for political causes. My broken record's repeating the vile tune from two days ago. I concentrate my thoughts on trees: Why do they spring branches? And how do they decide where to place them? Some branches even sprout further branches. Do they receive a delegation to make this decision, or is the central brain of the tree still calling the shots?

Another man in the gang of straight dudes interrupts my thoughts. He didn't notice me earlier, as he was busy drunk-talking to the group in front of him. He looks like a big, reddish-blonde-bearded Viking; all that's missing is the horned helmet. My long-legged, blonde, pink appearance excites him greatly. He howls: 'WHO ARE YOU? YOU ARE BEAUTIFUL! YOU ARE MY PRINCESS! KISS ME NOW!'

He wraps his arms around me and powers my entire upper body towards him. I react just in time to turn the other cheek like some Jesus wannabe, obtaining a firm lick instead of ingesting a forced saliva smoothie. One of the guys in the gang is a bit less drunk than the others. He says, 'I'm really sorry about my friend.' Me too, it isn't very fun to be expected to deliver kisses at a man's beck and call. Well, at least he didn't yank my head towards his crotch as some strangers on the streets have done before. The attention these straight men are lavishing upon me is quite unlike the sexual obsession coming from tranny chasers. I feel a bit confused, maybe this is inching towards what it means to simply be desired, not fetishized: *Don't care who you are, where you're from, what you did, as long as you're a tranny, baby.* My focus turns to the relatively sober guy, who brings up his impending trip to Rio de Janeiro. Last year I was there and visited the newly inaugurated statue of Clarice Lispector at the Leme strip of Copacabana beach. She lived and died in Rio, and I decide to invite this boy to the story of the first time I read her amidst my debilitating spring 2010 depression... each sentence cavorting from the page, tattooing itself across my skin, then delicately settling inside my veins, merging with my blood. Clarice wrote, and I pored over it with all my six senses, alongside the truth of everything I don't know – there where I could finally rest sprawled across a lawn, shielded from the wretched chasing of myself. I inform the boy about her final interview where she said, 'I guess the question of understanding isn't about intelligence, it's about feeling.' I tell him that my fellow sad clown, the blue god of ballet, Vaslav Nijinsky, wrote extensively about this subject in his diary. Unfortunately the boy I am talking to is not my synergy-soulmate-husband Nijinsky, but at least he seems interested in my deliberations. Hopefully this interest will exceed snapping a beachside selfie with Clarice's statue and actually involve reading one of her books. Then he would understand that her jaguar stare means No Smiling and Posing. The minutes pass by at a speed sensed differently by a god, a statue and a sad clown. After perhaps 45 of them in total, I finally reach the front of the line. The time has come to enter the club. *We shall see if I can be reborn...*

Inside, the dudes immediately rush into fast-forward mode. They push towards the bar to buy me two drinks, oh lord, pennies saved, pennies earned, I haven't been this happy in hours! But before I even have time to utter *Cheers, thanks a lot*, they all jump up on tables, take their shirts off, and start dancing. I don't see any faggots behaving like this, and certainly no women or in-betweens. My mood microearthquakes and I can't determine if I hate them for taking up so much space or love them for entering a queer night with such an unrestrained embrace. I decide that it's ok to hate them a little and love them a little. The same goes for the blend of music being played: As I mentioned, it's nice to escape the hip pretention and monotony of German techno. Still, don't they understand that Rihanna, Silvia Night and Nicki Minaj are *much* more enjoyable to dance to than this stereotypical homosexual crowd-pleasing succession of Eurovision winners and runners-up randomly followed by 'The Scatman'? Obviously not, 'cause here comes Sisqó's 'Thong Song'!

Other establishments in Reykjavik must play better music, but I'm in no position to leave. Everywhere will already be filled to the brim, and I refuse to wait in line for another 45 minutes. My mistake is beyond fixing. I cannot dance. The floor has been bespattered by liquor. It's too sticky. If I attempt a Nijinsky ballet leap, I will most certainly break open the soles of my low-quality shoes. Then I will be unable to take a single step into nature, thus demolishing the main purpose of my trip. The dance floor is filling up. The crowd is indeed a blender of genders and sexualities. Yet, I believe I'm the only t-girl here, which could be good, attention galore, or horrid, they all know to stay farfar away. I am not ignored. Every other straight man seems to be gaping at me with that customary combo of sexual curiosity and collective neuroses. The ballad of cognitive dissonance plays inside their minds – *she's hot but I should think she's not*. One would imagine the environment of a Pride night might assist, but even here macho men tend to relish 'trying something new' clandestine, while protestant PC 'nice' guys fear stepping out of line. Yes, tolerance is best *performed* at an arm's-length distance, and though they've read their Nietzsche, they repeatedly stick to the herd that trans girls left long back to forge new paths. Eating my own rebellion from the trash, my unnamed emotions mourn this unwillingness to dance. I recall the times I've walked down the streets thinking of Nijinsky. My body has sprung to life and I have done pas de bourrées and chassés along the sidewalk followed by a grand jeté with arms extended to the sapphire sky. During these breaths of life The People gawk at me for other reasons than The Usual. I am graceful and deranged like the mad Nijinsky of 1919, but with a slight connection to reality that always yanks me back. This is often an unfortunate attachment.

My embitterment experiences an expansion as a group of gay men tell me to stop sulking and 'release my inner diva queen'. I lack interest in being a fabulous and castrated puppet. For years these faggots have thrown me to the throngs of tranny-chasing hounds *woof-woof*ing and stalking about on the streets after closing hours, always after closing hours. *Tranny chaser* – I'll say it again: I hate that word, but what else should I call the man who got off a moving bus in Berlin and ran 500 feet after me just to pant, 'I've only seen your kind of girl in porn before, you want siiiiix?' I shook my head. He said,

'I'm so horny, help me please.' I drew circles with the toes of my feet. I thought obsessively about triangular pyramids and my magic number three. I shed a tear for the me and the Nijinsky no one would understand; I recall another day walking down the Reeperbahn in Hamburg on my way to a ballet about his life. A wad of spit splattered onto my left cheek, oozing dangerously close to my taste buds. A curse word wandered out into the open: *Kurwa!* So many different languages. So many different body fluids. Cum in face, spit in face, same shit different name? That was a question. I wiped off the spit and walked on, for if I didn't I'd drown into an amoeba, and after the ballet everything meant everything to me, which meant I was blown away by my strongest emotions, which meant I felt ready to die without wanting to die.

This is not how I feel at this party. Like all parties it behaves more like a masquerade. The pounding music interrupts my thoughts. I wonder why we put ourselves in situations that diminish intense engagement with the world? I flee to the second floor of the club, where the music is slightly less loud. I lock myself in the ladies' room to remove my always already thin mask. I have an urge to do a number two, but there's no toilet paper. I won't ask for more. I refuse to use any more of the Earth's limited resources. I'll hardly poop myself. My desperations lie elsewhere, Else-Where, all the men who kept me as The Other Woman have led full lives residing in that land called Else-Where. I gaze straight into the sad eyes of my reflection for several minutes: *Is my suffering beautiful, is my pain still worthy of love?* My reflection decides that I've equated masochism with self-care one time too many! She jumps out of the bathroom mirror to change my state of mind. Together we leave the toilets in order to live the Here And Now & Seize The Day! The day has passed: I am Queen Of The Night! I start talking to strangers regardless of my attraction to them. I smile. I laugh. I don't cry. I am welcomed into the warmth of different circles of friends. Had I been 20 years older and less pretty, this would've been impossible. *Stop it, Alvina! I'm not about to waste my entire life on your nagging critical thoughts! Can't you see, I am busy chatting with my new bestie – first name Carpe last name Diem?!* There is a man from New York who lives in Japan. He is 27 years old and works part-time as a model, part-time as a commercial actor. The upstairs DJ plays the song 'Summer Nights' from *Grease*. I tell my fresh acquaintance I used to play Rizzo, while my sister was Sandy, inside a living room of infinite tiptoes across eggshells to not disturb a mother who painted our world with strokes of a Complex Choleric Extraordinaire. I make the brash decision to skip all small talk. It does nobody any good. Somebody is getting into trouble. That somebody is *me*. I don't care. Self-careless, I'd rather hurt myself than others – granting myself forgiveness is easy. Still, my mind's eye whisks me back to the untamed California beaches of my childhood, where the riptide flowed like highland river rapids, to that time when I was perilously close to drowning at sea, and I feverishly reached out for a friend to cling to. Kelp was that friend. Kelp saved my life. But kelp isn't attending this party. My forays are rooted by the visceral without the protection of conceptual metaphors. If I jump into a current, I will drown in the undertow. If I am vulnerable in front of a man, I'll be stomped on once again. I see thick jet-black hair and contrasting blue eyes. I see a sharp, well-defined cheekbone. Two to be precise. All the better for slicing my aorta and chopping off my head all at once to make sure I'm truly dead this time.

I have no idea where I'm heading. I didn't even start this conversation with the intention to flirt. Who is this man? I suddenly find myself interested in knowing all the answers. I find the conversation digging deeper. I am digging my own grave. He is telling me about his parents. They were emotionally abusive. His mother loved in the vein of all four seasons – the Earth's, Vivaldi's, Stravinsky's Spring! She'd get along splendidly with my mommy, who used to blast Beethoven's *dun-dun-dun-duuun* 5th Symphony to accompany her shouts at a husband who'd always attend without being present. My future partner lays a soulmate egg by unveiling how his father resided in a separate stratosphere, unaffected by seasonal change. I am careful to keep our egg warm and together, uneaten and uncracked. Our kinship simply must hatch as it is following the narrative blueprint of Hollywood films that rarely fail to bring tears to the eyes of foolish little girls like me. *He* often feels fairly depressed. *He* has problems for me to solve. Alvina, don't be such a silly cosseter. I am dying for a poultice to soothe my own wounds. I am certain I'm capable of returning the favour. He does not like New York City. My demeanour brightens, I can show him how much I agree: 'Exactly! Take me down to the hashtag city, where the rents are high and the girls & boys are busy, where art's as watery as a can of Campbell's soup, and vapid ambitions elbow out all original ideas. New York City provides immense amounts of light but *never* warmth!' He laughs. He nods. He adds: 'Yeah, most people move there just to say "I've made it!"' He much prefers Tokyo. I have never been there. I'm looking forward to visiting him soon. Yes, the deep end always provides a smooth bed for us to create snow angels in fine sand. We take our conversation out for some fresh air. We smoke a cigarette to ruin the health gains that fresh air can provide. My mother does not approve of this action. Don't worry mom, I only smoke about a pack every other month. However, this boy seems to smoke nearly a pack a day. I am very worried about him. I look straight into his deep-set eyes and say:

'My intuition tells me you're an emotionally volatile being who's constantly attempting to keep it on an even keel. You do realize this can't be sustained for long?'

He looks straight back at me and says, 'You're right, absolutely right.' He does not begin to cry in my arms. He doesn't need to. He has already succeeded in eradicating the presence of everyone else at this establishment. Our eyes meet, halt, and hold. Whenever this event takes place, a box is unlocked, and I believe there's a brief moment where souls jump from bodies to embrace one another, generating an inaudible blaze. Some people are able to disengage from this process and recover relatively unscathed. I am not amongst their ranks. If I fall, I will lose another 1 of my 9 lives. If we are two sphinxes, we can only be saved by devouring each other. We speak of the pathetic meaninglessness of beauty. I am thrilled when he acknowledges mine!!! I make an effort to create an air of confident romantic exchange. I whisper to myself *I am engaged in a flirtation with a man* – as if it were a success akin to landing on Mars. We talk of literature. He writes down the names of Clarice Lispector, Violette Leduc, Arundhati Roy, Ingeborg Bachmann and Alvina Chamberland on a napkin. Yes, I have told him I'm a writer. Yes, he is interested in reading my words, which means he'll be launching a voyage into my heart's centre. No, I haven't forgotten that every man in his right mind would be completely turned off after reading just one page of my broodings. It is alright. I'm not searching for a man in his right mind. And this man certainly isn't, I can already tell, and now: I want more – All & Everything. Our shoulders touch and neither of us bothers to move. This too is a definite sign. My insides turn all mushy. My body says: *Ahh, I remember this feeling. It is the feeling of another body.* Little things often have the tendency to awaken many things. I look at him again, and my bedroom fantasies are not limited to getting down on my knees and sucking his dick until he cums. I have transformed from a bad feminist into a good one. I have been liberated. Being on constant lookout was a heavy chain; the Allied forces have stormed in and sledgehammered it to smithereens. My body? It's a city of celebration. My veins? The streets of Paris in 1944. My blood cells? Each of them a person in that cheering crowd.

Fiona Apple sings the strophe of my longing: *SEEK ME OUT, LOOK AT, LOOK AT, LOOK AT, LOOK AT ME, I'M ALL THE FISHES IN THE SEA, WAKE ME UP, GIMME GIMME GIMME WHAT YOU GOT IN YOUR MIND IN THE MIDDLE OF THE NIGHT!*

And my future boyfriend? If he's not singing 'La vie en rose' or 'L'hymne à l'amour', then perhaps he's busy composing something new? Staccatissimo Subito Lentando, he changes tempo, putting on the brakes by initiating ironic banter. He tells me he's never been to a gay party before. I don't mind. If he's not gay my chances are arriving! He asks me if I shave my pubic hair? *No.* Groom? *Yes.* These are very intimate questions. I am not thrilled by the topic of conversation. But it does at least imply interest in my body. He is being forceful. He is a man. 'I also groom my pubic hair,' he jests. I don't care. It is beneath us to be talking about such corporal trivialities. I look the other way in hopes that my protest shall be noticeable and reel us back into the bigger things. We don't have time for silly games. In 65 years we'll be ashes. If things proceed smoothly these ashes shall be placed beside each other in a cemetery or spread out in the same sea. *No they won't!* His next words put an ocean between us: 'I'm gonna go back inside and hit on some dykes.' *We are worlds apart.* I retort: 'Then I'll head downstairs to go dance and pretend to be happy.' He looks at me like I'm a black widow spider, dangerous, yet easy to crush. He is correct. I attempt to mesmerize him with my eyes again. The attempt is futile. He is searching for dykes to hit on. He is pretending to be stupider than he is. He is an asshole. Oh, if only condemnations such as *he's an asshole* ever saved me. It is too late. I've been singing the song 'Bloody Motherfucking Asshole' on near repeat since I was 19, with no salvation: *I WILL NOT PRETEND, I WILL NOT PUT ON A SMILE, I WILL NOT SAY I'M ALRIGHT FOR YOU, WHEN ALL I WANTED WAS TO BE GOOD, TO DO EVERYTHING IN TRUTH, TO DO EVERYTHING IN TRUTH, YOU BLOODY MOTHERFUCKING ASSHOLE, OH YOU BLOODY MOTHERFUCKING...* No! That simply will not do. *I will bottle up!* I will head down the stairs, dance and Pretend To Be Happy!

When your emotions reach the point of overflow, you no longer just dance to the rhythm of a song that's playing. A powerful force exists, stronger than music. It cannot be explained, only felt. And I'm feeling it; I am Living In The Moment, my insides are expanding, my heart's leaping through my throat in order to commit suicide by throwing itself from my mouth, aiming to die like an asphyxiated fish on land, flapping about in a tiny puddle of its own blood. I must get away from this sticky dance floor AT ONCE. My feet stamp on a table, scaring it to death. My hands pound against the ceiling, daring it to come crashing down. I jump higher, higher. My tear ducts are activated. To cry on the dance floor is to allow both full-blown depression and ecstasy the space to exist within one body, simultaneously. It can never be sustained for long. I am becoming depleted. Panting. Panting for breath. I sit down to rest.

I don't want to be here anymore. Six miles away lies a landscape covered in moss. It would provide both a mattress and a soft pillow. All I'd need is a blanket to shelter me from the cold, and I would be complete. I am so close. What brought me Here instead of There? The promise of love? Is it a lie? For a girl like me, most likely. Oh, was he frightened by his desire for a tranny, or did he realize I remind him of his ex-girlfriend's cat that once smacked his smartphone into the sea, or-or-or?-?-? All these navigations... so familiar – to think I could be like everyone else for an instant, a basic error. *LoveLove,* I am back where I belong, to blood spewing from the glaciers of my own dominions, private properties waiting to be liberated. My mind has regained its purity; it is no longer distracted by its various neuroses. I have travelled beneath the surface with this particular man. I don't need any of the boys on dry land. I am focused. I am missing out. I do not care. I shout. I continue shouting. It appears as though I'm very engaged in the lyrics of the song being pumped out of the loudspeakers. I am not. I am living the moment of understanding the meaning of a moment after the moment has passed. I am feeling things stronger after the fact. Why does this grief repeat itself? When someone sneaks up behind you and yells *BOO*, you don't name that feeling 'surprise' until several seconds later when the shock subsides.

I start searching for *him*. *He* is nowhere to be found. Is he hiding? Gone forever? Or just on the toilet? I can't call out his name for I don't know his name, but I love him all the same. I've known many people's names and not loved them, so why can't the opposite be true? My desert is experiencing a sand avalanche. The dance floor is full of sloppy-drunken couples smooching as if they were hyenas gobbling abandoned carcasses and guarding them from the potential threat of lions. No doubt, moments ago he too was a participant in one of these mindless make-out sessions. Now he has gone home with his girl to avoid disturbances from a frantic lioness. Will he wake up tomorrow morning and find my name scrawled upon a napkin? Will he do whatever it takes to find me? No. A two-second search on the internet would do the trick. Even that amount of effort is too much for this man, and it's because he's fully disinterested, not because he's my hero who boycotts goggles & apples & amazon-deforestation.com.

My own tried and true search engine called eyes find him talking with another woman. I make a swift decision: I won't compete with her. I don't intend to be the jealous girl who views women as rivals for the attention of a man. She leaves on her own accord. She isn't interested in him. I don't have him all to myself. I don't have him at all! He sees me and lets out a laugh, 'She wasn't a lesbian, but she was married.' I don't find his joke the least bit funny. I refuse to laugh along. I ask, 'Can we talk?' He rapidly assesses the situation through an analysis of my tone and expression. He understands that I have driven myself into some serious topographies during the 20 minutes we spent apart, while he just kept 'having a good time'. He has no interest in taking part in this conversation. He has a verdict: 'It doesn't matter anyways, cuz I'm not gay.' My riposte delivers a statistic, 'But... dear, I haven't been with a gay man in six years.' He remains stiff-necked, unmoved by persuasion, with no trace of our preceding flirtations. There is only one thing between us: *unease*. It never happens to me follows me always. I was in for the All Or Nothing, yes, the All Or Nothing that leaves you with *Nothing* in 90 percent of *All* cases. So, what now? Is he just going to stare at me with a blank expression or is he going to open his mouth to say something that matters, if not to me personally then at least in relation to the bigger picture: the consequences of the fall of the Soviet Union? *No.* Svetlana Alexievich? *No.* We-Need-To-Build-An-Economy-Not-For-Those-At-The-Top-I-Think-About-This-A-Lot? *No.* Marx? Spivak? Keynes? *No. No. And again No.* Well then, whatever it is you have to say, just say it!!!

'Well, it was nice to meet you. Hope to see you around,' he declares in a monotone voice. He is mocking me, patronizing me with the dull charity of day-to-day courtesies. I plan a spectacular sentence. My mouth opens wide for the final say in this devastating encounter: 'Now that we've met, would you mind never seeing me again?'

If I could change one thing I would've looked him straight in the eye while I said it. I didn't. I was too much of a coward. I looked between his eyes. I don't care if it gave off the same impression. Impressions are just the thing that reality spits out of a photocopy machine.

He heads towards the door. To leave? To have a cigarette? It no longer matters. I go to the bathroom again. I splash cold water all over my face because everything feels a bit better when cold water shock-kisses the pores dotting your skin. My makeup smears. Who gives a shit? I'm a bit intoxicated by alcohol. I'm much more intoxicated by adrenaline. My despair looks in the mirror and sees only scar tissue and shards. She knows she is grieving the 7 heartbreaks, the 8 rapes, the 10,000 trampling stampedes... Yes, I know exactly how cruel the world is to girls like me, yet I stand before each new he naive, raw and alacritous as a sweet sixteen. An anomaly axed to smithereens. I scream at my stabbed lungs: *WHY ARE YOU STILL BREATHING?*

It is 4:30 a.m. The club was supposed to close at 4. It's breaking the rules. It's still far from empty. It'll get along just fine without me. I look around the club one last time to see if he's returned. No. He's gone. Just as well. This whole endeavour wasn't planned and it certainly did not go as planned. He&I have both had enough of my mood swings. I escort myself to the nearest exit. The sun has risen. Good news: it'll get progressively warmer during the 45-minute walk back to my den. If I increase my tempo to that of a power walk, I won't have to freeze at all, while simultaneously decreasing the amount of time spent outdoors by 8 or 9 minutes. I am ready to embark. I look up and see the face of...

Him! Again? How can it be when he already assassinated me? Is he following my soul around in heaven? No. He is not! Cease, wishful thinking, cease! He sees me and calls out:

'Alvina!' I am flooded by buoyancy. He responds with a facial expression that is flippant and casual and nonchalant. 'Ugh, I just went out for a smoke and now the security guards won't let me back in,' he states plainly instead of crying in front of me. A guy he knows exits the club and walks straight by him; 'Pff, that motherfucker didn't even say goodbye.' I am listening to his voice. I am frantically grasping onto the last strand of hope. Each word coming out of his mouth cuts five centimetres from that strand and now he is beginning to slice into my fingers. *Ow!* He offers me a cigarette. Alas, my right hand has lost all its fingers. I try my luck with the left. I succeed. Barely. My entire forearm is shaking with pain and despair and the chemicals inside me that always insist on acting as enemies. He wonders if I'm freezing from the cold, proving that he doesn't understand the roots of any of my problems. *He* lights my cigarette in an attempt to compensate for the lack of ignited fires between us. It is an insufficient substitute. I look up. His face is expressionless. *IT'S A SIN!* He looks in another direction. *How dare he!* His precious gaze apparently deems me unworthy of even ten seconds of its time! I say: 'So you're mad your friend left without saying goodbye? Well, so will I!'

My steps away are not gleeful skips or sashays. I kick my powerless walk into gear with the fuming engine of a feeling incapable of any lasting joy: Pride. I know this heartbreak by heart; I have been known to allow men to swiftly pull me back on a slingshot and then let go, as I catapult into the air, hitting the ground, *THUD*. That's how I've defined *A Fling*. Pride. I refuse to look back. I wish for him to come running after me; FAST! I know he never will, so I stride at that speed: (FAST!). I smoke at that speed: (FAST!). I-hate-myself-&-I-want-to-die

at that speed: (FAST!). NOT SO FAST, I STILL HAVE MANY THINGS TO LIVE FOR?! I can't think of *any* right now. My imagination celebrates my moment of death without actually killing its body. It's a win-win situation. Highly boozed-up people are lingering on the sidewalks; some of them even wobble about in the middle of the street. There are no cars since practically everybody is either asleep or intoxicated at this hour, and Iceland has very strict laws against drinking & driving. At the end of the dewy horizon, I see the towering mountains where they filmed *Game of Thrones*, but for now I am stuck in a Zombie-Zone. I zigzag around these drunkards like an Olympic Gold Medallist in Slalom without skis. I smoke my cigarette to the very end, since I once heard a Greek trans woman in a documentary say, 'If you don't smoke your cigarette to the end, you don't know how to really live.' I KNOW HOW TO REALLY LIVE! I use my skin as a fire extinguisher. It barely stings. It delivers an ecstatic instant. I am in my own world. I attempt to draw a portrait of a feral cat with the glowing ember, right below the space where doctors inject vaccines. I fail miserably because I lack the talent to draw accurate portraits. My old tried & true tradition of wrist-slitting is being replaced with arm-burning. More bruises, less blood; still, a little trickle escapes the prison of my own skin, only to be killed instantly by coagulation. Are any of the drunkards noticing my actions? I DON'T CARE!!! As long as they leave me alone and keep their inebriated opinions to themselves, I DON'T CARE! I am in my own world. I am living one of my many moments of complete interior focus, where public becomes private. I am free and can't see you or anyone. You may see me, but your general consensus is look-at-those-wild-eyes-stay-out-of-her-way.

The fire has vanished. From the cigarette, not my innards. No, in order for that to be the case, my insides must first be burned to a crisp: allow me a few more shocks: that should do the trick. I find a trash can and rid myself of the remnants of this cancerous stick – if I were on a balcony seven stories high, I would revel in watching it fall before immediately regretting my littering deed, rushing down the stairs to retrieve-retrieve-retrieve! I look behind me for the first time. I have walked 700 meters straight. I remember the troubles that brought me here. Where is the boy? I cannot make out his silhouette. My eyes don't belong to an eagle, and my pathetic attempts at flirting have nothing to do with the precision of its claws. Imagination: You must make up for the lackings of my vision. I know! He is still standing in the same exact position. He is not allowed back into the club. I know! He is not sorry that I'm gone. He is awaiting his destiny. His destiny is completely separate from mine. I continue my walk in the opposite direction from his position. I pray I did not hurt his feelings with my curt emotions. His face remains expressionless. It refuses to give away any answers. I have left without saying goodbye. I am reading his mind. He does not like drama queens and rapid mood swings. He thinks I am crazy. He thinks I'm a pain in the ass. Oh, why can I never manage to be one of those non-threatening lite-feminist simple-girls?! Instead: Emotional Vagina Dentata, it would take a superhero, Catwoman, to not find me impossible! I go from independent-witty-manic pixie with a hint of the-sexy-kind-of-darkness to voilà: FULL-FLEDGED HYSTERIA – ejaculations of tears, feminine sperm, in only a matter of minutes. Now, *everything* hurts me. BUT IT'S NOT FAIR THAT THE MORE HORRIFIC SHIT YOU'VE LIVED THROUGH

THE LESS PEOPLE WILL WANT TO HOLD YOU! *ElioElio-Elio-OliverOliverOliver-Yuzuru&Javier-Dalida&Luigi.* I am inhaling the life that always brings you to higher spheres, but often leaves you there with nothing. Yes, the girls who take magic and run with it must be punished... My complexion is gaunt, nearly cadaverous. I am the trembling body of a nervous rat. I shall survive off scraps flung towards me. I will outlive all the flingers. I no longer have any interest in going to dance floors to pretend to be happy. The ocean would rather drown us than be a stage for dancing. I look across it and behold: the sunrise has reached peak beauty! My mother told me she never saw a sunrise, but many sunsets. Given her years of recurrent insomnia, I don't get how this is possible. I am interested in once again singing my favourite songs for the dawn with my sobs serving as instrumental interludes. I wish I could begin every night and end each morning with the cold caresses of this specific ocean's water covering my face – that this now-instant could become a forever. I am in the rooms of the beyond happy. I am Clarice Lispector barking at god: Oh to hell with it all, there is something terribly wrong with the comfortably successful! I am the woman who wore a gigantic poofy ballroom gown to a casual party in order to impress a man. Needless to say, she succeeded to fail.

'How's your life with an ordinary woman,
without the god inside her?
… Now you're grown cold to magic, how's it going
with an earthly woman, with no sixth sense?
… How is it, living with a postcard?
You who stood on Sinai.'

—

'What shall I do, singer and first-born,
in a world where the deepest black is grey and
inspiration is kept in a thermos? With all this
immensity in a measured world?'

MARINA TSVETAEVA

5 —

Hello from the other side *(Other side!)*,

Due to an intermediate hangover, the full orchestra playing in my brain has seen a reduction in its numbers. *30-year crisis. Budget crisis. Budget chaos.* Chamber music replaces my mind. My now is thankful that I didn't order more drinks. It would've made me feel very vomity, totally maimed and incapacitated. Instead I find myself rising from bed at 1 p.m. The air is stuffy. I open the window and greet the Earth's yellow fireball patron way up in the cloudless sky. I ask her: *Who's afraid of the big bad emotional vagina dentata – all men or 97.7 percent of them?* She responds: *I share your heat, so don't ask me, ask your planet's inhabitants!* Two huge houses pigheadedly block any conversation or view of Reykjavik's surroundings. I police myself with a cross-examination regarding last night's fiasco. My exit was swift, efficient. I have no means of contacting the boy. I was a bit drunk. Very good news, all of it. It reduces the risk of sustaining long-term brain damage from tormented hopeless devotion. The truth is, this moment is telling me it was an intense flash that needs no future in order to exist. Yes. I refuse to turn myself into the scapegoat of my own empty hands. I won't fantasize about shared moments filled to the brim with paragon pleasures flushed out by the agony of the misbegotten. I won't repeat this pattern for the 33rd time. I can forget him simply by refusing to give him a story. This works similarly to the way you wake up confused and shaken after a dream. It may spill into your day and affect it deeply. But it seldom remains for days on end. Unless of course the dream becomes recurring. But that, my darling, is another story altogether. On an average evening you'll begin to cook dinner and honestly recall none of yesterday's dreams, despite 'scientific evidence' proving that an average night's sleep contains 3 to 5 of them...

Reader, I have so little to give today. It is already 4:30. I sit and mope on the sofa. I'm too busy feeling sorry for myself to compulsively think of *him&himonly*. At least I have that going for me. I point my feet and stretch my legs towards the ceiling with an outward rotation. My mood is elevated by the elegance and elasticity of ballet. To be simple-minded is fine from time to time. Otherwise you'll soon burn out. My words are ashes of thoughtfeelings burnt beyond the bodies of different beings without connection to find symbiosis: *All...* Yes, as ashes we all look the same. At last, a rebellion against visual obsessions! Proof that I have felt love for this life that I've cursed and cursed. Tomorrow I shall venture into the Icelandic wilderness, the great outdoors, where the world shall draw into me without effort, kicking open a gate to the perfect environment to be alone with my thoughts. Dearest booklover, I know I've been treating you like my therapist. Our session is complete. You'll see. I'll provide you with ample evidence that I'm capable of shreds of happiness and positive thinking. *How dare I while the world is still so fucked up!* Don't worry, I'm not about to motivate major CEOs to push aside their guilty conscience and increase productivity by practicing mindfulness and meditation every morning like some Steve Jobs. But perhaps once I've convinced them to actually quit committing atrocities they could begin... I'm your writer and I must explore *each&every reality* in rigorous detail, trying with all my might to grasp the vital differences between judging and having an awake, critical mind. In less than 24 hours, I shall find myself on a guided tour of the waterfalls and glaciers and cliffs and *oh my lord*s surrounding the southernmost point of Iceland. And force *you* to come along. Look out! I may become exalted. I may act like an annoying child at the beach splashing about when you just entered the ocean for a tranquil swim on your first day off in ages. This is not some fluffy self-help rhetoric, as self-help guides teach you to have no expectations. And my expectations are sky-high. Yes. To be surrounded by striking nature is to be pure in whatever emotion you experience, which is a better way of defining joy. I have never stayed long enough to make any statement regarding whether or not my feelings would remain if I built a permanent home at the foot of a massive waterfall.

I investigate all the different south-coast tour offers and start a heated argument with my wallet. This wouldn't be necessary if I was with Ronaldo The Rich Crybaby. I settle for a mid-priced tour called 'The Beautiful South Coast', just in case the others were to focus on exploring the ugly south coast, although the ugly south coast also sounds rather interesting. No. It might mean studying discarded plastic bags and soda cans at windy, desolate highway gas stations. So, 'The Beautiful South Coast'-trip it is. It begins at 8 a.m. Ick! When an odious alarm hollers at 7:15, my body has never succeeded in feeling anything but *Leave Me The Fuck Alone Before I Strangle You Herr Clock*, no matter how excited I was for today to arrive.

I decide to give yesterday's drama a purpose and allow its depletion to help me fall asleep. 1, 2, 3... I count the sheep. There are over a million on this island. I zoom in on the black sheep. They are few and far between. I count only 37 before I slip into that other reality, where it is always enough to do nothing, and I am freed from the wearying duty of being my own shepherd.

6
A Hot Ice Land is its Own Romance

8:19 a.m. A minibus screeches to a halt two feet from my face. A door opens. 'Don't look so stressed! The sun won't be going down for another 14 hours and 22 minutes, so we've got plenty of time.' The assertion is delivered in an endearing Icelandic accent, sprouting from a tiny woman with short red hair, warm red clothes and square green spectacles. Drivers are to vehicles what the Wizard was to Oz. Once placed face-to-face with them, they're not as impressive or frightening as they were when you were nearly run over. Our bus-driving tour guide looks like a cuter version of the Grinch, though I suspect she's never stolen Christmas. I estimate her to be 61 years of age. I could be wrong. I don't care. I don't care that she arrived 19 minutes late or whose fault it was – the passengers', the company's, the traffic, the roads, the cracks in the glaciers? They have all been instantaneously forgiven. 19 minutes late? That's my average we're talking about. Today, I skipped my meal, makeup & hairstyling and still arrived panting, 4 minutes past scheduled departure. I have the good fortune of being saved by other people failing more than me. It's rare. And I feel such peace, love and understanding at this moment. Skogafoss, the first stop on today's breaking apart of ordinary life, lies 2 hours into the horizon. Will I sleep in the meantime? What if I miss an important view of a natural wonder from the window? The return trip follows the same route. I won't be missing anything. I can rest easy without a guilty conscience. I set my alarm for 9:55 and sink into my seat.

When I rouse at 9:53, we pass by the town of Selfoss, population: 6,512. I glance out the window. What I see registers inside my mind and creates a life of its own there. I see stone mounds near the top of a hill and believe that fabled Icelandic trolls must have carried them up to the summit. The humans wandering on the sidewalk have no idea I'm studying their every move. It is an unseemly habit of mine. Like that time at the library in Berlin when I did not dare strike up a conversation with the auburn-haired, arch-eyebrowed, mismatched-clothed mathematician whose peculiar mannerisms I'd been noticing for weeks without him noticing mine. One day while leaving, he threw away some papers in the trash can. My curiosity felt an urgent need to learn new answers to the question *Who Is He?* As soon as he vanished from sight, I hoped no one would notice how I followed in tow to retrieve what he discarded. I bent my knees, discreet-discreet, keeping my arms parallel to my body. I clasped the paper in the bin as if my hand was a paperclip. Success! No one in the library saw my deed. Or were they just pretending to be busy reading their books and typing on their lapdogs, while actually taking notes to relay the situation play-by-play to The Mathematician the very next day? My face turned red even though I wasn't caught red-handed. What was revealed on his papers? A whole new world: several lengthy mathematic formulas scrawled in multiple directions and an A4 paper in German with echoing poetry that did not resemble the 'redrum' repetitions from *The Shining*. No, there were zero signs of frightening aggression, but 33 signs of naive romantic passions and cryptic idiosyncrasies. I don't know if I'll ever find a group I belong to which feels like 'my people', but if I do it'll be more important that they are freaks than queers. And while bisexuality and heterosexuality provide my only chances to gain his affection, my deed taught me nothing of his sexual orientation; however, it handed over ample evidence that he's on the same side of strange as me.

(Later that evening I purposefully burned my bare legs on nettles. I fall in love with everyone only when I actually love no one. I hope to see him again when I return to Berlin. I have no idea what my next step should be. If one even exists?)

Meanwhile, in Iceland, our tour guide launches into a comedy routine for her 12 passengers. We pass by an airport: 'There's a landing strip. Some people are even using it! Speaking of flying, my favourite bird is the Arctic tern. Hopefully we'll be seeing some later today. They migrate all the way down to Antarctica each year, and during the course of their lifetime they will have travelled to the moon and back 5 times.'

I am impressed by this bird. Actually, I'm more than impressed. I am enthralled and beguiled! I know so many difficult words. What good does it do me? I wonder if an Arctic tern would shit on me like that malicious seagull did the other day, if the fact that my mathematician has much friendlier eyes than the guy at the club means he's a better person? I want to let our tour guide know that her sense of humour is providing me with more happiness than all of my one-night stands combined. No. That would create an awkward situation. Instead I'll convey secret messages to you, my dear reader, so you'll know criteria bores me, and laughter is never my top priority.

The condition of the road is good. This highway could take us around the whole island. We are turning to the left, heading off-highway, driving on a dirt road, abiding the law by wearing our seatbelts. The bus shakes like airplane turbulence, but I'm not afraid as we're not 10,000 feet above ground. I understand that our detour is a clue: Just around the bend a something special shall appear. Our tour guide shouts: 'We're near.' And as we turn another corner, there it is, surrounded by green meadows and mountains: *Skogafoss*. Virtually all waterfalls look like veils in paradise, but no whales have ever swum up one. At least not as far as I know; Google cannot provide the answer because whales have been around 28–33 million years longer than the internet. The bus stops at a parking lot. I run out the door to greet the crashing sound of falling water with devotion. I comprehend, but do not understand, how someone once surveyed a waterfall and immediately said to himself: 'That must be able to produce electricity.' I feel its energy pound through my entire body, making me leap and clap my hands. I grasp an essential difference between poets and engineers. The former poses the question *What For?* while the latter asks *For What?* Their jobs must be conducted with the utmost of care: One risks exploiting our resources, the other our souls.

I reach into the river to collect pebbles for a shrine in my room. Rocks, novels and wilted flowers can transform my home into a place where my heart is. A plastic bag from a grocery store is being put to work, storing stones; as long as I'm living it'll never become litter. I begin to run up the short trail to the top of the waterfall. People in the way impede my pace. I mustn't get impatient with anyone who's old and slow. Soon I too will be old and slow. And at the point of death: *Standstill? Same nothingness for us all?* I cannot hear myself talk to myself since the lightning bolts of water are roaring louder than thunder. I try to assess how tall Skogafoss is. It would be an easier task for my mind to handle if I climbed straight up the cliff face, but I lack that physical strength. My rough estimate is 160 feet. Perhaps the exact information can be found on some www-dot, but I am freed from Wi-Fi connection for another 8 hours. Yes, I suppose writing always entails the possibility of taking notes that you'll later enter into that google thing that in fact systematically searches you... Ugh, this thought turns my mood towards darkness. I cling to my feminine emotional intensity, as it may be the sincerest form of resistance to our cold, digital world of apps, facts & fake facts. I can't fit into a system where people send more messages than ever, and must insist on the depth of length instead of all the 'hey, what's ups?' on WhatsApp.

The sun has emerged from the fog and from the top of Skogafoss a new light spreads across the entire terrain. Two feet away the river blindly bounds over the precipice without fearing the drop-off. No, water doesn't feel such things as fear or panic, but undoubtedly these are the names of the final emotions experienced by most humans throughout history who've found themselves caught in that current, coldly sweeping them towards a fatal plunge. Yes, every position between the here-at-the-top and the there-at-the-bottom is a rapid journey to casualty. I won't be traveling down this road. I am enjoying my view, its green&green stretches for miles&miles all the way till it embraces the big blue&blue as the river carves a path through the centre with a tint that resembles the eye colour of a Siamese cat. But the colours I see are only reflections of what these entities reject. Within, they're actually every shade that I can't perceive. I thank the bursts of wind for irregularly tossing water splashes out from the cascade. Without them the symmetry of the waterfall would be as frightening as delicately holding a white rose without thorns. Several rainbows reside inside the mist. They astound me. I am speaking in hyperbole, but not in the US American way, where everything from sweatshirts to salad dressings to hairstyles are AMAAAZING. I am reminded of the danger of being transfixed by beauty and the cheapness of my efforts to lock it up inside a poem or a novel. I do it because of a wish: to convey a splendour that hopes for a life outside of me, hindering me from submerging myself in the body of water that lies at my feet, forbidding me from joining the ranks of those who plunged to a bone-crushing death. Oh *death*, you vulgar word for the unknown. I must reach the bottom via slower methods. I will be safer there. And the monster within, which forever pushes me to jump, shall be silenced for once, though not for all.

My favourite games to play are the ones where I'm the only contestant. That way I get to experience the feelings of both the winner and the loser, without having to feel envy for the winner or pity for the loser. The game I'm about to play with myself is called *get wet from the mist without becoming an outright swimmer!* Don't fret, I have won the race to the bottom and am now out of danger. By the foot of the waterfall, I enter the fog. I am physically experiencing nature on my body in order to merge with it. The sensation of millions of ice-dancing ants crawl all over my body. Water, why is a woman like me never granted permission to land? At times I wish to quit rowing upstream and allow myself to just fall. I take another three steps forward to a point where I can nearly reach out and touch the plunging cataract. *Crash-crash-crash,* it says in the pitch of shattering glass. I dare go no closer to its neck-breaking force. I am dealing with a roaring lioness on a daily basis. I stretch in a direction where I can cup my hands and fill them with more placid liquid. I take a gulp from the stream. Satiating my skin and throat in an immersion with these intense elements eradicates the forced barrier between my body and its surroundings that life has placed upon my soul. Just for an instant I stop thinking. I allow this moment to go on for a sustained flash that cannot be measured in time. Then, I back away slowly and return myself to a human form… A So Long Farewell.

Time is running out, and yes, in a mere 10 minutes we must get back on the bus to our next destination. I step out of the thickest mist. I can once again see the waterfall in its entirety. It evokes a memory, three years back, by the Narvik fjord in Norway. Ceaseless clouds cockblocking the midnight sun. I was Maleficent, Queen of the Moors, trekking up mountains and down hills. Hating myself. Loving myself. Speaking to no one for 4 days and wailing at unreachable eagles perched at the summits of jaw-dropping cliffs. I hiked far uphill into the forest until I reached a stone mound in front of a waterfall. I observed without drawing any conclusions. And there, I kneeled, and began to shiver again and miss my ex-lover for the first time in over a year. My mind was a peaceful disorder. I closed my eyes and, like magic, the waterfall transformed into his naked body. I pulled down my skirt, opened my mouth, and felt his dick growing hard inside it. An ignited inner fire increased the outside temperature by 15 degrees… *Needle-like nails nimbly erecting hairs across torso, wet throat tightly vibrating around dick, the pulsations of his gasps, moans, thrusts, musical notes, fingertips grazing eyelashes, collecting rare tears of bliss. I open my gaze to the outside world. He is no longer standing before me. I am sucking off the waterfall now. Working us up to a climax, unlike 4th of July fireworks, volcanic lightning bolts slicing through an iceberg of oceanic solitude, shaking my knees, cramping my hands, syncopating my mind, leave-taking my full body in convulsions upon dew-covered grass. The water meets the lava, shaping it back into a solid form.*

Reader, look at me, right here, right now: as wet inside as out. I cannot relive my Norwegian experience at the foot of Iceland's Skogafoss. There are too many people around, none of which are The Right One. And it is not possible to relive or redo anything anywhere other than in your mind's eye, which in turn, like the eye of a storm, tends to see things in a shifted form. The man I met two days ago never held me. His traces are all immaterial. My only ex-boyfriend is long gone forever. We broke up after just six months due to personal differences. *No.* Those are judicial terms from a press release. How can I explain? His name was Kay. He meant nearly everything to me, and I meant close to nothing to him, for I am a life of isolation and he is a someone who connect-collects existence through a string of love affairs. But I know there was a love there, as he existed on his own and inside me simultaneously. I touched his hand. It was *a pure joy*, a sense that existence doesn't always have to hurt so much. And I was not thinking of conclusions.

(Why must men fall apart when falling for us? Why can't we be granted equal access to the number of reasons why relationships end instead of having 90 percent of them end due to social stigma? As they fight tooth and nail to reduce love to anecdotes, our curse: breaking fully free only to find ourselves paired with the most unfree people in this world.)

Reader, please follow me, I am down on my knees begging for you to follow me. I apologize for my sidetracking of the story again, but only hurricanes storm louder than my innermost thoughtfeelings. Oftentimes when I see all that's going on around me, a violent reverberation occurs inside my heart-brain-body. *Everything* must change. *Everything* is the name I must listen to. **<u>I am overwhelmed.</u>** Is this the story I am trying to tell? I don't know. I just continue. I try to bestow equal amounts of honour upon everything that takes place. And you, you are overhearing me talking to myself. Suddenly, I begin to sing Regina Spektor's arrangement of a Boris Pasternak poem in Russian. *A thousand blackbirds, ripped awry from trees to puddles, knocking dry grief into the deep end of the eye.*

I hop on re-al-i-ty: *Goodbye, dear Skogafoss.* I am back on the tour bus. I push myself to photograph that which I just saw. I have no camera, iPhone, or smart-anything: not practical, not well prepared. I get off the bus with my startled lapdog wheezing in tow. I open its screen. I am planning for the future instead of living in the moment. I have not taken any photos since I was 9. That year, a summer camp leader at Point Reyes National Seashore taught me a new way of connecting to my surroundings. 'Take pictures with your heart instead,' she said, as I cried over spilt milk and complained about running out of film... Shortly after, in a pile of autumn leaves, I wrote my first serious lines, as I knew I had to find out all the *whys* behind, and leave the pictures that could only *present*. Iceland, your beauty is manipulating me into breaking a 20-year pact. I aim my lapdog in the direction of the waterfall. I take four photos. Three good pictures and one spectacular image featuring a photobombing moth whom I hardly even noticed fluttering by. She closed her Bible-paper-thin wings at the perfect distance from the lens in order to resemble Half Dome in Yosemite National Park. Now she's flown off, heading back to the Stade de France or my den in Berlin. I decode a message left in her wake: *Alvina, good job breaking that pact, today's the day you shall start trusting your ability to leave one extreme without speeding straight to the other.* To take only 20 photos per year: It is a protest that has been liberated from dogma.

Now our tour guide starts the bus engine, and we leave the parking lot for the next destination. Reader, I am at the edge of my seat; I am about to meet my first glacier! A far bigger event than the losing of my virginity, for yes, Sólheimajökull sounds like the salient name of a someone to love. Our treasured tour guide informs us that if the Katla volcano underneath Sólheimajökull were to erupt, the glacial flow would form into a river more voluminous than the mouth of the Amazon, and Mr. Climate Change could cause landslides that trigger city-sinking tsunamis! She seems to know everything. She's our tour guide. She simply does her job and does it well. I am preparing myself for the act of shaking hands with Sólheimajökull, 36.8 degrees °C greeting freezing, as the bus drives through a landscape of lush hills filled with grass and sheep who won't become meat-market fashion victims if I have a say in the matter, which I don't. Our tour guide tells us of the half-mile bridge over a no-longer-existing river, which disappeared due to the decreasing size of Vatnajökull, Iceland's largest glacier. **It makes us look like a bunch of lunatics who build bridges over nothing. Without *ice*, Iceland will be just *land*,** she explains in another memorable quote that is too important to put in quotation marks so I put it in bold. And now the bus steers onto another bumpy dirt road...

There are no signs of glistening white blocks of ice sparkling in the sunlight. Instead, great, big, dusty, black pillars ascend seemingly out of nowhere from a mile-long barren landscape. There are times when reality pops up like something out of a big-budget, action-adventure feature film. This is a horrendous beauty; it overwhelms my response systems. Our tour guide speaks: 'The ice monster you see here in front of you is up to 700 meters thick at her summit. And you might be wondering about her dark colour? It consists of a thin layer of ash from the Eyjafjallajökull eruption 6 years back. At the turn of the millennium, this parking lot was situated at the very edge of the glacier. Now, you see, we've got to hike one full mile through a desert; fine, it's good exercise, but the melting spells bad news for *all of us*. It has very little in common with the melting Wicked Witch of the West at the end of *The Wizard of Oz*, except for that both the glacier and the witch scream, "You curs-ed brat, look at what you've done, I'm melting, melting, oh what a world, what a world."'

The tour guide herds us off the bus. It's time for her daily power walking routine. Whether I like it or not, I am forced to follow her workout pace. The alternative: to be abandoned in this sterile landscape left in the wake of the treasure chest of a melting glacier. It is beyond desert-like. There are no cactuses blooming. There is not a single trace of a shrub or a reed. There are only about ten blades of grass growing within sight.

Regina Spektor says: 'All the poets in the alley coughing up blood and their visions and their dreams are coming up red, they can either wake up or go deeper, but it's so dangerous to wake a deep sleeper.'

After 12 minutes of near-running, our group reaches the threshold of this gargantuan, black-ash-covered ice mass. Intimidation and anticipation shake my body from its core to its borders. The surrounding soundscape lets out a whisper: *trickle-trickle-trickle.* Every 11 minutes you can hear the crash of tiny breakdowns from within the frozen fortress. I imagine the booming sound of a gigantic collapse, which must occur from time to time. A stream of water seems to be coming out of nowhere, but one does not have to be a genius to understand that *the somewhere* is melting ice. In some parts of the world a stream can also flow out of rocks or firm soil, reminding us that we have no idea what is going on just feet below us. Right in front of me, a tiny patch of bare glacier reveals a structure clear as a mountain lake. I brush my hands against its subzero stone body, caressing my new giant friend. I must feel each specific element against my bare skin. I gather volcanic-ash deposits from Eyjafjallajökull and rub them on my face. I kneel down to rinse everything off with a shock of freshly melted glacial water. This must be the ultimate face-exfoliating spa treatment. It could not be recreated in exactitude by any spa in our world.

I rest my cheek against the ice giant and begin to weep for her mile-long retreat. My saltwater tears join forces with her meltwater dittos, lamenting as they bid farewell to their respective sanctuaries. At this rate the entire glacier could be gone within 50 years. I realize human sadness is nothing in comparison. Have you listened to the sound planet Earth voices out into space? *Yes? No?* No human being can run the 1.8 kilometres between Sólheimajökull year 2000 and Sólheimajökull 2018 at full speed. I don't think you'll find a clearer moral of the story even by turning over each and every rock in your path, some of which will end up in my plastic bag destined for a big city life in Berlin. All around me the muddy soil is littered with puddles unlikely to return to their preferred state of ice for millions of years. This rapid melting is not the act of a witch or the Katla volcano with her immense surprises. Humans can't even predict volcanic eruptions. They're too busy bringing about their own disasters and dreaming American dreams. What can you expect when a whole nation, a superpower, is built upon the principle that not being a millionaire is just a temporary circumstance, an embarrassment soon to be overcome by hard work. I am ashamed – ashamed that we are letting our dreams be used as mechanisms of control, instead of profound freedom.

(Reader, can literature prevent the murder of nature or just disturb a too comfortable person? I'm typing these desperate words into my lapdog keyboard the way one plays my most beloved instrument, the piano. Despite my efforts, the sound that comes out is less like a musical sonata and more like the pitter-patter of rain. What a

lacking instrument, these words. Yet they are amongst the strongest tools gifted to us. Some words are secret soulstorms birthed deep inside a me-you-us, longing to be liberated from the prison of one body. If kept from ourselves or stored in the form of too-many-broken-promises, some words can cement us all into statues.)

I advance a few steps away from the dirt and begin to hike up the glacial icecap. Our tour guide hollers: 'Stop dead in your tracks, Missy, the ice monster will eat you if you treat her like a walk in the park!' I obey. I am in a situation where the sturdy voice of knowledge is to be trusted more than my inner adventurer. It is dangerous to stride any further lest one should slip and fall between the cracks. My body would be very well preserved there, freezing with no shivers; however, I'd risk providing the agents of global warming with an argument for their misdeeds. I can already hear them saying, with a Texan accent of course:

'In order to fetch this here body of an Uh-Mer-Ican, we must melt this here whole chunk-o'-ice.'

No. This isn't true. I'm no president. I'm far from that (in)significant. I can die in peace here if I want to. If you can have a smile on your face while imagining your own dead body, something good has happened in terms of separating yourself from your ego. Death is one of many ways for the Earth to remind us: *You don't own me.*

I wobble down from the ice slope without falling on my butt. Or flat on my face. This can't stop new teardrops from forming inside my corneas. They know very well they won't be granted access as members of the UN Security Council or deemed acceptable in government cabinets or boardrooms. However, is there any better way of reminding the powers that be of the dangers of overflowing water sources than storming their meetings with a choir of sobbing faces? I am hopelessly naive. I am hopelessly naive because I am desperately searching for a plan that could work. And in this search I must try each and every thing that has never been attempted before, until I find something that does the trick. I do not try on tears like one tries on clothes.

The last century was a psychopath. This one is still a teenager. In the city I'm forced to be an object, and my rebellion: a flood of tears. I am: a crying object; crying, screaming to survive her own life. Bloodied by their belief that we do not share the trait of breathing in oxygen and breathing out carbon dioxide. In nature I become a mother. If I watch a flower for a full day, I can follow its cycle rhyming in tune with the sun, while gaining the trust of bees. A water lily in the Amazon lives for only 48 hours. She changes colour from eye-white on day one to violet-pink on day two, and her gigantic leaves can carry the weight of a light adult like me.

I am sorry reader, when describing an island filled with both fire and ice, I simply must expand the storyline from chamber music to a full orchestra. An island can do much more than just carry its own weight: My words expect the same from their readers, my world craves the same from its humans. I am not the author of a scenic brochure. I have greater ambitions than boosting tourism. Nevertheless, one must always return from the retreat of a fantasy back into the material world that surrounds us. My return is brought about by the arrival of a hailstorm. I cannot see the rainbow behind the rainbow as my visual sense is observing the formation of dancing ice bulbs swaying to the music of wind gusts, sometimes following one direction, other times crashing against each other like they're in a mosh pit. Thankfully we have now left the glacier behind us and are sheltered by the bus. I am hoping these seeds of ice are a premonition: a sign that a god, a president, or a fool on the hill has listened to my desperate pleas and cries and calls.

There is only one stop left on this journey: the black-lava sandy beach of Reynisfjara. Our tour guide puts the windscreen wipers on full blast. I think about how The Windscreen Wipers sounds more like a rock 'n' roll band from the early 1960s than a device attached to a motor vehicle. I remember that Icelandic weather often shifts every 15 minutes, like the temperament of someone who has a lot to prove. And sure enough, as soon as the ocean appears within our view, the storm blows over and the sun turns herself into a caricature, a smiling talking emoji chirping, 'Hello, hello.' One day that same grinning sun may die and drag us all down with her. However, more immediate threats have been brought to you by the sponsors of politicians with campaign strategies full of memes and GIFs and reality-TV scripts. Always spying on the people, calling that *listening*, always ready to serve double faults, calling that *serving our best interests...*

Swelling ocean waves are creating rhythmic hammer blows that crash into beaming ink-black sand – they differ from accurately reflecting intense life only because of their regularity. Besides, an intense life is not defined by the outward size of explosions. The bus has dropped us off by the beach. I rush to the shoreline, squealing, jumping, rubbing my hands together in a reverie of electric elation, wading no deeper than inches above my ankles. The riptide is strong enough to tear off my legs at the knees! I dash 50 meters away from the water to the base of a 100-foot cliff that resembles numerous Roman columns glued together. I scratch one of them with my nails to participate in its age-old carving and commemorate my 7 times dying by jumping before knowing if he'd catch me. I find a crevice that tempts me to crawl in and stay forever. A cave at a black beach. Like Frida Kahlo, I want to be inside your darkest everything! Mrs. A. No-Wind & Mrs. A. Panoramic-View-Of-The-Ocean warmly state: *Welcome home!* I wonder if I am permanently fixated on details that escape most people. If I became a fossil inside this cave, I would be at peace. From here the sea appears to be lifting the cloudless sky. And its surface glistens with a magnitude that would make pure gold blush. I have everything my eyes need. Leaning into a crevice has become my default position. The sharp rocks of the cave walls massage my back. I am engrained in the humility of the southernmost tip of a tiny island, enwreathed by an unruly deep blue that drowns all hubris into polyphonous silence.

The last time I felt this at ease was in February, when Alma-Rapha kissed me for one full hour. Alma-Rapha? Yes, dear reader, that's correct, I haven't mentioned him yet. He is the boy with the Nijinsky spark in his eyes and Kahloesque paintings who brought me the closest I've been to love all year.

Facebook told me that today is his birthday! I must take some more photos with my lapdog to send to him With Love From The Black-Sand Beach Of Iceland ❤. No, after our kiss I sent him a loving, poetic message. He didn't reply. I sent him another. He hid his heart behind a no-word-wall. I can't send him a third. He doesn't care how much we have in common (introspection, sensitivity, love of Harvey-Björk-Galás). Damnit! My emotions have been stirred away from tranquillity. My body wishes to jump up and rush straight into the cold ocean and be washed away by its waves, then drowned in its rough undercurrents so I can end my life now, just get it over and done with: At last, dead forever!

'*I swore on your eyes that I considered a gospel, to turn your stab into laughter – I'm burning, I'm burning, throw some more oil on the fire. I'm drowning, I'm drowning, cast me in the deepest sea.*'

I stay put in my hiding place from extremes. For at the same time as I was thinking these thoughts, a third part of me started the process of building a new world. Our snug little grotto is the church of a secret, not-yet-known religion, a temple that comes with a risk – there's a danger, a danger of stones falling from the roof! Yes, I know that both male lovers and religions have shackled and killed countless women. My secret-not-yet-known religion decides not to write a bible or any other doctrine so we may keep people out of harm's way for a few thousand years, knowing that all we know is that we don't know.

As for a man to have and to hold – if he ever dares display his heart to wild cavewoman me, Nina Simone and Chet Baker shall serenade us with outsider psalms, and I will wed and bed him right here inside my tiny church cavern ♥. And he may not be Alma-Rapha, *he* may be an even more special Rafa, a Rafa with as many on court OCD rituals (e.g. pedantically placed bottles, no stepping on lines, never squashing moths – that's love, not OCD) as Grand Slam titles (19!). Oh, Alma-Rapha would be SO jealous if he ever saw me sitting in front of the TV watching a glittery, neon-pink-clad Nadal hit another inside-out forehand winner, making it *Game-Set-&-Match*! I could fix this very easily, simply by going 'Live' on Facebook. No. I refuse to stoop that low. I abhor that narcissistic application. I shall deactivate the whole Facebook instead! And then, as in reality *I'm tranny not the kind of girl you marry*, please spread my ashes on this coal-black shore where they can fuse with their true element: the residue from a volcanic eruption.

My dear reader, I hope you enjoyed the Rafa Nadal anecdotes. I realize my recurrent musings on the topic of death must be more concerning, so please, allow me to expound: I did not come to this island to meet anyone, neither did I come here for the victory, surrender and defeat to at least be buried or burned in a woman's body. Aside from being an endangered species hunted to near extinction, one third of my kind have tried to off our own heads. My case is not unique. I have a long list of reasons. I have a Clarice who convinced me of the awful responsibility to last it out until the very end and attempt to breathe each breath I can, slowly, quickly, deeply, even if I at times must hold it for 33, 66, or 88 seconds to feel able to survive.

Yes, I believe I shall allow death to seize me by surprise instead. I must hurry back to the bus. I don't want to be late. I don't want our tour guide to worry that I've become a big wave's takeaway dinner. I don't want to cause such distress. What time is it? FUCK-SHIT-FUCK!! I LEFT MY DUMBPHONE CLOCK ON THE BUS!!! I CAN'T SEE ANY OTHER PASSENGERS! THE BUS MUST'VE LEFT WITHOUT ME! Oh me, oh my – so long, dear den, chasm, cavern, grotto, cave, cabinet, crevice, lair! I AM NOT READY TO LEAVE, I DON'T EVER WANT TO LEAVE!!!! WHY WON'T ANYBODY *EVER* LISTEN TO *MY* NEEDS???? CLIFF FACE, SAY SOMETHING, DO SOMETHING!!! (*Cliff face says nothing, does nothing.*) My hot temper is working itself up again. It is its own romance. My drama forms into a swift sprint across the beach, throwing a tantrum at the affront the traitorous headwind is causing me. I fling handfuls of black sand at it to exact revenge. It all blows straight in my eyes. *Stop laughing at me, wind! Damn you, I don't have time for your shenanigans! My tears are merely a physical reaction. I'm not having a complete nervous breakdown! Wind! I don't enjoy combatting your 25-mph speed. I don't enjoy pushing against your force. You are stressing me out. If I miss the bus, it'll be all your fault!* I reek of panic. My mouth tastes of blood. Through my dry windpipes, I detect the feeling of a burgeoning sore throat. My health is deteriorating. I worry this time it'll prove deadly. Hypochondriac diagnonsense 1: *The first sign of HIV!* That virus no longer kills, and I haven't partaken in any activities that present plausible risks of infection... I better tell these things to my emotional response system; it's never a good listener. Diagnonsense 2 and 3: *Terminal cancer! RABIES!* They'd be certain assassins to do me in! I wonder if I will die with many regrets. I see the parking lot. I see it still contains the bus! A small triumph has been won by a failing body. I rush into our vehicle. I see my dumbphone.

I have arrived three minutes before scheduled departure. Phew! Saved by stress.

My plastic bag has enough time to gather a scoop of ebony sand and some volcanic stones; their total count is now 43. Will airport security give all of them boarding passes, or will they force me to leave 40 behind? My thoughts subside as the breakers crash-land onto the beach. Each wave is a life. And the foam: a corpse. It all reels back and becomes a part of the oceanic ultramarine. This is what death must be like. At the very least it is a thought that instils calm within my agonies. How do I know the human mind is terribly limited? Because we can't imagine infinity or a fixed beginning and a fixed end, or even consciousness without a body attached to it. I am tirelessly working to change all that. It would provide an immense relief. Our tour guide counts, 1, 2, 3, 12, 'Good, none of my newly hatched little ducklings have been drowned by some sneaky sleeper wave.' Then, we drive away, all in one piece or perhaps not.

The bus traverses through landscapes so plush they could render the entire beauty industry jobless. I am terrified by the guillotine I unleash upon these mountains, meadows and streams of tears each time I close my eyes. I am overloaded with an exhaustion that needs *nothing* to be cured: Take me home to no one. Luckily I only have to walk 35 more steps today. Total. Does this mean I won't be resolving my battle between naiveté and bitterness today? I suppose. Everything is going too fast. Next time I *must* take it slow. On the first date: hand-holding with eye contact. Second date: soft kisses only. Third date: intense make out-session, lips focused on tattoos, scars, burn marks, tears. Fourth date: sleep together naked without sex, wake up, lip touch, eye gaze for one hour. Fifth date: hug for ten minutes straight then let the lioness loose from her cage... The beauty of allowing oneself to take a step back, oh reader, the wildness inside my head was always more vital to me than the wildness experienced through actions! I'm lucky that way, but all my men have treated me as a zoo animal, forcing me to shrink my steps in order to fit into an enclosure. Tell me reader, why do they fear freedom? I am 28 days away from turning 30. At the age of 20 I never thought I'd live this long, but that was only because at 20 one is comforted by considering 10 years to be *A Forever*. This is no longer possible, although some days continue to feel like never-ending years spent in darkness. Don't worry. I have grown to realize that it's dark where it's deep, I've outgrown the goal of self-improvement and individual liberation. The buzzing bus transforms my body into a vibrating bumblebee. I listen to myself existing, affected by nothing but the threads gently lifting my lungs. This tranquillity is interrupted by an earthquake of shattering crystals within my veins. Going about in the world feeling too much is such an internal bleeding! I try to find my way back to peace of mind by getting lost in the lives of the other passengers. But alas, a mother has been annoyed by her two children since morning and is impatiently kicking the seat in front of her, waiting for today to come to an end, fraught by the fact that it shall be reborn again as soon as the birds start chirping bright and early. All three members of this family wear separate thorn crowns, leaving their bodies trembling with unspoken anxiety and claustrophobia. 20 years ago I too could not breathe within a plastic bag...

A cold sore starts growing inside my mouth because little miss Sore Throat demanded to have a cellmate inside her jail. I am getting lost in another mood-spell that renders the preceding moments useless and seemingly unattainable. I start thinking of the boy from the day before yesterday. I wonder, is he another person with experiences in the range of 75 percent to 25 percent, but no experience of 100 or 0?! I catch myself mid-sin. I vowed to banish him to a place called forgotten. I have broken a promise to myself. It is better to break promises to yourself than others. And whether the answer to my question is *yes* or *no* or *I don't know*, I can still feel relieved by the reality of a *too late now*. Meanwhile, I am playing another sonata on the grand piano of love affairs unable to come to fruition. It is the mute swan song of eggs being eaten by foxes, by snakes, by otters. It quivers with each and every up and down that never saw the light. Indeed, all my loves continue to live their own lives within the realms of my subconscious. From time to time they present themselves in my dreams, as a reminder that they're still alive and well. There are love affairs to be had with people. There are love affairs to be had with cities. There are love affairs to be had with nature. Nature has never told me I'm too intense. Nature, I'm not glorifying you. It is impossible to exaggerate the truth. And the truth is. And the truths are, you bring me closer to solving the mystery of my chronics: anxieties, emptinesses, illnesses. I am not being overly dramatic. I must do whatever it takes to prevent my life from being dominated by awful social games like 'hanging out' in groups of people I've only ever hung out with in groups of people, therefore never getting near anyone's maskless existence. That would be the death of me. Save me, nature! Save me from a bad-natured fate named *A woman named Alvina killed by a woman named Alvina!*

My legs rest against the bus seat in front of them. Sometimes I feel as if my organs, especially those residing in between my legs, don't belong to me. Sometimes I wonder if something must belong to you in order to provide you with pleasure? My heart doesn't belong to me; it belongs to everything. If I let it go completely it may cause me less pain. My eyelids succumb to gravity, and I fail to take in the mossy landscapes I missed this morning. The tectonic plates of my inner core reach a standstill, which is necessary to avoid the stagnation of constant movement. Do any living beings other than humans experience impatience? Yes. *Cats.* True, I've seen that in action. However, the further question is if they have learned this behaviour due to their close proximity to humans?

I lean to the southeast, the direction of sleep; I am aware that I never snore, so I won't be disturbing anyone. Dearest Alvinitsa, I now grant you the permission to *Just Let Yourself Go.*

My dear reader,
We are both exhausted after this long day. Let's spend the evening apart. The bus just dropped me off safely at my bed & breakfast, and I used my last iota of energy to give my beloved tour guide a sentimental goodbye hug. I shed two tears and let her keep one. Now, I am stepping inside my room and can happily reveal that I don't care how I or anyone else looks. I'm too tired to experience vanity. Perhaps tonight's dreams can be an attempt to envision who I would be without mirrors.

My sore-throated, virus-wrestling body feels love for one thing and one thing only: the ideal environment for a deep sleep: a bed: an invention that hasn't changed much in the past thousand years.

(Another town, another bed, another time, 1995: housebound, backpained mom yells 'Tom!' Dad responds, 'Goddamnit,' quiet enough for everyone to hear, then upping his volume to 'Comiiing!' At the record player tonight, mama teaches us drama lessons. The time: 2 a.m. The song: Beethoven's 5th Symphony. The volume: Full on. The melody: Dun-dun-dun-duuuuun. She screams along, volcanic lightning bolts, aimed at father, ricochet onto earthquaked-awake me, 8 on the Richter scale, stress-sweat and piss in bed, slow down think of tiny snail, till the next dun-dun-dunduuuuun spears the snail from beneath the skin, leaks more pee. The first movement of Beethoven's 5th Symphony lasts 7 minutes. Mama's stamina lasts the same. She treads up the stairs, her footsteps feeling guilty, very guilty, there's no way they'll bring her body barging into a child's blue room to deliver her midnight shouting speech. She's done it 25 times before. She'll do it 25 more. But not tonight. Tonight is game over for the nuclear family nuclear war. Tomorrow mama's psychoanalyst says, 'Good for you, you needed to get that out of your system.' You can always count on your psychologist to be on your side, just like your family and friends, the bedbugs that bite in a bed never made by him or her or you. I believe the whole world's pain is on my shoulders. I am incorrect, but it does little to improve my situation. My knife-nails draw-blood from limp-wrists to pain-kill. The white sheep can't clear the high fence at 3 a.m. An overdressed black sheep dares to leave her hiding spot, makes her way to the high fence, clears it by three feet. The white sheep, former bullies, start a party in her honour. She can't enjoy it. 2018. I've forgiven everything, I've forgotten nothing, blame it on the past, don't regret the past, it made me what I am today, which is what? What can the past-tense explain about the present-day but... everything... that we already know... Today I laugh at all the camp elements of

'Mommie Dearest', daddy lives his life as a coward at half intensity, answering my coming out with the wall behind walls called no reply – every intense woman's skull-shattering Achilles heel – meanwhile an intricate love story between mom & spawn, I'd need a whole novel to tell you All About My Mother, the true artist, the freakish warrioress, the chocolate-box embraces, born on Duras' 33rd birthday. I colour-in her illustrations with a deluxe box of crayons; she's lived alone for over 15 years now, she walks up to a random ambulance and knocks on the front window. The driver rolls it down. She inquires: **Excuse me sir, can you tell me what happens when I die?** *He gapes at her, thinks:* **Who's this crazy lady, who does she think I am? God or a thanatologist?** *She reads his mind, clarifies:* **I mean, do you just let my body lie there rotting forever or do you kick down the door?**)

7

I wake up to a trapped existence inside a bubble called apocalypse, encircled by an unkindness of ravens, a murder of crows – clairvoyants. Slowly my bed & breakfast den's white walls emerge from darkness in a floater-eyed silence, tainted by the foul scent of a struggle between infection and antibodies. KNIVES STAB ME every time I dare to swallow. KNIVES STAB ME with no blood drawn. Dear Virus, there's no way I'll allow you to stay for a week just 'cause you barged in and trashed the honeymoon suite! My throat is not some fucking hotel! Unlike the heart with its ribcage-barbed-wire-fence, it is completely out in the open and susceptible to attackers. No wonder people wear scarves and turtlenecks.

Today goes by three names: No Rabid Mouth-Foaming, Still Getting Sicker and Time To Go Home. Thank god for the rare 9 p.m. checkout time at this bed & breakfast. Curse the devil that my red-eye flight isn't till 4:30 in the night of morning. How will I manage to stay intact till then? The clock strikes noon: I should try to get up now. It would do me good. *Oh, what good would it do?* I believe my depression is returning after a few days' vacation. I feel it deep in the centre of my stomach, where it always begins or ends up. Being depressed is like trying to chop a pineapple while using the surface of a lake as your cutting board. Not easy.

I wax neurotic over one life problem and then move on to another. Such are most of my mornings; this morning has decided to carry on the grand tradition. Meanwhile, my facial hair continues to grow by the second despite my constant hatred and condemning protests... Oh, I don't want to write anymore! These 3 hours a day spent in front of a keyboard, hoping I'm getting somewhere, growing tired before ever reaching any *there*, sapping all the energy out of the remaining 21 major *ticktocks* of the clock. For what? All my words fall off cliffs anyways, shattering too many conventions because they did not know what to promise, and failing to stir up revolutions from the bottom. Is this really the best I have to give to the world?

> *'Only the solitary seek the truth, and they break with all those who don't love it sufficiently.'*
> **BORIS PASTERNAK**

My electric shaver doesn't carry the fervour of a letter from Boris, but he still does his utmost to comfort me. He traces his edges across the stubborn stubble of my cheeks as I shout commands at every single hair follicle: *Lose your fighting spirit! Realize the futility of your actions!* Despite being lawnmowed obsessively on a daily basis, their motto remains: *Never give up.* A sorrow: I can't even affect the actions of my own body. Still, one last stroll into the city should be doable. I begin applying my armour named makeup so The People won't see me as an ugly failed tranny who's lost all control. A broken heart whimpers: *Please, let me be ugly & failed, please let me lose control...* An engorged oesophagus roars: *Cough-Cough-Cough-SpitPhlegm-Cough!* Indeed, the tranny has lost control over her body and fails to leave her room. She drinks cups of lemon tea: 1, 2, 3. She glances out the window: *Look a birch tree, look a honeybee!* She reads & writes, reads & writes & curses her bad fortune: Ugh, *if* I were outside, I could've run into Björk, praised her work, and hurled my book manuscript into her speechless arms like Violette Leduc once did to Simone de Beauvoir! It would have done me no good, she's no publisher, and my words would be burned or cast into a bottomless crater. (Or just the nearest wastebasket... Oy vey! Drama queen! – 'The opposite of love is not hate but indifference.')

    I wish I could transform into a flowing scarlet dress that breathes on its own and treats air with the same patience as a jellyfish treats water. This feeling preoccupies my mind with a distraction from loving the impossible. I think of my mother shouting: *You're spending your whole life wasting all your talents and callings!* Is my mother right? I don't know. Reader, I wonder if I'll rapidly wither if I'm ever given everything I want. Maybe I'm better off remaining inane as a wave far out at sea that keeps slamming up against itself. I know that being denied love can make you want to alter the ways of the world. I think of my library mathematician in Berlin; could he help me solve an equation: *How do you change the entire world when you can't even make it to work on time?*

    Saving the world certainly doesn't start with self-love or romantic love, but I'm still drawn to the passion of synergies. To fall in love with a plant is simple; it's a bit harder with domesticated animals, some more so than others; humans are nearly on the same level as wild animals, because they can't be tamed. Every time I fall in love with a man, I'm on the verge of committing myself to an insane asylum. I wonder: *Can visiting a dating site take me there?* Well, at least it'll interrupt this HBO Special 'Conversations with Myself' – so boring it could single-handedly make any TV channel go bankrupt (what potential!). Every journey off the beaten track begins with a sense of boredom or restlessness, desperation or adventure; and now, reader, all that lemon tea has invigorated me, certainly I can leave this house, make lemonade and meet someone special! So, let us now shift storylines to one much more exciting and action-packed, as I get down on my knees to pray: *May the shallow pool have a deep end with a hidden exit to the open ocean.* Yes, let's try to make this one of those movies with a rough beginning and a happy ending!

Plot: *Uncertain of her own destiny, a single woman experiencing a pathetic 30-year crisis sets off searching for a soulmate, but ends up spoon-fed with overdoses and chased by a swarm of horny bees.* Wait... that sounds like some action-adventure flick, and we were aiming for romance! Okay... Let's begin with a brief introduction of our protagonist: For over a decade, Alvina shunned the world of internet dating. She tried her luck at meeting men out in the wild, but since she is fully unable to play games, or play stupid, or play cool & casual, a string of disasters gouged her bowels. Andrei, Peder, Paulo, Robert, Shawn – she kissed them a few times then spent months crying over spilt milk and the lack of flying sperm. Oskar and Kay – one fucked her once, the other a few times more, before running fast as they could, with feet touching their backs, howling, 'IT'S NOW FORBIDDEN TO BURN THE EMOTIONAL VAGINA DENTATA AT THE STAKE, BUT WE CAN STILL GHOST HER!' as she sent a search party of 20 desperate text messages that could've been

200 to zero replies. 7 men, 7 failures: *The truth can lie in numbers.* Will her luck change? After 10 years of half-love affairs she decides to try that luck on a dating site:

She crafts an intelligent profile, but her brain scares men by the dozens and has won over exactly none. Luckily her beauty lures many more, and her six pictures quickly provide a promising date. A match made in heaven: 2 bodies considered perfect according to modern beauty standards for the respective genders. *He* is 28, lifts weights obsessively and consumes jars of protein powder. *She* is 29, does water ballet and used to have an eating disorder. *They* arrange to meet at a bar in Berlin. She's 15 minutes late. The bar looks like a dusty antique shop. No one under the age of 48 is in sight. She searches behind a life-sized portrait painting and a Titanic-style chandelier, but he's nowhere to be found. She discerns: *He must've stormed out without even giving me the chance to sing my theme song – 'I'm always here when you call, but I'm never on time.'* She calls her date. A phone rings. It belongs to a 73-year-old man who's been looking her up & down since she arrived, as if his pupils could produce masturbatory strokes. The phone rings and rings. His eyes stop jerking off; they dart about till they pull his full body out the door. Our protagonist collapses to the floor and cries. Slapstick. 73-year-olds know their way around the internet better than her. Curtain call. The audience somersaults with laughter.

Onwards and forwards, to the present day, in first person:

Dear viewer,
I've had a dating site account for months now, and despite receiving thousands of messages, I've yet to exceed a few meet

& greets. My experiences would be enough for most romantic selves to suicide and surrender to the dictatorship of Perpetual Bad Luck, but 16 new messages here in Reykjavik are making me contemplate a voyage beyond my Observer status. Dick pics start prancing into my inbox, like dead rats 'gifted' by cats to their owners. If this were a video game, they'd equal Game Over; but what happens on the internet lies somewhere between a video game and reality, so the rules are blurred. I am unsure. All I know is that I don't give a shit about the size of phalluses, as no dick could be harder than my life or larger than the hurdles I've had to overcome. Still, there may be 200 frogs, but also one prince behind these dick pics. *18 new messages! 19, 20!* The hunters are trying to pick up my scent through the screen. They are intent on transforming my romcom fantasy into the only genre where *we* make big bucks in starring roles: Porn. They raise hard, deep questions:

- 'U still got a dick? Is it big?'
- 'Are you a trans? Cuz if you're not you're very hot!'
- 'Hey sexy, got any XXX pics, ass & tits?'
- 'Let's fuck! My cock's 9.5 inches and I've got the stamina to pound your ass for hours!' (He sends a picture of his erect penis next to a yardstick. He didn't embellish, it's precisely 9.5 inches!)

I'm like: 'Hours spent getting fucked by a 9.5-inch dick? That sounds like a nightmare of soreness with possible multiple haemorrhoids on top!'

Both he and Mr 'are you a trans' block me 9.5 seconds later.

Like most men writing to me, Open-minded123 has no profile pics. But at least he sends a face photo. He's cute. He says he's in the closet, so we must meet in the basement of his apartment complex RIGHT NOW! *Basement.* That sounds like horror-film material, with me as the first victim of a future serial killer, or the first person to fall down the stone staircase in slow motion, hitting my head 5 times, drowning in a pool of my own blood!

Curious4trans says he can only do cam since I'm his first transsexual – he's too afraid to meet me. I say: 'The only thing we will do on cam is sort through the reasons behind your secrets, ok?' He stops responding. Hottranssexnow looks pretty good; I am slightly aroused. He writes: 'Send nudes!' I refuse. He blocks me after responding, 'Sorry Ms. Prude, I don't do blind dates!' Apparently, six pictures of my face are not enough for modern dating. I feel: *I need to be touched!!! Perhaps I should meet the guy in his basement after all?* He reads my mind and writes again. He digs deeper into WHY the basement: 'No one'll see us. I live with my gf. Iceland's tiny, if one person spots us on the town, my gf will know by tomorrow. Let me just give you the code to our apartment building's basement and meet you down there.'

I'm like: 'Sounds very complicated, don't you see a problem?'
Basement boy's like: 'LOL don't worry, it's simple! No one ever uses that basement, so she'll never find out... My profile's totally anonymous here... and I'm not planning on telling anyone I like trannies any time soon.'
I'm like: 'Bitch, fucking inside a closet is the antithesis of simple, it's cramped, the darkness is fine, but it shouldn't be based on lying to the light, which, you know, closets break easily... and

to be hidden in yours when I broke free of mine long ago was *never* what I fought for!'

He sends over more photos, tempting my loneliness to annihilate my principles... I wish to kiss his five yellow, flirty-faced emojis. And him, him as well, he's *so* handsome, blonde hair, green eyes... *STOP! Let us use our imagination.* He sends a picture of his hard dick right after it's shot sperm all over his chest. *UGH! STOP! IMAGINATION!*

Me: 'GOODNIGHT, I walk a tightrope over hell with no safety net each time I leave home, and you and your tyrannical normal li(f)e and lily-livered secrets are who&what kills us and keeps me there and it's not fair, so leave me the fuck alone till you fucking change, just go where the pepper grows, yes, that's a saying in Swedish, no, I don't care if that makes any sense to you, why don't you just shove that pepper up your ass motherfucker how'd you like that???'

He: 'Relax madwoman, I just wanna fuck your sexy asspussy Rocco Siffredi-style!'

Musical nr: *All I wanna say is that they don't really care about us.*

Oh reader, so this is the place where Icelandic trolls come out to play! I swear to fucking god, white, middle-class, 'feminist' guys are the rarest finds in my inbox – they're seemingly less sexist, but more transphobic than macho men who'll go for it, and take risks, while politically correct nice guys say 'If I can't fetishize, I'll turn a blind eye,' fleeing when unexpected events and cognitive dissonances arise. They perceive us as too filthy and intimidating – the Whores to their librarian-looking

Madonna cis girlfriends. They either won't tell anyone or dare try anything or even admit we exist. Oh, how they dread that desire that grows biologically inevitable with our hormones. Or surgery. Or goddess-given-top-model-gorgeousness. Stealth post-op t-girls I know prove my point by revealing that they've had sex with hundreds of men who couldn't tell the difference, with rejections appearing only *if* they disclose their history. It's not preference, it's prejudice... And what I've learned from trans friends and straight men from Turkey, Brazil, Iran, Greece, Argentina, Italy, Morocco and India especially is that male heterosexuality that excludes desire for trans women is a Protestant Northern European colonial concept. In these places, particularly among working-class men, we're seen as an eroticized category of women, clandestine and confined to sex work, with gender not defined by genitalia. Yet, where the desire for us is the strongest is also too often where the violence is the steepest. Liberal Western culture, however, refuses to make room for trans girls as full womenhumans with needs beyond half-lives as asexual othered third-gendered symbols of tolerance. This isolation from intimacy is at least as oppressive as being a secret sex symbol, Aphrodite After Dark. In fact, my Iranian trans friend told me that straight men from Iran would have affairs with her if they were new to Berlin, but after 5-6 years they'd stop, for they'd learned that's not how it's done in Germany.

Love, where have you taken your medicine? I risk everything and they risk nothing, and I have almost given up completely, torn to pieces by torturous penalties for destabilizing heterosexuality. Heightened misanthropy in an already acidic world hardly boosts one's joie de vivre. But the global total of 97.3 percent secret keepers is not 100, so: ONE LAST

TRY! I decide to find the 27-year-old source of a dick pic. He softens. He tells me he is new to this site. He apologizes for flashing his genitals. He thought that was how communication was conducted nowadays. He may be correct. He writes: 'I just wanted to make you horny.' I reply: 'Well, that was hardly a success story.' He sends a photo of his face and torso – long Bambi eyelashes, chiselled abs and a prematurely receding hairline that will probably be highly noticeable within a matter of five years. His expression exposes a slight discomfort with posing for cameras. Now he looks friendly and innocent, kind of naive and vulnerable. A wave of empathy flips me into an opposite emotion, and I replace scorn with compassion. I forgive him for being a flasher. He says his name is Victor. Dear Victor Hugo, I'm sorry, but I can't meet you, I feel empty like a flame that can't ignite upon dry barren earth, not a nude posing for an oil-on-canvas in 1845 hoping to be portrayed in a flattering light. I must retreat back to myself.

Dear viewers, the popular jocks from high school who used to bully me now want to fuck me, while my dreams star feminine men whose straight varieties usually fear emotive trans women, so what do I do, stick to the bullish Belgian Blues? I receive 13 messages from 5 new ones. I'm all stress hormones and no sex hormones! They quantify sex in inches, hours and positions. They obsess over my physical entrance points, yet *I'm* the one labelled *hysterical, too intense.* I stare down my lapdog, my lapdog lowers its eyes. So what if I dive into everything with a vehemence of 100 percent, I cannot be a myrmidon dog lingering one millimetre from the door until Master comes home to bludgeon my nose by mistake!

Viewer, we are reaching the end of this little motion picture, and though it may have blended elements from romcoms, porn, action, horror and more, nothing happened except some clicking and typing and many disgusted facial expressions coupled with some lustful ones. The difference between lust and love – perhaps it can be defined by looking at someone's handwriting with trembling affection and not requiring erotic visuals to incur a sensorial response. Call it: *Men who pick partners primarily by beauty know nothing of a love deserving of its name.* My future wishes to be kissed up against a wall by the mathematician-weirdo who delicately hums songs to himself while reading at the Berlin library. What species of animals would this transform us into? *ROMANTIC NOSE-TOUCHING SEAHORSES!* This dating site is as suitable for *ROMANTIC NOSE-TOUCHING SEAHORSES* as a shallow, littered puddle in the middle of a metropolitan city, and I already get my ass slapped like herded sex cattle every week in the streets of that city! Still, I know, I know the tranny chaser who shadowed me for four miles one Christmas Day wasn't just a scary predator stalking his frightened prey but also *another lonely*, like so many, involved in an activity that further increased his lonely. I lost him amongst crowds & candles & carols and I couldn't find any open stores that carried trust in shadows or men. Time, save us from a future as rated & rating robots! Modern people live in the moment and go with the flow. Me? I drown in it. I can at least save myself by deciding to live in the past. I cast my visibly exhausted lapdog into the wall, and its bones and blood scatter and splatter EVERYWHERE. *No.* No scene this time. A proportionate reaction: I hit the delete button and wave goodbye to my dating-site self. By the time summer turns to autumn, Facebook too shall be thrown out like a drug from rehab. And once I've weaned off that speed, I won't become an Instagrandma, posting seductive selfies in the right lighting to gain new stalkers named followers, calling that 'trans visibility'. We've got 200 Tamagotchis beeping, needing feeding, distraction-surveillance-envy economy, tasks that can't be heavy or fly, 1.3 billion boast-posting brands. Social media sites are so dull that the entire internet is dying of boredom!! They bring us further from the angels of our better nature, not fully killing our ability to care, but giving it an attention span of 10 seconds. Brazen anachronism may be the best way to change our world – Amazons fighting Amazon wildfires & dot coms while lighting wildfire love letters!

8

My lapdog has been laid to rest, and with it the romcom/action/musical/porn/horror film. I have been glued to the screen for 2 hours. I'm far from in love, but I almost feel like checking into a mental institution and never speaking to anyone again. I take a look around my room and try to stop feeling like I've taken speed. It is 8 p.m. It's time for me to check out of the bed & breakfast. My heavy bag *bang-bang-bangs* down the stairs, ruffling the owner in the kitchen. She glances at me with hesitant eyes. 'I've been –' she stutters, 'I've been wanting to tell you this since you arrived... but I really believe you are a unicorn.' Her positivity startles me. I respond, 'Cheers, thanks a lot,' even though terminal uniqueness rarely provides a home for anyone. She takes my keys and blows me a kiss as she leaves, allowing me to sit and wait in the dining hall until I must go to the airport. I turn my dialogue towards the tiny food scraps spilled underneath a table. One tells me she's been lying there since lunch. Another wishes to be swept up. A third hopes to provide a meal for a starving mouse. I hide this one in a secret place that brooms and vacuums are likely to miss. My job is done; sit back & relax. I sink down silently with my teacup and achieve something close to a blank mind. There is so much that one does not need to say a single thing about. At roughly 15-minute intervals, I pull my own hair like a toddler playing with a life-sized doll in order to not fall asleep. The brain must constantly remind our eyes that we do not own everything within sight. And meanwhile, though we haven't even been able to create eyesight for a blind man or a gravityless room on Earth, many people still believe technology can solve all of our problems.

My hours left in Iceland are in the single digits and decreasing by the second. My solitude tells me: *Be content.* I change my position in my chair. The imprint left on the grey cushion bears the shape of a narwhal: tusk, torso, tail fin. I will be very hesitant to leave my newfound narwhal friend all alone when I depart for my flight. It'll be alright. I also have a friend waiting for me at home in Berlin. Her name is Banafshe. Before I left, she told me: 'Maybe you'll fall in love on your vacation, isn't that what people do on vacation?' I have failed to fulfil her prophecy. I do not belong to the category of people who can play that game and win. I am returning home empty-handed. *No.* Enough of these melodramatic antics. She was not delivering a prophecy. She was merely making a joke. Nevertheless, what would I do with a boyfriend, or perhaps more accurately, what would a boyfriend do with me? Oh dear, look at me, reader, committing the sin of two consecutive simplified questions. Still, some people believe they're able to water down the world's greatest problems into 15-minute TED Talks. Meanwhile, I may be mourning a lack I've never truly felt. Since childhood, I've been sufficiently amused by hopping between stones alone. I'm not continuing on purpose, but I suppose certain pasts do not erase themselves in the present; *I need it heightened, All The Way!* I find it on stage or writing in a book. I've yet to meet the man who can trade magic-potion recipes... Passion – it's always bubbling inside me. Reality – only when blended with fantasy are you a full existence. The future is stored up in a bottle with contents only a genie can relay. But for the time being, an icy breeze whistles *shoo-shoo-shoo*, propelling me in the direction of the airport.

9 —

Keflavik airport *reeks* of Scandinavian Design. As I head through security, my nerves start sprouting worries like stacks of unfiled tax returns. It's not that I'm late or agonizing about whether the staff will feel me up to see if I'm a man or a woman. No, my fusspots are growing due to the 23 rocks in my bag. I want the staff to give them 23 boarding passes but fear it's strictly forbidden to bring so many. If I say I need them to make a circle around my shrine, the staff shall laugh in my face and call me a new-age hippie. If I say I'm uncertain of their use, but many steps in life would never be taken if we were required to cognize the exact destination before embarking, they'll say, *Shut up, Socrates!* Instead, I'll stick with the plain and simple: *Earlier today I spent a great deal of energy reducing the number of stones from 43 to 23, and upon counting I envisaged 23 as the perfect number for nothing horrible to happen to the aircraft, so please don't force me to give any up.*

Ólafur and Soraya from the security staff let me through without a single question asked. I breathe a sigh of relief for every battle that remains inside my head, never to meander into the terrain of an unpredictable reality. I've got no idea what it means to feel protected there. When I grew up the one who held my hand used the other to pull my hair as everyone else used both hands to train their punching skills on skin that bruised easily. I never liked having my blood provide nourishment for those who were not deficient. So, when I was a child, I used to tell myself I had 5 months left to live if that was how long it was till my next flight. It almost made me excited to get on the plane.

Nowadays there are a million ways I'd rather die. I've made a list of them, and flying ranks at the bottom, with no added benefits. I board the aircraft. I recount the stones: 24. One broke in two!! An omen: The plane's likely to crash within 15 minutes. If I am lucky, my spot will be in the back, as far away from the windows as possible. It's the safest place. 36C. Such good fortune. It's an aisle seat at the very rear. I remember the clueless rich-bitch Harvard professor who said her aviophobia only allows her to fly first class. Privilege shrinks your deep knowledge of the world while expanding its surface area. Yes, unlike on ships, first-class plane passengers are first in line to die. And the woman here in 36A shouldn't be greeting me with such a laid-back smile either. She is by the window, and in merely a moment's time, she could be sucked out into the atmosphere at 30,000 feet just for insisting on enjoying the view. A woodpecker glances at us through the glass, tries twice to jab through it, then flies away. Another warning. My frightened state distracts me from feelings of *I don't want to leave Iceland...* Now I just want to reach the other side of the sea in one piece. If that's too much to ask for, I might as well die. The plane creeps towards the takeoff strip. I brace myself by tensing up my whole body. If that won't save me in case of an emergency, I know what will: strapping my seatbelt tightly and ardently holding on to both armrests!

I break into a sweat which blends with the scent of my perfume, spreading itself around to all surrounding passengers. If they were predators, they would smell my fear loud&clear and pounce! The jet engine gears up, and I sharpen my ears so as to hear any and all possible irregularities. I don't like this. There is too much going on. The flight attendants seem calm, *phew*, the passengers too, and the pilot hits the gas pedal; up, up, and away, MY GOD IN HEAVEN, HERE WE COME! I fear for the moment when the up goes down turns nosedive. If I could travel 7 days back in time, I would've split my last Valium-sister in two instead of swallowing her whole. Oh Laika, you poor little stressbombed space dog. I am starting to understand how you felt up there, glancing at the moon with only the fumes of your own perspiration as companions. *Alvina, what're you yakking about, you're surrounded by members of your own species!* Yes, I know, I could just open my mouth and speak to the relaxed woman in the window seat. Chatter always provides an escape from intensity, but I suppose I prefer to face *everything* head on. Turbulence shakes the airplane to and fro, forcing my pulse to slam against my skin in a desperate search for a way out. I envision the sound of the engine increasing to a roar before exploding, as the aircraft splits in two, leaving no space in between for any survivors. The Earth is angry at us for engaging in an activity that hurts her. All of her revenges have the potential to be triple-fold to any of the damage we've inflicted. *23 stones, 24: Who cares, age isn't the thing that's just a number!* Stop transforming plain setbacks into catastrophes! I gently start tapping specific pressure points on my body and close my eyes so I can return to becoming that long, flowing, golden dress which breathes with the swimming rhythm of a jellyfish in a splendid loss of sense of direction. Ok. I have made peace with dying now. I realize this decreases the risk of its occurrence, as death prefers its prey panicked.

The turbulence subsides. My brain ventures past its skull. How does a person's existence change at this altitude? It is not like being a bird, it's closer to being inside the belly of a gigantic robot bird that can only land properly in certain designated areas. I can't understand what all of us are doing up here in the sky? It is something that demonstrates a large root of many of the world's problems: Humanity's spiritual evolution is ages behind our scientific and technological evolution. A potentially more catastrophic case in point is the invention of the atom bomb. Or, for that matter, the innovation of every tool with the sole purpose of destruction, often framed as 'protection'. Are you still not convinced of the truth in my first statement, reader? Well, let me provide a few examples that shall make both our heads spin & boggle: *Our bodies contain hydrogen from the Big Bang 13.7 billion years ago, and while there are more stars in outer space than grains of sand on Earth, they still don't outnumber the amount of H2O molecules in 10 drops of water... Go ahead, blink your eyes and there you have it: a moment as long in relation to your lifetime as your lifetime is in relation to the history of the Earth, so you better make it count! 1, 2, infinity – look, an Alien 66 million light-years away just saw a Tyrannosaurus Rex!* And many people today are starving. And that's not 'just the way it is'! If we left Sweden's 187 billionaires 100 million each, the resources for public spending would double. In the meantime, 7 billion hearts are pumping blood through a human body. And I have no one here to talk to about my fear of flying. How can a life be sustained and a body not completely disintegrate 5 miles above the next plot of land? I do not understand. Then again, how does an e-mail or a phone call work? I have no clue. And what about the printing of this book? I would like to learn the *how* to *everything* I do, but I wouldn't have any time for anything else if I seriously attempted that task.

(My thoughts drift to Icelandic horses. If one of them is in the plane's cargo hold, she will be leaving home for good. That's the law. In order to prevent all diseases but homesickness, Icelandic horses are not allowed re-entry into the country. They can only be boarded with the aid of heavy sedatives. They have no part in the decision.)

Reader, I'm writing to you in order to do my part in levelling the harrowing gap between our spiritual and technological evolution. Since humans probably can't create souls inside of robots, technology is no replacement for spirituality. Nownow, this isn't an argument of for-or-against, but for a side-by-side, far from the Big Tech Four. I'm cerebrating questions such as: *Which wounds require stitches, and which need caresses?* And: *What disentangles curiosity from greed?* I once heard a story about an artist who began hiding her innermost depths in order to get ahead, forcing all other artists to do the same until no one remained to unmask the truths. Each time I introduce a razor blade to my wrist, it wishes to talk to my blood so that I won't reside at a comfortable distance from my scars.

The plane begins to descend upon Berlin. My fear of an accident almost makes me pee in my pants. After takeoff, landing is the most dangerous portion of a flight. I'm too tired to deal with death once more. I won't risk my life up in the air again for a very long time. I shouldn't even be here to begin with. Why won't some politician confer with leading scientists and just decide the number of hours each person can be allotted on an airplane without destroying the climate? It would be a sigh of relief. It would make God stop targeting passenger planes at random, punishing both saints and sinners with death penalties. The air shuttle shakes. The landing gear is unfolding. A crash from 1000 feet can choose a few passengers who get to survive (*Pick me! Pick me! Why me?*), unless of course the engine decides to explode, in which case we're all cooked... In 10 hours' time, will I be engaging in an activity that commemorates life, like placing 24 stones upon my shrine or doing the dishes after dinner? I close my eyes and let my heart go sailing. The wheels reach out for some material to grip onto. Our captain proves to be competent. No swerving. All those hours spent in a video-game-like simulation did not go to waste. The brakes are doing their job properly as well. We are slowing down. We are on the ground. So: Life continues. It goes on.

(PTSD, it sounds like some sordid high school, like a cheerleading chant I know by heart as it's stuck on repeat, which doesn't mean it's all I ever hear, it's an abbreviation for when the world hurts you badly, and you add a C for Constant & subtract a P for Post when history won't leave you B, as I continue to react to nothing like something, and something like nothing. Petaluma hasn't been the chicken capital of the world since 1933, and my cameo in that chick flick was Chicken Little getting her wings clipped by popular crowds and gangs of outcasts alike, and my 2018 may still be an outsider among the outcasts, but hopefully no dodo sprinting from extinction!

1999, life year 11 – a year off in Torslanda, Volvo capital of the world – a child wants nothing more than for mama's back pain to be cured, and that girlyboy finds her only role at school, the jester – dressed as Lene in Aqua, singing 'Barbie Girl', calling Dr Jones, with no sticks or stones or rotten tomatoes thrown. No, I made the children laugh and play, so they crowned me class clown, and the boys fondled my cotton tits, and the girls sang along to all the lyrics, and the moms & dads told mama, 'I know what your son's gonna grow up to be,' and their hahas had a different tone than the kids', and after-school was spent hiding out with seagulls and ducks at a waterlily pond surrounded by sloping stone mounds where I was free from the entanglement of entertaining human relationships, till the water got drained, and my tears tried and failed to refill it, and the fox and the cat and the badger sauntered across the mud, stealing the eggs from the bird's nests on Hourglass Island 'cause I couldn't stand guard 24/7, and time passed, it wouldn't stand still, and I didn't return till I turned 14, and flew from P-Town to Sweden for good after a celebratory disco dance over mom & dad's overdue divorce. But we're older now, and my drag queen manners make the big-muscled, brown-shirted boys wrap my old nicknames in a new language, Bögjävel-Tjötkärring-Tjejhumor, in a Torslanda called Nazilandia where I hide at home on weekends trying to follow the wide world of sports, cursing my attraction to Alexei Nemov and the Goran who finally won Wimbledon, and everything's wrong, and something's the matter, and it's never been quite right, and I'm acquiring the words for it, but it doesn't mark a vast improvement – **Mama, ooh, I don't wanna die. I sometimes wish I'd never been born at all...** *Today, I write from a Berlin library where I'm the only one who ever does ballet stretches and jumps, just waiting and waiting, for a what, for a who, for a boy more magical than therapy (easy!), and as dreamfullystrange as me (hard!), to rest beside somewhere other than in my reveries – is it you, can it be **you**, reader, I beg of you, stay with me, I can be so kind, and maybe, just maybe, I can create a bird-of-paradise nest for an us in this life that no longer resembles the sound of a cell phone ringtone.)*

HOMESICK
Berlin

1 —

My dear reader, my darling glósóli.

Why not take a minute to think about all the things around us we don't see: viruses, bacteria, particles, protozoa, plankton, one-celled, two-celled, three-celled organisms... I'm at home listening to Björk and Sigur Rós after returning from a vacation in Iceland, and I seem to be having a 30-year crisis. I'm nowhere near as unique as I think I am. Then again, neither is Björk or Jónsi or anyone else for that matter, but that doesn't mean we can't be good people. Being a good person is the profoundest meaning of life, the only real reason for our mothers to not abort our foetuses. It should be the definition of *good enough*. And Björk sings the mantric lines: *The pleasure is all mine to get to be the generous one; when in doubt, give...* Before wondering: *Who gives most?*

My poor physical shape doesn't allow me to be distracted by Berlin's city life. The day of rest in Reykjavik wasn't enough for my Judas of a body. My illness has built an impenetrable wall of mucus and inflamed my throat. Stuck inside the nothing of my couch, I enter the time that is no time. Could I have streptococcus? If so, will the bacteria unroll into rare rheumatic fever and infect the centre of my heart? Oh, this was not what I wanted from the things we don't see! Grisly hypochondria, thou inheritance from my mother, leave me be. Arrive household remedies gifted by that same her: *Turmeric, cinnamon & cayenne. Garlic, ginger & honey. Add Bioperine & pepper for better absorption.* Sickness, I know you're punishing me for getting soaking wet by that waterfall. How predictable; we're always forced to face consequences as repercussive responses to that which makes our hearts flutter with life. Now even jumping in a puddle could kill me.

Reader, mainly two forms of existence can spark senses of immortality and purified magic, of life-meaning intensity and serenity: absolute solitude and all-embracing communion with an equal. What am I to do with this unblendable blend, devote every other week to each? My body is very weak at the moment, but I still hope my honesty will comfort you if you are disturbed... I'm sweating profusely, though I wish I was weeping. The only task I can handle is watching the Olympics. I manage the 5-meter walk from bedroom to living room and call that 'an athletic achievement'. I turn on the TV and giggle my way through water polo, ping-pong and football. If aliens were to tune in to these competitions, I'm sure they'd perceive them as brilliant, flamboyant comedy sketches. I sigh! Oksana, Goran, Tonya - the enchanted tennis players and figure skaters who saved my childhood are nowhere to be found. I don't know if this Olympics shall bring any new idols to mix in with the stones, books and dead florals of my shrine. I turn off the telly and look inwards towards myself. It changes nothing. All I find is stiff joints and a manic brain - entirely unproductive, allowing everyone with half my intelligence to surpass my achievements...

Lucid dreams. Arrive. Deliver me from this sick and sticky body that gets dry-humped by her living-room couch.

There's only one man who can rescue me from my depression: *Ronaldo!* In a reverie between asleep and awake, I lose myself in his journey, creating both a sandcastle and a tidal wave. My imaginary self escapes from my body to shout from the rooftops: *RoRo, I am Catwoman hear me roar, let me be your Yoko Ono!* At long last RoRo, here I am, ready to send paragraphs of booming poetry without you reciting lines I've heard before: *Stop robbing me of my male role as Seducer in Chief!* Like Yoko, I shall never hide my assets as if they were defects. On the World Wide Web, I squeal with glee at your bold style, labelling it *Batman meets Lolita*: rings, pink short shorts, tight rainbow-colored sweatshirts, plucked eyebrows, flowers tucked behind your ears. And your opponents' fans, they always yell *Maricon* as you take to the field. *Maricon*, Spanish; it sounds like a passion fruit or a picturesque beach resort. *Maricon,* it shares the title of The World's Most Beautiful Word for Faggot, making love to the Portuguese word *Bicha* – the even more feminine form of bitch... No, the feminine form of animal, *bicho*. Oh, RoRo, when a fellow footballer called you a *Bicha*, you responded: 'Uma bicha? Sim, mas rico!' – *'A faggot? Yes, but rich!'* Ronaldo, the Rich-Bitch-Bicha. Bitch, I'll go on a sex strike if you don't properly pay your taxes!

ROROROROO, I'M ALONE, ALL ALONE, SO ALONE, I HAVEN'T HAD ANY SORT OF SEX IN 6 MONTHS, HAVEN'T EVEN BEEN KISSED, OH, THAT'S NOTHING, NOTHING, NO TIME AT ALL, LAST TIME THE COUNT OF MONTHS WAS 11, I GET TOO MANY NEW OFFERS EACH DAY, TO SAY YES MEANS DEBASEMENT AND HUMILIATION, 6 MONTHS AGO I GOT DEBASED AND HUMILIATED,

11 MONTHS BEFORE I GOT DEBASED AND HUMILIATED – DEBASED AND HUMILIATED – I USED TO GET DEBASED AND HUMILIATED ONCE A MONTH, WAS IT BETTER, WAS IT WORSE?

Alone, RoRo, we're meant to be a *We* because we're meant to be alone! Yes, in your own words, in your own documentary, you said it, said it well: 'Most of the time I'm alone. I consider myself an isolated person. I come home, completely disconnect from the world, because I know the next day I'll be pulled back into that world again. I like to be quiet. I like to enter my own world. I am at home and I am at peace with myself.'

But... RoRo, from this moment when I'm lonely to that time when you need someone: What can I do to make you love me, fuck me, cry with me, hold me? In that order. Over the years I have perfected my feminine sex appeal. It's as meaningful as snow finding its way underneath a parked car. It has given me nothing. Will I miss it when I age? It has brought me only trouble and harassment. *That was before I met RoRo, who gave me everything*, I shall assert at the next World Cup, which will coincide with the release of my new bestselling novel, solidifying our position at the top of the world of sports and culture! Forget *Brangelina* – they are in the throes of a divorce case. Make way for *Rolvina*! Behold, as we enter the realm of politics and rise to a position of greater power than both Billary Clinton and the Perons, ushering in a New Left era that combines justice with peace and ecological sustainability! DING-DING-DING: REALITY CHECK!!! Reality, why must you always insist on being so cruel, forcing me to recoil into a world of unfulfillable fantasies? RoRoRo-your-boat is on a luxury yacht off the coast of Monaco, leaving Yoko far from rocking the boat. Oh RoRo, if we meet, will you be loving and playful like a boto dolphin or stiff like a roll-on/roll-off ship? And what if I tell you I can sensually deepthroat dicks up to 22 centimetres? Will you invite me into your lair? Will you do more than just cum, throwing me out together with some stained sheets to cherish as souvenirs? Will we stand on tables and scream to Diamanda Galás & PJ Harvey, skipping your Ricky Martin & Elton John? Will we start a life together on the island of Lesbos? Will I bear you a daughter? You're a Rich-Bitch-Bicha; you'll surely find a way to pay for the first ever successful uterus transplant so I can give birth to rows and rows of mini-RoRos of all genders!

(In the most ornate caverns of my own mind, I caress all that I'll never be granted access to. These are the irreplaceable gifts you can send to yourself if you belong to a class of women that has never been protected.)

Reader, have I lost it? In the real world I mope my runny-nosed body to my bedroom, and RoRo The Crying Terminator doesn't care if I love him or hate him. He says: 'Your love makes me strong, your hate makes me unstoppable.' I condemn him for sending objectifying messages to women on social media! I berate his empty macho power trips with fancy cars, a.k.a. male stilettos, and numerous rumoured flings with fashion models! I don't care that I have the legs, the cheekbones, the ass of a Gisele Bündchen; I still won't put up with this shit! I will have to change him. I must feign indifference. I must ignore him completely. That'll get to that narcissist's massive ego and force him to look up from his tanning salon of 150 million followers!

Reader, the thought of RoRo working as Mark Zuckerberg's favourite robot servant just brought me back to the simplest, most complicated question: *Is life meaningful or meaningless?* I've decided to cast my vote for a life governed by the principle that *everything* is meaningful. If I stare at an ant for a considerable amount of time, I realize she has a life that I don't want to ruin in any way. What is painful about the world is that it's impossible to live one's entire life without inflicting any injuries on any living beings. On the opposite end of the spectrum, fishermen kill sharks who kill seals every day, and we're all going to die soon anyways. In 100 years just about everyone living today will be deceased, save for a few trees and turtles if they're not driven to extinction. So, here, nothing really matters, and then we find ourselves flung into passive nihilism with hedonism becoming the order of the day. Very boring. As painful as *everything means everything* is, at least it's not empty. On an average day, I get two friend requests from anonymous men on Facebook; they like about 50 of my photos, and many proceed to send headless pictures of their sixpack abs. I understand what they want from me, but I don't understand what they want from life... It's a very complex question to begin with, yet still a much more preferable starting point. Does my body attract only machos? Should I change it so *you* can see my mind? In which ways does acceptance drive us? Do I have an inner voice? And if it conveys many opposing opinions, which one should I listen to? And what if one of those headless torsos turns out to be RoRo's? Perhaps I should write back, and then he can hold me in his arms as I continue brooding over both my singular issues and the survival of all species. Reader, I vow to do my very best to not live a life that leaves a garbage trail the size of a massive dumpsite in its wake and to have RoRo tell the world about our relationship. It may take a while for me to succeed and ascend to my throne as *Queen Yoko Ono – Feminist Havoc-Wreaker Of The Football World!* But for the time being, if you see him lying in the sun on that yacht off the coast of Monaco reading Violette Leduc, Clarice Lispector, Sylvia Plath or Angela Davis, the moth has delivered another message. And RoRo will throw his smartphone into the sea as his team sends out a press release attacking human chauvinism: *Why is everyone obsessed with prioritizing humanity, yet at first mention of apocalypse they speak of grieving the end of bird chirps, green meadows, and blossoming trees?*

I have now stayed indoors for five days. At this very moment, I'm lying in bed staring at the off-white ceiling. The off-white ceiling is doing a poor job of consoling me. A yeast infection in my asshole has insisted on adding to my ailments, picking me to pieces, and then throwing me into a trash can of self-loathing. I feel like the scraped knees of a fallen cyclist after running over the neck of a poor little decapitated sewer rat. Dear nervous-breakdown brain and virus-afflicted body, please apologize to my readers for disclosing every story in its entirety: the more insignificant, humiliating and mundane, the merrier. Don't force them to watch Tonya Harding and Yuzuru Hanyu land triple axels on a loop for two hours. Just explain that Yuzuru is a Nijinsky on ice who owns no cell phone and cries when he sees Winnie the Pooh. It's enough. Now, dear body, I have given you all you've asked for: *rest, endless rest, garlic, water, ginger, honey, cayenne, curcuma, sauerkraut, pepper, apple cider vinegar*. And still you want more! You've repaid my efforts by starting a nagging night cough that forces me to take sleeping pills called Stillnoct that still don't knock me out but strongly affect my already poor judgment. Yes, thought patterns always take on an own particular form when you lie awake as the hours pass and your bed turns into a private version of hell. At 6 a.m. this morning, I spent 20 minutes believing I only had 20 breaths left to breathe. At the rate of one breath a minute I typed out a tearful farewell email to my mother. As soon as I took my 21st breath, I realized I wasn't dying. Since the letter remained unsent, I didn't have to write another apologizing for the inconvenience.

2

Reader, the ginormous nonsenses and petite wisdom teeth of the past 7 pages have been brought to a halt. I stop. I think of the day when I was 13 years of age and had just decided to stay in the straight closet of shame forever. It was the same day that my mom and dad yelled: 'You have no friends, all you ever do is stay home and pet your guinea pig!' That day my relationship to myself became something hidden from the world, completely separate from my relationship to other human beings. No one at Petaluma Junior High School liked me. My strangeness got its face flushed down a toilet called *too feminine*. All I had was a guinea pig, Sylvia Plath and several tennis players and figure skaters. I recall that morning two years later when I woke up in a Swedish hospital, hungover as hell, after a stomach-pumping, heart-stopping alcohol poisoning, praying I didn't tell anyone I liked boys or felt like a girl. I had not. I had kept all my secrets safe and sound inside a never-ending stream of vomit that nearly choked me to death. Locked out of class, out of town, out of state, isolation cell; a kick here, a kick there can quickly escalate to a kick everywhere. Oh, those years spent secluded with no one to turn to for fear of hammers and zoos; oh, the intangible residue that remains well after tearing down a wall, which proved itself to be a dam giving way to a torrent of new upstream struggles. What do years of constant heckling, of fractured homes, do to our psyches, our spirits, our souls?

Ceaseless need for attention, affection, admiration, affirmation?
Depression?
Overactive imagination?
Self-destruction?
Preoccupation with people's views of us? Stark rebellion against it?
Bitterness?
Thin skin? Feigned toughness?
Heightened empathy?
Obsession with being understood?

Does 'rising above' mean receiving a significant amount of attention, affection, admiration, affirmation? Or does it signify the splendour of being unable to turn a blind eye? I don't even think we have words in our vocabulary for what happens to us when trauma becomes everyday and never-ending. How do different animals experience exclusion?

I think of the discrepancy between the way sand looks and feels, the way a clock ticks and the way time passes, the way one fantasizes about passionate lovemaking and the way one stares at the incongruent forms on the ceiling when submitting to sex with the wrong man. Oh reader, I have no need for a lacklustre together to replace Alvina Alone, it better be better, it better be much-much-better or better-off-alone with solitudepassion as my secret hiding place!

(A boy once thought polyamory would solve my woes. He said, 'Love is like juice concentrate, drinkable only when blended with 4 parts water.' I answered, 'When I was 15, I mixed 4 parts vodka with juice concentrate & my heart stopped, what's water to you is vodka to me.')

God, I will not pray for you to rescue me from my bodily infections and loveless affairs. I know that you are far too busy. Still, please help me, I'm sorry that I'm always tardy, but you know I try my best to be a good person, and I never lie. So, please help me! If I don't leave my apartment by tomorrow, I shall start tearing off the yellow wallpaper and become the furniture that I've already begun to talk to. 'Good day, couch!' Couch: 'Shut up, you lousy lay, you're far from my favourite human & I'd prefer you were a gerbil.' Me: 'Fuck off table, get outta my room, my house, my life, I never wanna see you again!' Oh god, that poor innocent table, taking the brunt of my bad mood due to Mr. Couch's rude reply. If I were in the Outside World instead, dear God, I could find an upside-down beetle struggling with her feet in the air and turn her right side up, saving her from starvation, bird beaks, or other sadisms of nature. I could fall in love with a man who smiles at me at the red light of an intersection; who understands my returned smile as a cue to strike up a conversation before it turns green; who isn't smiling just 'cause he thinks I'm a brave tranny in bright colours; who walks by my side without the horny air of a stalker; who already has two kids he's raising on his own; who welcomes me into a world of domestic bliss; who teaches me the meaning of the six-letter word *family* and provides proof that the words *mutual* & *love* can be combined. And I'll finally have something in common with everyone wandering around hand-in-hand. And I won't end up feeling suffocated or trapped or captured or bored or dead inside. Or, I'll end up feeling all of the above...

All I know is It Gets Better rarely applies to trans women. As evening makes its way past midnight, I worry that I might lie awake thinking negative thoughts about the future again. I wish instead to live in the moment of a dreamscape that isn't driving toward a certain goal. I pour apple cider vinegar into my anus and ease into a land of less itch. To provide further motivation for sleep to fall, I play the song 'I'm So Excited'. I pay close attention to the lyrics: 'Tonight's the night we're gonna make it happen.' I disregard the parts where they cite activities quite separate from nodding off. My purpose for the night is nothing other than leaving the world of liveliness. An Icelandic troll sings: *Sleep, you black-eyed pig. Fall into a deep pit of ghosts.*

3 —

Reader, a fly died in my dream, as did a 43,000-year-old Pando tree and I too, yes, *me three*. Apparently death was what was needed to finally put me to sleep, but it certainly did nothing to help cure my illness, as my sinuses feel like a snake pit at breeding time. If you found that line inventive, remember it's likely a mere fluke. I'm not talented and interesting and new and innovative. I'm untalented and boring and stuck in the past. It's a good thing I hate prizes and artist residencies, because I'll never win or get accepted to one. The highlights of my 7th day trapped inside my four walls are: *A hot bath and the Olympic synchronized swimming duet final.* I set my first activity into motion, and the horror film of my nightmare repeats itself: two fruit flies get caught in the faucet stream. I rush to scoop them out of the water; I place them on the bath mat; I fetch salt from the kitchen and sprinkle it over their bodies. According to a video on the internet, this is supposed to revive them through restoring the balance of their bodily fluids. So far, I see no positive results. They continue to lie completely motionless sprawled across the bath mat. All three of us are *very* upset about this outcome.

Their star-crossed fates plummet me into the history of my love life – a lush oasis endlessly performing monologues from *Romeo & Juliet* for a desert, with not even an ocean to listen. I christen the two fruit flies Ms. Romeo Montague & Mr. Juliet Capulet and grow jealous of their deaths... Reader, I already told you about my 7 half-love affairs that ended before they ever really started, leaving me mourning what never was for months, sometimes years of haemorrhaging. I also told you about Alma-Rapha, the boy with the Nijinsky-glow in his eyes and Fridaesque paintings, who kissed me, then refused to reply to any of my messages. But I didn't tell you about the man I fucked six months ago. Well, he went and got himself a cis girlfriend like they all do. He wants to pass me over to his brother. I am not the least bit attracted to his brother. I am a platinum blonde Rapunzel imprisoned inside the tower of perpetual bad luck, waiting for a prince who busies himself with feeding ravens and saving dying trees.

(Another story within our story, another once upon a time, 2006, 7, 8, 9: a first love or a first obsession, a strawberry-blonde freckled Shawn showed me that sex may not always shatter you but a kiss sure can. After 20 or was it 33 he'd already had enough of my public Courtney outbursts, my Kahlo-drama haircuts, my kamikaze-wristslits; the last straw, our big night of fights, my one-page love poem framed by his bedside, the panther's stare I stabbed into his pupils as I shredded the paper sheet, crumbling-chewing-devouring it three feet from his face with one promise: 'I'll get over your eyes by the time I shit this poem out!' Shawn welled up and cried, while my intestines they died, and I poured out my teardrops in private to water forget-me-nots for two years past that hard-stooled poop – and then, and then – that last time we spoke, that why-oh-why he told ME, not his girlfriend, of his first attempt at death... I, dancing atop a porta-potty, crashing through the roof into the lap of some poor shocked shitter, then sprinting full speed straight into Shawn, he, singing to the sky, shit-faced beyond belief, shock-cries: 'You

shrew who shares my enemies of hungry & full, I tried to kill myself on a train track last week, the last week of spring!' And me & he began to flood the world with living water as I used my hands to mix the trickles of two skinned tomatoes who must unite to survive. But he ran to fuck his much younger girlfriend. So I ran to cut myself in the forest. So there was no next time, just a phone call five years downstream, the last week of fall 2014: Shawn has died by suicide, by hanging himself in a cave in Spain at the age of 27, and all I could do was crouch to pee in the middle of 42nd Street, for the thing is, reader, he still didn't want me to stay or else I would've till the end of forever, and the thing is, reader, he was a happier person than me, he just did what was always on my mind in the same place where I wish to be saved by an us, by a we... What follows: an intermezzo of 50-dollar hand jobs to johns in alleys with rotten-shrimp-stenched frozen sperm to numb my many long texts to the Kays the Paulos who smashed me past my gradual movement from never-was-a-man to what-is-a-woman(?) – a girl who takes everything too seriously and doesn't know shit about how to watch the Netflix & chill or have fun affairs or be casual without becoming a casualty: SHAWN WAS ALWAYS A HAPPIER PERSON THAN ME! NO, I think, can't ever know, can't even measure a thing like that: what I've been through and if my fights actually keep me away from a grave where only hurricane rain can sweep me off my feet? Perhaps the answer is in you, reader, I'm telling you, I look inside myself and it is ever-so confusing. Shawn! Shawn! Shawn! Your autopsy read only logos: 'Death by self-induced asphyxiation after substantial consumption of alcohol,' as your obituary quoted your pathos, 'In a world where start should be stop we've already reached our finish line.' Shawn!!! I've changed so much now, I cry in front of audiences of hundreds, I cry at first dates & public libraries & awful* *parties, invisible branches tear at the fabric of my being, and I bleed, I cry, I surrender to the stream of life, and maybe that's the key to the why I'm still alive, but then whyohwhy could sobs not save you? _____ silences fill in the blanks that empty words cannot, deleting his number used to be meaningless as I knew it by heart – 0708???, I've forgotten, I've forgotten, It's gone, It's gone, It's forgotten.)*

*(Reader, a shorter saga now, suitable for children up to the age of 5: Once upon a time, 22 months ago and 5.3 feet away, my eyes led a he to an unforeseen place, my bed, for 24 hours straight, and he called it 'mind-blowing spiritual lovemaking', but then, a reveal, a girlfriend, and a me whispering in his ear, 'Please don't be mister number 100 million to profess loyalty to the normal life, please be that one guy to stay by **our** side.' He went back to her and I went back to black. Just a one-night stand, get over it, happily never after?)*

Collapsed across my bathroom floor, I hug a cold stonewall that refuses to hug me back. Not even the dark end of the street has two ways when I'm the one doing the walking. *Stop complaining.* Things could be worse. But things can *always* be worse... I think of an excited stray dog that finally gets adopted. Upon arrival in her new home, she immediately sees a glass Coca-Cola bottle underneath the bed and mistakes it for a chew toy: her saliva drools, her teeth bite, the bottle bursts in her mouth, and she swallows a thousand shards which pierce through her throat, her stomach, her intestines. She explodes in desperate yelps between vomiting fits and dies an internally bleeding death, slow and teeming with agony. I cry. I think of the military authorities that have utilized even worse methods of torture. I cry some more. I would be exaggerating if I said love or life had maimed me like said sad dog. However, if I said it hasn't been too far from it, it would be the truth of all the ghosted and stood-up trans women, street breeds he feared might pee on his white picket fence. Reader, a forensic study of my own abyss shows that men's silent walls have hurt me more than men's rapes, for I never truly felt vulnerable underneath a rapist's gyrating body. At times it is better to be treated like shit than air.

4 —

Stop complaining you dumb slutcunt! Go read a self-help book! The sun is shining, and I finally feel strong enough to leave my flat. At dusk, my dear friend Banafshe brings me to the river Spree for a witchbitch ritual. Our aim: to reverse all conjoined negative spirals: in physical health, in romance, in artistic recognition, in discipline, in sleep patterns, in feelings of self-worth, in light-hearted joie de vivre, in tranquillity of mind, in financial stability. We hold hands in a dewy meadow. No other humans nearby. We cast three Icelandic volcanic stones into the Spree. We light a bonfire upon twigs and sacrifice a dried rose. Then nine photos of football players. Then five heart-shaped chocolates. We rub our hands and arms across the silky-smooth ashes. The scent of melted chocolate hearts intoxicates us. Surely our efforts must lead to something. Yes... the bond of our friendship is further strengthened. It means *Everything*. It keeps us above ground, away from a premature burial. Human warmth – it can kill, it can save.

Reader, I am back home alone in my den. I have stopped speaking in words in order to be understood in a new, necessary way: Scream-of-Love – *AWWAAOOOWWW* – Multiphonic. In the language beyond thought, from schreiben to schrei, from écri to cri: Scream-of-Consciousness. I am a sorceress who's bathed herself in a magic potion of sauerkraut and apple cider vinegar for days. And at last, a victory! My yeast infection is declared dead by drowning. Its final words from my solitary, antisocial anal walls: *Yesterday-very-itchy-neeein-keeein-sauerkraut-Today-not-so-itchy.*

5 —

When the walls cave in, I am not crushed. I am flung into the outside world where there's too much going on, too much commotion, and I cannot do the locomotion without getting stared at. Since returning from Reykjavik, I haven't spent a full day out in Berlin, and I seem to have forgotten that people stare at me no matter how I behave. Some are confused, others are shocked, a few think 'how cuuuute', the majority are horny. I stare back at *The People*. I intimidate some of them. I provide many with the hope that today is their lucky day. They whistle. They praise my legs. I try my best to get rid of them. And after a too-long-while they finally tire, but that don't mean it's over. No, the only thing out here that could shift the spotlight would be a fat lady singing at full operatic force in the middle of the street. Eight people are gaping at me as I wait by the crosswalk. One of them is literally salivating. Two are laughing. Three men stare at my stems. Two women give me nods of approval. I stand up to deliver a silent shout: *Hey, I may appear hot, baroque, or maybe even brave to you, but if only your easier existence knew what I go through every day, your gawks and ha-has and friendly smiles would be replaced by tears in a jiffy! Besides, I might be the only one here who's not wearing a costume.* Is it possible to remain fully unaffected by their giggles and gazes? No. And since I'm no superhuman, perhaps I should have stayed indoors. Think positively: At least I haven't been raped in two years. However, when I go to Paris to perform in a few weeks,

I'd better watch my back, as it is the Sexual Harassment Capital of the World. Meanwhile, strolling along the willow-tree-lined canal in Kreuzberg, I see several men I'd let make love to me consensually. If only four of them could line up together and walk down the nearest sidewalk abreast, the *Sex and the City* theme song would start playing in my head, advising me to flirt with them by asking: *Which one of you is Samantha? Miranda? Carrie? Char...*

I become fixated by one beautiful man in particular who also looks interesting. I'm fooling myself. It is impossible to *look* interesting. It resides in the interior. Young club kids in New York City have astonishingly creative outfits, and they vapidly captivate without content. Yes, hyped aesthetics are so simple for capitalism to embrace. Today everyone who's anyone wishes to be linked with the two easy progressives: Gay Pride & Fine Art... The beautiful man's eyes head in every direction but mine. He is winning an Academy Award for the role of a soulmate who doesn't notice me. I do not know him. He's got just one thing to say to me: *Stop holding an innocent bystander hostage in your fantasies.* Hardly the first time, but maybe the last, for yes, it may all be different this time, for *look*, now he's entering *the library*. So what, who hasn't been to the library? Everyone who sets foot in your place of dreams can't be your dream person. If that were the case, I should spend all my days camping outside the arrivals gate in Iceland, going to the bathroom between incoming flights to touch up my makeup so I'll always look my best. Still, perhaps I should enter the library and walk straight up to the beautiful man, tapping him on the shoulder, then opening my trapdoor: *Excuse me, are you looking for Sylvia Plath? I mean a book by Sylvia Plath, not the person, but if you're looking for her, I may be the closest you can get, not that I'd stick my head in an oven, I mean I've thought of it maybe a thousand times, but, umm, anyways, let's change the subject; have you ever spent any time upon a Victoria Amazonica lotus leaf?*

He'll stare at me in shock or disbelief. He looks like a good guy who won't spray me with filthy propositions, so it's unlikely he's interested. He'll say, *Sorry, I'm not into trans.* I won't yell, *I AM AN ADULT FEMALE HUMAN BEING NOT AN ICE CREAM FLAVOUR!* I'll think: well, the last guy I gave my number actually worked at an ice cream parlour. As I cut through the sightseers at Alexanderplatz, his striking face lit up and tossed a firecracker at my desire. I sauntered into the parlour and received ten compliments and one free scoop of vanilla. He was even flirting with me openly in front of all his colleagues!!! 8 hours later, at 2 a.m., I received a string of text messages confessing that he has a wife, asking if I've got a pussy or a dick, then answering his own question: 'It doesn't matter, I love your ass, let's fuck at my place at 6:30 in the morning when my wife's gone to work. But, no kissing!' After I deliver a stern telling-off, he quips: 'Wow, are you dominant in bed!?' That's it, I'm never giving my number to a man again! I am left libidinous, yet refraining, 100 percent neurotic, bordering on schizophrenic. The Ballad of Sexual Dependency. Suck-him-off? Bite-it-off? The conflict of The Piano Teacher: *Erika Kohut can't have normal relationships with men and is completely frigid.* I DON'T WANT TO BE THE ETERNAL OTHER WOMAN, I won't be the one they *fucked and left*, I'll be *the one that got away*, the one they desperately wanted but never had! Or: I WILL FUCK THEM ALL! Poorly. And full of awkward inhibitions. Just to kill their expectation that trans girl = sex goddess!

I think of my beloved idiosyncratic mathematician-poet from weeks past. He seems so shy and awkward, his long eyelashes extending like sequoias from his mountainous mind. He must be a loner who reaches peak human contact by having 300 strangers surround him at the library. His mismatched clothes draw me toward his body. But *why* am I always forced to take all the steps with *all* the men who are not complete oglers? I imagine him glancing at me with his thoughtful eyes, his fawn eyes, those eyes ten times more tender, ten times kinder than the deep-set eyes of that moody guy I met in Iceland – the model/commercial actor with one of the top ten most meaningless jobs, after CEOs, stock speculators and 'influencers'... My math whizz solves his shyness, yes, he springs up from his godlike calculations and rushes to my side, he sings: *Crazy girl I want you, Crazy girl I need you so, Crazy girl I love you, more than you know!*

Boy I want to hear you sing it!!! Glorious passivity (the world would be a better place with more of it), what a joy that this situation at least gets to exist in the form of wishful thinking ❤

Alas, reader, my mood has shifted since the last paragraph, it is speeding down a steep slope, and I must head home at once. Luckily my Neukölln apartment is only a 30-minute power walk away. I stride along the canal until it forks up towards Weichselplatz. With teardrops falling down my face, I bid farewell to the hidden fish and visible geese. Today has seen my stress levels increase triple-fold and my shoes get worn out unevenly like the leaning tower of Pisa. I'm tired of the pedestrian somebodies, and I have no interest in replacing them with celebrity nobodies who say yoohoo on YouTube. As long as I'm endlessly unheld, everyone had better stay the hell out of my way, yes, that includes God and *all* my 37.2 trillion cells!

(Reader, please keep in mind that when I'm writing to you I am both spewing out the embarrassing truths of my frail psyche and trying to imagine a more ideal organization of the world. I firmly believe we need both to deeply realize anything and stop putting quotation marks around our lives. There are so many terrible things in our present day 'civilization' that I hope one day will be deemed as atrocious as the gladiator games. Meanwhile, my private life kindly reminds you to refrain from dissecting and judging my feeble-minded retreats into fantasy. All romantic love is a projection; I'm just taking it one step further. Mustang horses escape from the protection of domestication, and I am an Amazon warrioress who knows that wild mistakes are more heroic than rigid correctness. I persist with miraculous risks through endless battles, ceaseless fiascos, relentless disasters; and if I recoil permanently into my own two million imaginary worlds, the real world's repression shall have hurled me into exile!)

MY NEEDLE-EDGED NAILS ARE FOR THE PLEASURE OF MY LOVERS AND THE DESTRUCTION OF MY ENEMIES! OH, I HAVE SO MUCH MORE LOVE TO GIVE THAN JUST PETTING A CAT TILL SHE PURRS!!! Will I always invent new hopes and dreams to follow to impossible destinations, harbouring something within myself stronger than that which can be received or even given? If I stay at home or hover in corners or dance on tables, I shall remain alone in a domain of transmutation, limerence and shadow selves where no one can or dares approach me. But reader, is there really no man who's able to find me lying down in a crevice between the tectonic plates of Iceland? The only threesome I wish for is this *gender-fluid-someone* gently fucking my front while the rock undulations caress my back. Is that really too much to ask? *Have I ever had sex with a man with six-pack abs?* Yes, I have. *Does it mean anything?* No. Not even my 15-year-old self would be that impressed by their lavished attentions. There will always be different sides of me conveying different messages. I must decide which side to listen to. I remember being a bit happier when I didn't believe I had so many choices. Ugh, I do not enjoy bouncing between extremes that actually reside very close together: *hyperventilate or hold my breath?* Both will quickly lead to death. Instead I will bring an exhausted honeybee who can't fly to a corner store, getting her sugar water so she can eat and restore her energy. And if she stings my hand, I shall provide her enough time and space to unscrew her stinger in peace so she can fly away and not fall to the ground disembowelled and dead. This usually takes somewhere between 30 seconds and five minutes. If I get ideas that I'm unable to write down on my to-do list during this time period, I shall not angrily slap myself in the face, as it could startle the creature to death, hindering her from resuscitating the planet, mouth-to-mouth, flower-to-flower.

One block before I enter my den to call it a day, a German man detects me. He lets out a panicked holler: 'BASTARD! DU ZER-STÖRT MÄNNLICHKEIT!' – *YOU'RE DESTROYING MANLI-HOOD!* If only it were that simple... I put my keys in the door and leave the streets.

(Reader, stay with me in the now-instant of non-linear and I will grant you my all, my everything, in chunks of raw, heavy, glittering gold as we unfold or unravel or fall to our deaths from a blood-red magic carpet in real time, disrupting the live coverage of the Oscars... But... A miracle! We saved each other's lives by letting our soft parts cushion all the vital organs enclosed within the entangle of our embrace. Now, we are revived into a new beginning in the middle of nowhere... If I couldn't heal my mother's back, I must make sure to heal the whole world; if I couldn't keep Shawn alive, I must make my own depressed life worth living. So bring it on CPTSD, F33.2, GAD, misophonia, MTF, are they Western nicknames for thinking-feeling different, WTF; reader, what's your diagnonsense? My list of useless talents includes a lifetime of giving 30 superb blowjobs to men who'd kill me if I kissed them in front of their friends (I naively hope to have blown my last asshole) and out-analysing ALL psychoanalysts (the patient's IQ is 169 – this level of intelligence always risks banishing a person from the world) before going back to my I don't know, I don't know, I really just don't know, but I have this hunch that our inner universe truly could be as large as, and expanding as quickly as, the universe itself, and if so the hermaphroditic journey is a soul's step closer to our origin of Everything before Zeus's division – Gender Astronauts returning... home? Only to be burned on earth! Indeed, if deeply knowing life and the world also means knowing its darkest alleys, why are almost all gurus men and never the trans women who've seen three times more and spent twice the time immersed in inferno? Why does a male Buddhist monk write a book titled In Love With the World *while a trans woman names her novel* Love the World or Get Killed Trying? *And last but not least WHY do so many slightly feminine straight men think patriarchy's not about them, wilfully forgetting that taking responsibility is*

perhaps the most central feminine quality of all, as the occasional earring or manicure rarely alters anything?

*A deep embrace may be the surest way to save us from the mundane that home must not be, even though our inner emotions sadly can't seem to match the things that actually occur and tend to be misnamed as our lives. Listen, what is it you can hear from all the way across a mountain range, and what could make you cross it? I still believe in us enough to believe it's not a bad thing. Will you change what you can and accept what you can't and not cry **can't** too easily?)*

PARIS
late August 2018

1 —

There are many people who dream of a job where they travel a lot. It's true, I too enjoy traveling. I also love staying at home. In the end I have a tendency to grow unhappy with both. Yes, I suppose that, like Violette Leduc, I wish to do nothing and possess everything. Yes, reader, I'm truly fleeing the scene of home so I won't be forced to celebrate my big 3-0 amongst friends. My 30th birthday is in 3 days, and this bus carries me to a Paris where most of my playmates are dead dears like Violette. The trip from Berlin extends between 6 a.m. and 10 p.m. I can sleep for four or five hours. I can do nothing – or write. I can curse my lust for men – or look out the window and view the changes of scenery: new languages on new road signs, new tree species in new forests, new fields with new flowers, new farmlands with new crops, new dew drops, new rivers, new lakes, new mountains – all with names I indeed do not know, adding to the list of things I'm unaware of. It is 11 a.m. and my curiosity is challenging my exhaustion. Two nights ago I was playing music at a bar. I was drinking. I was handed free drugs. I still haven't learned how to say no to gifts that I'm uninterested in. I ended up wailing Chavela Vargas songs and 'Don't Cry for Me Argentina' from a bench instead of a balcony.

  I don't know what to do about the fact that there are three men on the bus I'm attracted to. I sort of regret that I didn't sleep with the cute guy who propositioned me on the street yesterday. I was beyond tired. Why must my inner neurotic alley cat insist on considering sleeping with a man who whistles at me, raises his eyebrows twice, then winks as I pass? It's not a serious offense when committed by an ugly man, and a compliment with delightful prospects when committed by a handsome fellow. I am a feral cat up for adoption, and he was just looking for 10 minutes in a petting zoo. *Love?* Each sexual harassment becomes further evidence that I can find 5000 men who want to fuck me, but no one to love me. *Love?* Take me away from hyper-stressful scatterings of lust, glancing hither, searching thither, never without an anxious aftertaste. *Love?* Was he one in a million? No, he was one *of* millions. *Writing?* Are you love's unworthy substitute? You are what opens up the possibility to dive the very deepest into life. I surface: *Where? Is it enough?* I will drown in my devotion to you. *Is it enough?* A writer must refuse to enter popularity contests. This authoress is a messy, overachieving perfectionist with no layout skills, a Virgo who can't drive. We don't know the narrative of her story because there is none. And we are happier without the things we don't need. And in the unlikely event that this book becomes a bestseller, the authoress will refuse to join Marina Abramovic's new church of scientology for celebrities. *Does compromise mean to water down?* Tears over meltwater ocean-overflows are the only techniques at my disposal within this department. How I long for Iceland, and how I long for a someone, a together, where we never hide our weak spot or ugly cry from the other or the Earth, for she granted us permission to exist with a *Yes!* And we must sacrifice some things to show that we love her in return.

For five hours I have inhabited a different world... Now, I shall take a short break so we can reflect beyond the surface of mirrors.

The bus reaches Paris. I size up its castle-like structures, heavily trafficked streets, and symmetrically trimmed trees. Birds soar about, with pigeons dominating all other species by about 10 to 1. Now, Alvina Alone steps into the new city and names it: Grandiloquent. The temperature: a tropical heatwave singing the swan song of summer. The air: it smells sweeter than Berlin's, though far from as fresh as Iceland's. I receive a Warm Welcome To Paris from a crazed fan: 'Très jolie, ça va?' English translation: *OMG, Alvina, is that really you? I've worshipped your body for YEARS, especially your long legs, OMG they changed my life!* He's the 600th fan to interrupt my thoughts this summer. I'm not going to thank him. For once my thoughts were not of a negative character. How dare he steal my fleeting moment of curiosity, of serenity! I am wearing a Do Not Disturb sign, but he does not care. I hurry my body away from his gaze, crossing an avenue broad as the river Ganges. Like magic, all vehicles leave me alone. From the other side I can barely make out my fanboy's silhouette. The metro I'm supposed to take is standing at its platform. Is it waiting for me? Will its doors close right in front of my face? *Ne me quitte pas, mon métro, ne me quitte pas!* It adheres to my pleas and allows me to rush in. Dear Paris Métro, you have such a gallant and kind heart. And now you are sweeping me off to my home-away-from-home, an apartment of my own provided by the theatre I'm performing at.

    I arrive after 25 minutes and enter the room. Its inventory list:

1 dark wooden table (I don't think it talks)
2 velvety red, throne-like chairs (I don't think they bleed)
1 multi-coloured rug (too small to fit Cleopatra within)
1 metallic kitchen counter with a sink (I think it can spit)
1 tiny toilet with no bathtub (I think it can stink)
1 couch bed, folded out and made to indicate that the unmade double bed three feet away is a no-go zone. (why? I dunno!)

Books line the white walls, and the ceiling's so high that only a worldclass high jumper could hop up and bump his head. The same goes for the checkered linoleum floor, but now we're talking long-jump champions, Jackie Joyner Kersee, 7.3 meters, but the breadth is just 5, a mediocre Warholesque artist's feat or the misstep of a Valerie-ish virtuoso. There is one poster of Cyndi Lauper and another of Dolly Parton, separated by a painting of a yin-yang. I suppose Cyndi symbolizes yin and Dolly yang. The room is spick-and-span, and I feel filthy after my day spent on the greasy bus. *I'm so stupid*, I stupidly think, *that bus was Lysoled clean, jag är the one who's lathered in oil!* I'm too tired to take a shower over the toilet or limit my sentences to one language. Okay, this room's no castle, but I'm sure it's vast enough to grant me some moments to rid myself of the world and create a new one. My life isn't taking any shortcuts. Perhaps one of these days I'll look out the window and write an essay on why it's dangerous to pseudo-spiritually preach contentment to the oppressed and absurd to say you must love yourself in order to love someone else, as so many love others but not themselves, and so many love themselves but not others. Case in point:

Donald Trump could be one of the most self-loving people on the planet... I fall asleep. Like a newborn baby. No. Like an aging house pet.

2

The sun plays a prank by waking me up with a bright light shining directly in my eyes. *9 a.m.* I have a stretching-in-bed course planned until 11. Tonight is the night of my performance. And not only that. Today is the day I will meet my husband Vaslav Nijinsky. You know, reader, the ballet dancer I've been talking about throughout this book. Well, he's here in Paris, too. I wish to look my very best for him: *perfume, shaved legs, pink lipstick, eyeliner wings, mascara, hotpants...* I hesitate between a crop top and a knee-length peacock top. I decide on the latter. It highlights my creative side, which surely impresses a sad clown like him much more than showing skin. My aim is to leave the house at 1 p.m. In order to leave on time, I need someone to push me. As usual I'm all alone and left to my own devices. When I close the door behind me, it's nearly 3. *I'm late I'm late for yet another very important date!* But Paris is the city of romance and tender caresses where everything's forgiven.

Vaslav&I decide it would be appropriate for us to meet at his grave. He spends a lot of time there and finds it peaceful. The cats and crows keep him company, the trees address each other through the underground fungus, redistributing surplus nourishment to saplings, the sun glows... the wind blows... the leaves and branches dance us into an inner-frenzy of freedom. We are now here together, husband and wife. I'm reading Violette Leduc aloud; he's sitting and listening, silent and attentive, in his costume from the Petrushka ballet. I stand en pointe to show Vaslav my supreme elevation. I am kissing his forehead, his neck, his left cheek. My kisses leave gifts of traces of pink lipstick. Vaslav doesn't describe me the way Genet once described Violette: 'She's crazy, ugly, cheap and poor, but she's got a lot of talent.' No, Vaslav believes in me, *all of me*, he assures my heart that we're worth neither more nor less than the branch of a tree. Then he presents me with an intense pre-performance pep talk:

'I will ask them a question about life. If they feel me, I am saved. If they do not, I will be a poor and pathetic man... In Switzerland people are dry because there is no life in them. I do not like Zürich, because it is a dry town. It has a lot of factories and many business people. I do not like dry people, and therefore I do not like business people. I know they think I am a sick man. I am sorry for them because they think I am sick. I am in good health, and I do not spare my strength. I will dance more than ever. I will also write. I will not go to evening parties anymore. I have had enough of this kind of jollity to last me a lifetime. I don't like jollity. I understand what jollity is. I am not cheerful and jolly, because I know that jollity is death. Jollity is the death of the mind.'

My husband knows what he's talking about. He choreographed the portion of my performance where ballet inverts into butoh: 'Danse Sacrale' from *Le Sacre du Printemps*. There are 122 jumps involved. He knows I must prove that there's nothing I wouldn't do for the world. He is correct. When I was 15 years old, my classmates made fun of me for every possible reason. A new opportunity arose when a girl in our class asked everyone if they would suck the dick of our 60-year-old math teacher in order to save the starving. All the boys and girls hurried to answer, 'No, I would never,' while I said: 'Yes,' without flinching, which resulted in the girl shouting to the entire class: 'OH MY GOD, *ALEX* WANTS TO SUCK THE MATH TEACHER'S COCK!' I hid my face behind my hands, mortified. I should have known better. But I have never known better. And I did not learn my lesson. I CRY OUT. I CRY OUT because my husband is DEAD. He was put into a Swiss mental institution in 1919 at the age of 30, and I was not alive to save him. He never danced publicly nor choreographed again, because he felt everything too strongly to function properly in the non-dancing portions of existence, which swiftly also rendered dancing almost impossible. The remainder of his life was spent in that own world, romantic only in print and moving pictures, like so many things... nearly unbearable to survive, yet a great storyline!

Tears are streaming down my cheeks. To my immense surprise, I am not alone. A retired 61-year-old Polish ballet dancer has joined in. He tells me he hasn't danced for over 30 years. He thought he'd given up that part of his life, but now, today, he stumbled upon Vaslav's grave, and all the emotions came flooding out, drenching his greying beard. Alright, my dear reader, let me recount some facts from the life of my Nijinsky. Descent: *Polish*. Age at time of death: *61*. Years spent without dancing: *Over 30*... The retired ballet dancer and I sit on a bench for 15 minutes talking to each other. We find mutual coordinates by switching between English, which I master better, and German, which he masters better. The time comes for me to leave. A performance awaits, and the audience won't believe I'm an avant-garde artist who decided to be absent from the theatre as a critique of Abramovic's *The Artist is Present*. The man says, 'People always see each other at least twice per life.' I don't quite believe this statement; sometimes we're lucky to have even met once. Still, I hush my protest so I won't be a magic-ruiner. We shake hands, but then he says 'komme hier' and we hug for 30 seconds. This is probably the best experience I've ever had with a male stranger in public space.

3 —

(Reader, though sorrow seems to scare us more than anger, don't worry about me when I'm crying. I am worse off when I'm not. After half an hour, I step into an underworld soulstorm where I embrace Persephone and forget what I was even crying about – without, I would still be colliding sideways into my own anxiety spirals. This is the most alive I get, the most consoled. And as long as I cry, I know I remain: among the living. Although it is too hard to bear.)

My performance takes place at a packed independent theatre in the 3rd Arrondissement. Upon entering the stage, I deliver vocals at a glass-shattering pitch, giving way to a multiphonic screech. Then, after crying twice during 10 minutes of silent staring at the spectators, I begin to *dance for you the war, the war that **you** did not prevent* – Danse Sacrale – a sacrificial eradication of self in the form of the complete physical breakdown of an exhausted body. 122 jumps. My emotions transform into those of an animal. I'm panting, panting, and I can't recite the paragraphs that build a more feminine world without the assistance of a someone else, who leaves the audience for the stage, who reads from my banner as I slowly-slowly regain the strength to resume and crawl across the finish line with sentences like: *If we love truth more than the myth of flawless we can break power with a together. Truly, trying to make everybody happy* *all the time is a noble yet unattainable goal that we've been taught to be ashamed of. There are other things worthy of shame... Such as eating calamari and telling Ursula not to take it personally!*

On the other side, the standing ovation will not end. My eyes well up, again, this occurrence as common as a horse's neigh. I cannot realize what I've done. I know I felt moments of ecstasy, rage, sorrow and hideous grief. In the midst of all this, something happened in space and time, and I was not the only one involved. I don't think I'll ever become a person who believes my words mean anything to anyone other than myself. My greatest solace is that this assessment seems to be incorrect.

    I decide to join the audience for a drink in the lobby and receive a storm of vocal accolades in return. I am gratified, my heart wrapped up in the warm, fluffy coat of utmost happiness. This feeling doesn't last long. Why not? There are both simple and complex answers to that question, reader. For today, I will let you ponder your own multiple layers, while providing an abridged answer: If unhappiness is your general emotional state, positive feelings have an exasperating tendency to rapidly transform into tragedy. Each time somebody tells me they love my work, I am reminded that I can find 500 people who are fascinated by my intensity at the safe distance of a stage or page and no one to hold me after the storm subsides. Still... Most hysterics, crazies, vulnerables, over-emotionals lack even this somewhere-under-the-rainbow to be at rest and welcomed at full force. Alone on stage is the only place where I can feel wholly at home with groups of human beings. And I am lucky. Luckier than my mother.

My dear friend Alejandro from New York is in Paris over the summer. He takes me outside to wax lyrical about my performance. The force of his quick-paced mode of speaking saves me from myself for an instant. He is not my lover either. This does not render a person meaningless; we all need friends in order to survive life till death do us part. One evening at a gallery in Chelsea, Alejandro encouraged me to nurture my poetic gifts, and I transformed into a someone who takes breaks from lamenting cries and worrying complaints in order to give birth to sentences. Can sentences outlive children? Eternity laughs at human hubris! Alejandro has a boyfriend. His boyfriend absolutely LOVED my performance. He offers to take us out to dinner at the rooftop of le Centre Pompidou, where we'll enjoy a view of the whole city, watching it attach itself to the adjective *breathtaking*.

Reader, follow me now, quickly, up the escalators, to the roof! I am at the top of the world. I am the toast of Paris. I sashay forward in my stilettos. You would almost think I am a young, self-confident woman. I am not. Nevertheless, the greenish-yellow lighting of the restaurant becomes me, complementing my tanned complexion and neon-pink-&-black attire. Alejandro's boyfriend must have quite a bit of money; the main courses cost 35 euros apiece. They are delicious delicacies. And the bottle of white wine? Its price is 50. It tastes ten times better than the 1.99 one at Lidl, which means it is not quite earning its keep. I only take very small sips. The last time I had a post-performance hangover, I felt like jabbing a knife into my everything, starting with my intestines. I don't intend to inhabit that emotional space tomorrow. Alejandro and his boyfriend gulp&gulp, then order another bottle. The boyfriend has many contacts: Journalists, Curators, Artists, Stylists. He names several that he would like to introduce me to in order to support my 'promising career that has only just begun'. I am getting greedy. Whenever I get greedy, whether for fame, sex, money, romance, new experiences, or 27 different food options on a menu, I become overwhelmed. I wish I could go home and cry Right Now & At Once but settle for fleeing the table for some Alvina Alone Time in the design-magazine-like toilet. I engage in a staring contest with the mirror. Who will start laughing first, me or my reflection? Neither of us. There have been enough smiles and laughter for tonight.

I think about why I abhor the concept of hedonism. It is because it centres the sensory pleasures of the self, while ignoring the everybody. Has this specific era of digital capitalism worn down our hope for another world? Is that why we're behaving this way? I believe we must instead enter a room and prioritize the well-being of the space as a whole. Besides, sense gratification isn't even possible; as soon as you get satiated you go searching for more. I hate hunting; intuitively I wish mainly to lie down. I splash cold water over my face and wrists. I decide against a reverse-narcissus attack on my mirror image. I feel replenished enough to resume social activities.

Back at our table, Alejandro and his boyfriend are very drunk. They're continuing to flatter me. Alejandro thinks I should finish my book. He speaks of writing as if it were something you *just do*. Meanwhile, I live side by side with my latest failures, sensing the simultaneous spasms of a still-breathing rat being swallowed whole by a black mamba. Oh Alejandro, stop tempting me to inflict words and true stories upon a non-existent audience! Why would *anyone* take notice of an attention-seeker whose sense of form resembles a toddler perplexed by building blocks? They're too busy hiding every failure and boast-posting their gratefulness towards all their successes on social media. And I hate them for it! I wish Susan Sontag was alive to write a book on this phenomenon. It could be called: *Instagram – Everybody's The Captain In Their Own Bathtub*. As I gaze out at the view over Paris, I experience a paralyzing vertigo combined with yet another compulsion to jump and let my heartbreak finally rest. Useless. I'll still never be invited to the parties of the posthumously revered artists.

Alejandro and his boyfriend turn their attention from me and commence flirting with the handsome waiter. He looks just like all the other waiters at this restaurant: David Beckham at age 28. Is this the hiring policy of le Centre Pompidou's delicatessen? I disapprove of it. I am worried that my friends are making the waiter uncomfortable. Don't they understand that he's forced to be here and put up with this shit just to receive a paycheck and hopefully a hearty tip to pay the rent for his overpriced Parisian apartment? I try to be extra nice to him to counterbalance my friends' thoughtless shenanigans. My exaggerated kindness doesn't seem well received. Perhaps he thinks I'm flirting as well. The situation can't be helped. He notices the scars and burn marks on my right forearm and rushes off with his face flushed bright red. I suppose he's of the belief that feral cats carry disease.

Reader, I just wish to whisper in your ear, *Psst, scars are the most sensitive area for a kiss...*

(My Icelandic tour guide visits my mind to ask a question: *How can Paris be considered romantic when it has no bridal-veil waterfalls or attractive trolls?* Her quirky sense of humour, her benevolent no-nonsense; they provided a protection that opened rather than closed a shell...)

4 —

I am lying awake at 4:48. Since the metro stopped running, I've been granted the favour of sleeping over at Alejandro's boyfriend's luxury condo in Montparnasse. I have a private room filled with Ikea furniture and classic antiques. The mattress is a comfy Tempur-Pedic. Three other culprits are behind my insomnia: Mosquitoes, Heat and Money. Anxiety gets along fine&dandy with money since neither ever sleep. And as for the heat? Alejandro's boyfriend offered me an escape, to join in on a poolside weekend at his family's countryside chateau. I declined the offer, citing my desire to explore Paris. And now the stifling air is causing me grave affront. Why must I suffer? Why can't I relax surrounded by the upper class and pool boys serving aperitifs? My much poorer upbringing is six-needle-mosquito-biting me in the heel. I cannot handle a tree that grows money in a deforested world. The Family would laugh at my ill-manners and peculiarisms, and I would run off crying, hiding in the garden, burying myself in Tsvetaeva's and Pasternak's letters, realizing all three of us rarely read contemporaries lest they curtail our style, while my favourite pool boy sneaks up and says, 'Hey girl, wanna fuck?' And if The Family catches us in the act, we shall both be thrown out to fend for ourselves in the endless forest!

    4:48. A startling revelation: *I am going to die relatively soon. And Alejandro and his boyfriend too!!!* I am comforted by the fact that time momentarily stands still during sleepless nights. This is the case whether you are in a luxurious suite or a sweaty night bus. My perspiration wets the sheets. *Sticky*. The pesky mosquitoes with their six-needle straw-mouths keep biting me. *Itchy*. Do mosquitoes in France spread any deadly diseases? Why do I always ask myself frantic questions to which I have no answers in the middle of the night? Besides: I don't hear any buzzing, nor do I feel the undulations of their stings prickling my skin. Perhaps the itches are just products of my own hallucinations. A bedside chair sits stiff as rigor mortis, providing me with proper proof that I reside inside reality. The mosquitoes emerge, circling my body in a gang of three. They deserve to be slapped, but they don't deserve to die, so I keep my hands to myself. I decide that my insomnia is best battled by focusing on breathing. I fart, silent but deadly. A cracked, rotten egg infests the stuffy air, forcing me to hold my nose. I experiment with having only my feet underneath the sheets as opposed to my whole legs. It is still too warm in this heatwave. I can't sleep wrapped in sweat. How about one foot above and the other below? It's a bit better. The sun is about to rise over Paris. I pace towards the balcony to greet it out in the open. I hope it has something important to say to me. The Sunrise Over Paris doesn't utter a word. It can only expose my own shadow. Nevertheless, if Clarice Lispector and Violette Leduc were able to both live and die without escape routes or emergency exits, so am I.

5 —

In an email to me, Diamanda Galás once wrote: 'A person who thinks too much generally finds resolution to the questions he asks himself upon the discovery of a filial soul. The end of terminal individuality is a great thing. One always returns to it, but then the music or the words of kindred souls can soothe the pain of maniacs or the depressed. And the number of those persons is not small.'

Today, Alejandro is saving me. I didn't wake up this morning, not due to any major health issues, but because one cannot awaken after a sleepless night. If you don't have a certain place to be at a certain time, you just decide, with great hesitation, to finally rise from bed and start your day. I open the door at 12:15, and Alejandro greets me with a whip of fervent, speedy conversation. Even with zero minutes of sleep, it suits me fine; the rhythm spins at the same tempo as my mind did all night. His boyfriend's gone to Lyon, and Alejandro is offering me a hand, helping me crawl out of the pitch-dark cave of my own cranium. Here, we're not glancing at the clock, no, time is watching *us*, holographic, and I move into my solar plexus. Alejandro's curly bangs bounce against his forehead like bedsprings as he obsesses over his next movie, *Medea, Medea, Medea*. That theme speaks to me, my mouth opens wide, 'Ayy, I am her, in house arrest, a quarantine queen rebelling against the main four religions written by men... Wait, apologies for these black-&-white

bitcheries, Ambedkar's Navayana Buddhism sees Nirvana as an injusticeless Earth!' Alejandro's hands gesticulate like flying birds, he's excited, wishing to quote precisely those lines in his film. I reply, *alright, yes, better than fine!* Our conversation continues: my body language expands my size to its triple, his fervour lands a quadruple-toe-loop, such power, this one-on-one – platonic, playful, pouncing wildebeests set on sleepless spiritual fire, are we two of the twenty thousand humans truly alive in the world today? This just means we'll feel more, cry more, jump for joy more, experience sadness in rage, curiosity in the city of Drama, and have intensity and serenity as our main hobbies. But... it also means Alvina is not actually alone! The metallic Ikea furniture disagrees, wishing I'd drown in a white dress, instead of painting it red with wild strawberries. Shut up Ikea, Alejandro is saving me, saving me from the violence of being realistic, rescuing me from the alliance between active violence and banal evil. Other days, Diamanda Galás has been my lifesaver in this tempest. We met in Stockholm in 2012. Our relationship grew into a kinship. A bond beyond jollity. She taught me not to fear pain, so I learned to sit with it, endure it alone, observe the multi-coloured darkness, feel the quivering vibrations, and then... a transformation: the form of euphoria which glows in lives that have made love to death and been impregnated with the alertness of a birth-scream!

6

Reader, a full day has passed since we last saw each other. Alejandro went to the chateau and I chose Paris. Anything else? Of course, but there are times when I realize I can spare you all the details and keep some secrets between myself and myself... I feel at peace. It is noon and I am chewing on some toast and crackers alone in my home-away-from-home. The 300 euros I earned for my performance are delighted to be given a long life inside a savings account instead of dying at lavish brunches. I contemplate the concept of Cruel Optimism, how we need to stop advocating for positive thinking when turning a blind eye to concrete problems only ensures continued inequity. I meditate upon open-feelings and shut-off-feelings and how it's off-target to state that 'people vote with their feelings' when they elect Far-Right politicians, as it's actually just their shut-off-feelings of *it happened to you not me*. And when you're accustomed to privilege, equality and confrontation can seem like oppression.

I go to the tiny toilet. My fingers flick a switch, and a fan wafts cool air onto my body at a seamlessly pleasurable speed. I quiver. Goosebumps and stiff nipples remind me to relieve myself in that more passionate way. My hand caresses my sex, strangling my agonies into a full-blown ecstasy akin to oxygen deprivation. I stick two fingers up my hole. I think of my mathematician-poet. He is so tender, doting and delicate in his kisses. He penetrates my eyes with loving intent, and I breathe fire as I bite into his neck. For the first time in 25 months, I allow someone to suck me off; my full head-to-toe forms itself into a glorious reverberating crescendo, funnelling from my forehead.

Dehumanizing myself is off the menu with my mathematician holding me after our mutual orgasm flowing into a mutual crygasm – a found stability in shared instability. I did not play porno girl to a macho man who just wants to shoot his load down my throat. I have been granted 30 seconds of hope for the future. I am reaping rewards. I understand: Alongside an element of feeling in control, my devotion to giving head derives from an aversion towards dealing with the dysfunctional, dysphoric relationship I have with my own body and its genitals. So, what needs to change? The world, my body, my mind, my men, all men, or everything and all of the above?

How am I supposed to talk to anyone about the totality of this? I'm telling you now, reader, and for just a moment it is enough as I Hop-Skip-Jump over to a more trivial thought that can be resolved straight away: *my destination for today*. I would like to find the best spot in Paris to be alone with my books. This place must be far away from the horses that constantly pass gas. Not silent... But deadly! A park contains no roads for them. I decide upon visiting the Bois de Boulogne, a green area located in the city centre. Vaslav Nijinsky and Sergei Diaghilev took walks there. So did Simone de Beauvoir and Violette Leduc. I imagine Vaslav throwing temper tantrums and running off into the woods. I hear Violette bemoaning her shortcomings: 'I'm an old, mad, ugly, neurotic failure. Alone, always alone. I've no money, no love life, nothing.' (*Moi aussi, chère Violette, moi aussi.*)

As I exit the metro station, La Défense appears far away in the distance. Its skyscrapers remind me of giant monster homes. But unlike the melting Solheimajökull, who has a volcano-monster named Katla living inside her, these sterile buildings house mainly businessmen. Many of them surely consider me the Bride of Frankenstein, to fuck, to fear, to pity. But their knowledge of monsters is next to nothing; for if I truly were a monster, my mother would be Katla, and I'd rise redheaded from the ash of volcanic lightning, yes, I'd stride inviolably into the world, immune to all this mortal brittleness, and I'd block all the stabs and punches and gunshots that murder us 400 times a year!

I enter the Bois de Boulogne forest as a human being with no one to complain to or run from. I let my feet become the enemies of each other. As they walk forward – one-two, one-two – they make sure to never touch. No shadows cast in the shade of the woods: 'Take up your pen, you can change things with it! Screaming and sobbing will get you nowhere – Writing will! Look at you! It's already changed the way you view yourself!' Simone said to Violette. I am still waiting. For a Simone to assist me. For a writing that provides us with all that we've thus far been denied in life... Feet – one-two, one-two – do you even know where you are going? No, you do not – one and two – thanks a bunch, as if it wasn't enough that I *feel* lost, now I literally *am* lost. I am a parasite. Yes. But a parasite who at least has the decency of parasiting on her own miserable existence.

    I keep trekking on. This forest is located in a city; it can't expand without end, can it? After 10 minutes or forever, depending on your perspective and flair for drama, I finally see three people by a parking lot in the distance. I am saved. I get closer. Two men in suits are grabbing a trans woman by her dress and refusing to let go. The world is a minefield of tyrannies for us to walk into. I attempt an altercation by trying to release her from their grip. Unsuccessfully. One of the men whines 'ROBBERY!' while the other flashes his police badge. He hurls abuse at me in French, but all I understand is 'Au revoir!' I refuse to obey his command. The policeman starts poking me with his baton. Harder. And Harder. I am not Pokémon, I'm no superhero at all, no, not even Catwoman. The baton hurts me in the places where breasts may one day grow. There's nothing I can do here but get myself into trouble, adding a plus one to an already existing equation. I decide to leave, to abandon my sister. That man was probably one of those johns who puts money on the dashboard and then takes it back once he's cum. I doubt he's as innocent as he pretends to be. And besides, if they're very rich and you're very poor, you have every right to rob them. Best of luck trying to explain that to Herr Constable. Last year, the policeman in Rome who randomly pulled up his car and stopped me on the street wouldn't listen to a word I said. He demanded to see my passport. He hid his heart behind sunglasses. I did all I could to still my mind, while my instincts screamed: THROW A TANTRUM LIKE SERENA WILLIAMS AT THE US OPEN! I stuttered: 'I-I'm just out for a walk in search of Ingeborg Bachmann's apartment.' 'WOAHAHA,' he roared straight in my face and proceeded to telephone the station and check up on my details. He didn't tell me to give him a ring each time I experience a hate crime, undoubtedly because he wouldn't want me calling him up every day. Instead, he said: 'Scram, you're in a sensible area with many churches and synagogues!' My walk away was no sashay. It was a colossal struggle to keep my back straight while my blood boiled inside a pressure cooker, burning with hefty shame at my feet and steaming with anger across the underside of my skull.

Dear pumping blood, you are the renewable source of energy which keeps my life company through thick and thin. Back in the here & now, I'm searching for a nice park clearing to sit on the lawn and read, but all I can see is trees and more trees. I stumble upon the Foundation Louis Vuitton. It is surrounded by fences and entrance fees. I bum a cigarette from a security guard and resume my quest. I trace a stray cat on my arm again to extinguish the ember. I utter 'meow', not 'ow', as pain is everyday and a kitty cat is a much-needed break. I give her a name: *Aurora*. Moments later my search for unbroken light bears fruit. A clearing 50 feet ahead. I take a seat. I read two pages in Leduc's book about two women, *Therese & Isabelle*. When I look up, three men are ogling me. I know, reader, I seem to be obsessed with repeating these anecdotes to you. It's not my intention. If it gives you a headache to read, what do you think it's like to live? Yes, for all the time I spend alone, I am *never* left alone. And Paris seems to be taking it one step further. Is this a cruising area or the red-light district? The rules of attraction lead me to straight johns searching for trannies. But I am neither a high-femme faggot nor a trans sex worker, though I've been both. And it really doesn't matter where I'm located; men consider me a living, breathing, mobile cruising ground anyways. Why bother going to a certain park or public toilet when I can be found wandering about everywhere with two holes that may soon become three.

(Books & whores... Every time I enter a fancy bookstore people stare at me with a look that says: *What is a street hooker doing here?* Meanwhile, a flirtatious man at a Berlin bar couldn't belieeeve that I was an author and my trans friend a university student. Still, he expected us to have a threesome with him...)

I sit on the lawn trying to read the story of a heated love affair between two women as three men zone in on my body with crude smiles, convinced that I no doubt look like a goddess and act like a cyborg. They view sex like Boy Scout training: *Always prepared.* They want it now and right now, never tomorrow. I am on the turf of men who easily expose their bodies and rarely expose their souls. It's been years since I was asked *what's your favourite song,* but I average about six sex invites per hour. Radical Queer Cruising, I suppose. Whose liberation goes 'Every Time We Fuck We Win'? Do you wonder why most trans women turn to sex work? Easy. How many job application rejections can one woman take, and how many hypersexualizing men can she stomach before saying, 'May as well get paid...' In the OkCupidian civilization, digitalized selves publicly post answers to 100 personal questions, and *No, never* is what 99 percent of straight men reply to: *Have you ever not had sex because you felt too unattractive?* I wonder how they do it or if it's even true? Have they never been sweaty after a two-hour workout, gone three days without showering, or eaten a shit-ton of garlic?

The three oglers close in on me with the use of their legs. Though I have nowhere to run, I use my stems to get up, stand up, and stride away. The oglers decide to not hunt me down this time... Perhaps tomorrow I'll finally give in, say, *Okay, fine, let's do it,* and 'be promiscuous' in order to prove to myself and the world that I too can enjoy recreational sex, that my 31st time with a secretive man provides both the charm *and* the prince charming! Until then, ice cream is screaming my name. Preferred flavour: *Mango sorbet*. Cost: *3.60 euros per scoop.* The costliness of this city is a disgraceful scandal! Since all love starts with hate, the ice cream tastes very good; it has little chunks of real mango in it. I never want it to end, and our human imagination still can't quite grasp space's or time's beginning, end, or eternity. At least not yet. I've told you, reader, I wish to be a part of this expansion of human consciousness. I'm not sure how yet.

7 —

Once upon a time, Sylvia Plath told me: *Any ole idiot can get a tan in summer.* Her words put me at ease as I stroll along the shady side of a Paris street. The temperature is 35 degrees. If I were walking in the sun, my face would transform from a prima ballerina's into a pig's. I begin counting my heartbeats: 1, 2... If I make it to 108,000, I will have made it around a full day. A good-looking young man whistles at me by the filthy Canal St. Martin. My heartbeat quickens. I know reader, I know, I said I'd wait till tomorrow to 'be promiscuous', but... I'm so weary of wasting my beauty on an endless string of *nays*. Nearly 108,000. For once, may I trust my *yes* and at long last make way for the potential of pleasure, of liberation!

I stop dead in my tracks and release a coy smile. The man is around 25 years old, with black hair, green eyes, a polo shirt, and three-quarter shorts. He grabs my hand, body contact, a momentary relief from unbroken aloneness. Before I can nestle into the sensation, he starts walking, swiftly, motioning for me to follow him towards the river Seine. His high speed ensures that he remains five steps in front so no one can see he's with a tranny till we arrive at our destination, the underside of a bridge. After staring at my legs, my chest, my face, he places his hands around my waist and tugs me out of the blazing sun. A spark ignites between my legs. A language barrier cuts off our voices, and I don't know how to tell him, 'Tomorrow's my 30th birthday' in French, *something-something mon anniversaire* – maybe I don't want to tell him anyways. There is just 1 meter of space before a 90-degree drop-off into the river. There are blankets, pillows, suitcases filled with clothes, and a used condom we could easily slip on like a banana peel. It smells of piss and shit. *Some people have no other option than to sleep here, they've got it far worse than me, and I am dumb enough to be here of my own free will.* Nausea invades my senses. This isn't a good place to faint. I don't trust that he cares about me enough to jump into the water and save my life. *Ohh what a way to go; hello Nijinsky, hello Shawn, I can see you laughing at me from above!* The man's facial expression changes. He takes out his dick. It rises. It is big but not beautiful – a dried mushroom – the opposite of a torch that lights my fire. Vomit and tears compete for the right to exit my body, but remain inside locked in a fight. I cannot do this again. I cannot put his dick in my mouth. It is exploding with veins. It stinks a bit, it might not have been cleaned for two days. I was taught to not put dirty things in my mouth for good reason. If he gets carried away fucking me hard, I'll fall into the Seine, drowning the lapdog who assumed she was safe-and-sound inside my backpack. And sure, I could contract several STDs from his sperm, but to swallow that unholy water must be akin to injecting snake venom!

The police pass by on a speedboat. They are all over the river conducting some sort of anti-terrorism drill. If they decide to abruptly halt it and arrest us for indecent conduct, I will end up gang-raped in a panopticon men's prison. It's a better idea to hide here and risk getting raped by only one guy. I search for a mastermind scheme. I find it: *Make a run for it! Right now. And whatever you do, DON'T look back.* I am a rolypoly hurrying across a paved road to the relative safety of a grass ditch. As soon as the sunrays make contact with my skin, I know: *You're okay now, bitch!* No swimming in the Seine. No arrest. No rape. No STDs. No me in the role of his favourite t-girl porn star. Not on the eve of my 30th b-day! I walk on sensibly and merge with the throngs of tourists. 15 minutes go by, and the cool river breeze nurses my level of adrenaline back to normal. One heartbeat, two heartbeats, three, thumping me, me, and me... A gay couple is holding hands. I feel attracted to both of them. They only have eyes for each other. They are in a mutual loving relationship; ohh, how marvellous it must be to feel one's love settling in another's body ❤ ❤ ❤

If I wished to present my life in an idealized light, I guess I could've described what took place under the bridge as 'he took me in his firm embrace and we nearly made love by the river'. But I would never lie to you, reader, and now I'm supposed to be meeting my friend Cecile for dinner at 8, all the way on the other side of town. That's in 30 minutes, and the trip probably takes well over an hour. See, this is where attempts at hedonism take you, to a place where you are very late to meet your friends! Debaucherous endeavours only serve to increase my tardiness from bad to utterly unacceptable.

It is 8:36, 3 hours and 24 minutes before my birthday. Cecile and I had decided to meet at her metro station, but she is nowhere to be found. I call her and apologize profusely for my lateness. She says, 'Don't worry, the birthday girl must always be forgiven, I just didn't feel like waiting around any longer...' Her home is near the station, so she'll be back in 10–15 minutes. We hang up. I think about using this time to paint my nails, but decide to do nothing and let my thoughts wander instead. The problem with standing still is you're no longer a moving target, you're a sitting duck. One man persistently rings the bell of his bike to get my attention. Another man asks, 'Are you lost, little lady?' and starts inching closer. My intuition tells me he perceives me as a 'regular woman', so I'd better not make a peep. My deeper voice could give me away, and he might lose his shit and punch my face in – oh misogyny, thou summer vacation to transmisogyny! Two women notice what's going on. They stand next to me, creating a protective shield – a rare act of solidarity. Generally, cis-jennys seem to believe I'm either dressed asking for it or that men would never fancy me... These two Jennifer Coolidges only speak a little English. This one Jenny Hiloudaki only speaks a little French. We manage to craft a conversation through body language and Google Translate. They friend-request me on Facebook. Cecile arrives. I am so very lucky to have three friends in one space. A bus passes us by. It leads to the Thai restaurant Cecile recommends. We depart with a swift 'Au revoir!' and make a 50-meter dash. The bus waits at its station. As we board, our pulse beats at a pace slightly short of out of breath. We inhale the stench of French fries and body spray. A gang of teenage boys stares me down and laughs. We stare back, point & laugh, which immediately switches their mood to *Very Angry*. I should've known to keep my head down, historically it's saved me multiple hospital visits. Now the atmosphere is ominous, and I've lost all control over where the confrontation is going. The presumed leader of the pack threatens: 'Who the fuck do you think you're tricking, you stupid, pink man-woman – stop disrespecting us or we'll break your nose and the cops won't do shit!' His sidekick proceeds to throw a full plastic soda bottle as hard as he can. A middle-aged woman lets out a shriek and begins bawling. She's been hit in the eye and may be extremely injured. *That bottle was meant for me!* I don't know what to do. I feel guilty. What if she can no longer see? The boys rush up to the woman and apologize profusely: 'We didn't mean to hit you!' They point in my direction: 'It was *its* fault.'

I hate myself and I want to die. *That bottle was meant for me!* Yes, but... No buts this time. *It was NOT my fault. I didn't do anything.* My thoughts are correct, but I must keep them to myself or I could end up punched. Thankfully, Cecile screams this sentiment in their ears while the distressed woman voices her agreement in between sobs: 'NO, it was not his fault, he didn't do anything.' *Oh, but don't you understand? I'm not part of the male class – that's what got us all into this trouble to begin with!* The woman has calmed down from her initial shock. Her eyesight seems to be fine, and the air becomes a bit less heavy. She goes to the bus driver. She wants to file a police report. The boys hurry off the bus as if they were a stampede of rhinos running from a stampede of hippos. Their ringleader yells from outside, 'Good luck with your sex change,' while gesturing to mimic gigantic tits. Surveillance cameras have captured everything they did. This isn't a good thing. But they also need to be taught a lesson. Three other women get involved. They support me with hugs and vocal condemnations of the young lads. I feel like crying, but my emotions are pulling me in too many downward-facing directions at once. I cannot talk. Once again, adrenaline wraps around me like a cape or a tortilla. WE WERE SUPPOSED TO HAVE A NICE BIRTHDAY DINNER, TOASTING AT THE STROKE OF MIDNIGHT. *HAPPY BIRTHDAY TO YOU, YOU LIVE IN A ZOO...* 'Well, at least it's not your birthday yet,' Cecile remarks, showing me the time, 9:45, then giving me a 30-second hug.

By the time we reach the restaurant, it's already closed. I am shaking. Being sexualized is so much easier to handle than this violent hatred. The former often takes minutes to recover from, chipping at my soul by way of sheer amount, while the latter may linger for hours. I try to think like a person who would write *#blessed*, but remind myself that I don't flee from troublesome truths. Cecile hands me a cigarette to calm my nerves. She suggests we go back to her home, 20 minutes walking distance from here. Oh, if only we had taken a walk to begin with, none of this would have happened. True. But perhaps another bottle would've been thrown; perhaps it would've been glass instead of plastic; perhaps it would've shattered upon hitting its target and I would be blind in one eye now... *Perhaps. Perhaps. Perhaps.*

Cecile tells me about her near-death experience. About 6 months ago, she almost drowned in Venezuelan river rapids before being saved by a trans woman who lifted her up in her arms and carried her to shore: *Safety*. Later, they made love. It was the trans woman's first time with another woman. Reader, this is another story that deserves to be told in full. I wish I could just lean in, relax, and let it stream across these sheets of paper for days, multilayer upon multilayer. But I can't. Because rulebooks state: *We lack space for a trillion-page world...*

Here and now we arrive home safe and sound with no new major mishaps. In a flowing red dress that perfectly matches her lipstick, Cecile serves me orange juice and makes us dinner: mashed potatoes, mushrooms, string beans and garlic. We talk about our struggles in life: of violence and rape, of self-destructions and redemptions, of disappointments and mistreatments, of love & hate and hate & hate and how rarely we've ever felt loved or protected. We invent new forms of laughter that could tear through the wet dawn. We are different, we are similar, we grow together in crooked directions of vast poetic elation and undecorated grief. Whoever said red doesn't fit with pink? I believe she & I are sad clown soulmates of some sort. I believe we all have 888 soulmates in the world; most we won't ever meet, and only 88, the number of keys on a piano, are meant for romances. My dear reader, in order to uncover the secret meanings behind this long moment's eye-to-eye may I please share our favourite verse by Nicki Minaj, and let it serve as an invitation to our havoc-wreaked beauty pageant:

> *Every time I write I'm precise in my skill, there's more to life than just ice in your grill. You wanna fuck me, blame me, fuck you, pay me, this is what you made me, say you wanna drape me, turn around and rape me, nah you ain't mistake me, where my girls at, where my girls at, if they be frontin' then tell them yo where my money at?*

Oh reader, these lyrics are so strong, yet unbearably heart-wrenching. They are the life I live in, not the love I long for – the lovemaking sessions that drip and taste like warm, ripe mangos freshly picked from sun-kissed trees, ending in a climactic collapse and a symbiotic embrace. At this very moment, I imagine those two men I saw walking down the street hand-in-hand must be cuddling like that. For this love to touch my reality, it seems I must transform into a completely different person. Not trans. Less intense. No overemotional fits. Maybe a lesbian. Most of the trans woman lesbians I know actually have stable, loving relationships. But, alas, it's impossible to flip your entire self over like a coin. Perhaps my little epiphanies come in blades of grass or studying the patterns of irregular water currents in a river instead.

Cecile walks me to the metro station and boosts me over the barrier so I can gain a free ride back to my den. Only after we've hugged goodbye do I look at my dumbphone and realize that I'm already 57 minutes into my date of birth. More important things than birthdays have taken place. I arrive home at 1:52, after experiencing just a few small nips of sexual harassment. Note to self: No eye contact with men, not even for a second... *Unless* you stare them down with the unnerving evil-eye Maria Sharapova gives her opponents before serving an ace.

(At 5 a.m. I am roused from sleep. The man who owns both this apartment and the theatre I performed at has returned home early from his vacation and brought a lover along. They begin to fuck. I won't despair. They are trying their best to be quiet. No, they're not. They are brushing me aside, despite my best efforts to stay out of the way. I am the sleepless guest lying on the doorstep of passion and pleasure. I am the 9-year-old child the parents mustn't wake up. They finish their moaning song and gyrating dance after 2 hours and 45 minutes. I let out a sigh of relief without actually sighing; I must not draw any attention to myself; I need to remember that I'm alive and can still experience positive things. Finally, and at last, I go back to sleep and dream of a Brazilian author who snubbed me at a reading two months ago. I'm not talking about Clarice Lispector. She would never do that to me. She broke my chair when I was watching her documentary. She sent her cousin's daughter to point me in the direction of her apartment one street up from the Leme strand of Copacabana beach. No, the author's name was not Clarice. It was Italo Diblasi.)

8

I am sitting at the renowned Café de Flore; she has seen Simone de Beauvoir write *The Second Sex* and doesn't care that it's my birthday. She believes I'm spending waaaay too much time inspecting my own navel, scribbling shit that interests no one. She judges me for being unable to afford anything other than a 4.80-euro tiny espresso. The receipt left by the guests at the nearest table shows 226 euros. I fold it and save it in my right shoe. My other shoe tells me: *You are a troglodyte, a cavewoman who should never crawl out.* The plants, the tables, the stains, the unused place mats, the folded aprons, the doors, the corridors, the carafes all urge me to accept my role. I will. I wish I could kiss a cockroach on the mouth right now; do they have a tongue or saliva? Alas, there are none in sight... A tiny mouse crawls across the floor unnoticed by both patrons and waiters. I feel more at home now. I have friends here who live and breathe. One does not have to be Cinderella with a future of glass slippers, fairy godmothers, castles and prince charmings to make friends with mice. The hours pass by midday: I have made it more than halfway through this hellish birthday, which has been nearly all my birthdays since childhood: focused microscopes expecting me to brag that *I am I*, when all I wish for myself is a transformation into a kaleidoscope!

I leave the café. I know where I'm going, and the higher I climb, the more I understand the city landscape: Lavender blossoms, main streets, towers, river forks, sunlight promiscuously dancing the tango with unnumbered clouds. One does not have to be like (or even like) *Amelie* to savour Montmartre. I have made it to the top. I did not fuck my way up here; I walked. But given the way the churchgoers are glaring at me, one wouldn't be able to tell the difference. Yes, this summit features a gigantic cathedral with a famous name. No, it doesn't matter how many millions of people inhabit a city (1, 2, 9) or how many thousands of quick-sex invites I turn down (1, 2, 9), I will always remain the town slut outside every church. I have the audacity to enter, and the luck of being here in the right year to not be met by a hail of stones. I have no wish to draw attention to myself. I sit down in the very back and listen to the mass in a language I don't comprehend save for a few words: *Le* & *Dieu*, as they used to call my Nijinsky *Le Dieu de la Danse*. And today, on my 30th birthday, I wish I could ask him some questions about life, but he's gone and he never knew the answers anyhow: *How does one survive life off stage or outside the writing crater?* He clearly had no idea, no protection, no 'coping strategies'. For years he didn't speak a word, instead communicating through bringing flower bouquets to his heart, then holding them up to the sky. Djuna Barnes says: 'The excess of his sensibilities may preclude his mind. His sanity is an unknown room: a known room is always smaller than an unknown.'

A spirit lip-syncs for my life: *You're not on earth to 'collect' as many experiences as possible, nor to 'participate' in as many activities as you can.* I sit still and listen to the church choir sing. The acoustics reverberate with a 10-second delay that provides goosebumps to a body and a momentary home for a soul. And then: *Silence. Silence and Wonderment.* A life is avidly burning inside me. Slowly the instants connect to each other, another... another... yet another! The moment – eternity's greatest rival. I see a moth fluttering about in the holy water, gradually drowning. Is she the same one who keeps popping up ever since I sent her from Berlin to comfort RoRo in the Euro football finals? *Possibly, maybe...* Her name is not a topic of relevance. Mass extinction of insects *is*. I ask myself: *What Would Jesus Do?* If I wish to pay my dues, I mustn't waste time praying to god or confessing my sins. I spring to action to save her soul. I play the Lord & Savior Jesus Christ by placing my finger underneath her moth-body, allowing her to walk on water and steer towards dry land. She shakes her wings in relief or disbelief. She stares at me or the colour of my clothes. We transfer a shared realization that our destiny has nothing to do with dying for someone's sins. The churchgoers pay no attention to this ongoing human-moth interaction. They're all facing the opposite direction, captivated by the preacher who's preaching. The choir chants... The moth takes flight... The chills multiply down my spine... Oh, those Bible-paper-thin wings! None of our actions will be recorded in history books. Just as well.

The church concert ends without knowing that it filled me with something without a name that I didn't know I needed. I would have preferred to receive it from another source. Did we really believe we could just eliminate religion from our lives without anything holy to take its place? Today owns property while searching for more followers. Tomorrow is unknown. But though the proceeding of time itself is predestined, the content of these proceedings is not.

Outside in the hot-air balloon-like 4 p.m. sunshine, I stumble upon a courtyard encased by lavish restaurants with outdoor seating. Every table is taken in order to not tempt me to sit down and see if I'll be served or shooed away. I thank the wealthy tourists of Paris for hindering this social experiment from taking place. It would have been a true lose-lose situation, unobstructed humiliation or 22 euros for a pathetic and unfilling appetizer, onion-breathed bruschetta/tasteless tomato soup. A young woman with tiny mid-90's sunglasses motions to a waiter and sentences a fish to death with the point of an index finger, a smile, and a noise-polluting US American accent. *Les poissons, les poissons, how she loooves les poissons.* I try to carry on with my day. In the next half hour, I count 30 cool people under 30 wearing those same sunglasses in shades of red, blue and green. Why do already ugly trends insist upon running a second lap around the track? Doesn't it feel strange to come back when no one's missed you? Fuck. Now I feel bad. *Dear Tiny Sunglasses, forgive me for my misguided insults, they stem from my own personal preference for gigantic bug eyes, yet you're the ones who waste the least amount of resources...*

I ponder heading back to the church to confess this latest sin but instead decide to zigzag my way down to the River Seine and park lakes that I'm used to. I travel at the swift speed of two clompclomps a second as the view of Eiffel Towers, La Défenses and Arc de Triomphes are replaced by simply being able to see what's right in front of me. Here, I am brought back to earth. At the bottom of the church hill, two cars in a row stop and try to pick up my short-shorts-sheltered booty. I will never understand why my feminine body garners so much attention, while my superpower, my feminine intensity, is feared like a rushing flood or the point of a needle. *Ugh, my ashes will be warmer than their sex!!!* How do I stay focused on my mind when my frame's always what's spotlit? As I age, the men of the streets will finally leave me in peace as my body begins to crumble without the touristic allure of an Acropolis or Colosseum. *Nice ruins...* I am a pink blooming cactus teetering on the edge of a cliff, juicy innards; around me just dust, sand, dry air. There's no one I need to apologize to for never being a happy, healthy, balanced, stable young woman. To grow older means finding ways to no longer hate yourself, to rest inside your most private catacombs. It does not mean 'there are so many things I never did': There will always be an endless number of things you never did: And most of the things you never did, you didn't do because you never really wanted to.

9 —

Life! Reader! Both of you, stop being so demanding! I've got2go now. Sharks must constantly move in order not to die. HUMANS ARE NOT SHARKS SO WHY DO THEY KEEP ACTING LIKE THE STEREOTYPE OF *JAWS*?!? I have a meeting with a businessman in the city centre. He is co-curating an art exhibition with a substantial budget of 250,000 euros. He saw my performance the other day, and now he wants to book me. I must be on my best behaviour! Oh, why must everything about being 'an artist', save for the actual creative process, be downright deplorable? Killer whales hunting great white sharks by turning them upside down, PARALYZING them and eating 85 percent of their time: the selfmarketings, the ass-lickings, the networkings, the gimmicks, the applying-for-fundings, the USPs, the grateful beaming beauty-pageant smiles for prizes and grants, the bohemian-lifestyle posings, the far too comfortable&privileged to create anything profound, the hyped mediocrities, the capitalist fear of content, the devotion to aesthetics, the cliques, the minglings, the packagings, the masks, the shields, the shields, the masks; art is the only place that thrives on uncovering shields and masks, yet there they are wearing masks and shields, until one day their whole face has vanished! OH TO HELL WITH IT ALL! I want NOTHING to do with it. I am doing it less and less, and one day I'll just STOP. Serving tea: None of the expert self-promoters I know make interesting art, 'cause self-PR and deep art cancel each other out and leave you to be *nothing*, wading in a shallow puddle, naming its bottom depth. And I, I'd rather stand still and find my way inside a pure *nothingness* – yes, as goddess is my witness, we will find a way to feed ourselves without starving our souls, and we'll NEVER be hungry again! Until then: I am a hypocrite who needs to pay her rent and take this very metro so I won't be late and unprofessional. *Ne me quitte pas mon métro, ne me quitte pas!* The doors close and jam me between them, digging into my skin and threatening to constrict my breathing. A girl pulls me into the wagon. She is very nice. The doors are not so nice – killer whales, sharks, snakes – they nearly decapitated me.

For a brief moment in time the Earth has allowed me to be perfect and unlate. I'm making a good impression, obtaining a free coffee and cake without even having to tell the businessman it's my birthday. Since Cecile hoisted me over the metro barriers at 1 a.m., I haven't told a single soul, aside from you, dear reader, the only guest I've invited to my party upstairs! I'm not about to let go of this secret to a businessman at 6 p.m. It would be very unprofessional. He's deeply impressed by what he saw me do on stage. He expresses interest in paying me 1200 euros to return to Paris next year. I can live off that for 2 months in Berlin... Berlin. Paris. New York. Mexico City. Oh, you cities with your violent histories, nearly every place on Earth once housed an exploiting empire. What are we going to do with that revelation? *Stop hunting?* No one has ever felt satisfied by greed; still it is one of humankind's most common dispositions... I don't know what the businessman thinks of my deliberations, since I haven't disclosed them. He simply pays the bill as I add some coins for the tip. We agree to stay in touch and bid farewell on good terms.

Oh reader, despite caffeine and the promise of money, I am still very weary, fatigued and sad on my 30th birthday. And the bouts of energy: they have more to do with irritation and manic anxiety than exalted states of serenity. My stomach is upset because I am upset. Perhaps all the shattering pain thrust upon me by my heartbreaks and others' hatred & lust is what feeds my need to change the world, my longing for anything other than history repeating itself... As I leave the café, I allow the broad avenues of Paris to take me in their arms again. I don't care for famous names; I am content with anonymous pulses. I see a billboard featuring the actress who played Violette Leduc in her biopic. Is it a sign? A hint from Violette that her spirit has chosen to stalk me? If so, I need never again miss a hand to hold as Violette shall carry me through life with her humiliations and embellishments, demands and embarrassments, her meekness, her hubris, *us* both steamrolling tanks of weakness, *we* two tiny squealing mice craving the world from our surroundings, scrambling our way out of cages and into traps: *Simone-Simone, please help us float upon our bloody overflow!* Violette! In Simone de Beauvoir's introduction to your memoir *La Batarde*, she indicated that you might have found a key to life towards the end. Was it so? Did you really find *it*? For behind the guard of her academic veil, I'm not sure de Bourgeois ever truly understood...

10 —

It. What is *it*? If we are *that* goal-oriented, the search party shall be called off immediately. The words you are reading create the sound of a soul being shattered. The authoress is writing wrongly to frighten off anyone who likes to click 'like'. So, who's left? I truly hope you're not expecting personal fulfilment – this obsession once caused me to completely lose my sense of purpose in life; in great distress I nearly jumped off a cliff: *One final thrill?* I'm more interested in paying attention to the force that makes me scream: *DON'T STEP ON THE LADYBUG!* A someone who wasn't me compared Clarice's final novel to Nijinsky's diaries, and I felt completed. I married Vaslav the day he pronounced his vision for humankind: *Eagles must not prevent small birds from carrying on with their lives, and therefore they must be given things to eat that will destroy their predatory intentions.* Perhaps we shouldn't let go of all attachments; perhaps we must be attached to every living being – or find out how to make them one and the same ♥

Neon-pink lipstick imprints shelter Nijinsky's forehead, his neck, his left cheek: homages to the statues we were better fitted to become than this pair of despairing humans absorbing an entire world we could not accept belonging to. A statue has no haste. It does not experience stress. Nor does it mind a seagull shit here & there every now & again. I stride down the Champs Élysées. I am not a film star, but several people want to take pictures of me, the polite ones ask *dearsirormadam* while paparazzi employed by make-believe magazines hound and click, sending a message that the hypervisible need bitter poison just to exist. The sun sets on this part of the planet. I wish for it to rise again only if it promises to burn me to death.

'When the human is born, a sorrowful longing is born. When the war has battered, the bloodshed is numberless. I'm burning, I'm burning, throw some more oil on the fire. I'm drowning, I'm drowning, cast me in the deepest sea.'

I make a list of what happens to me during my 53-minute walk through the 9th arrondissement: 3 *whistles & Hey babys*. 2 *I love you, marry mes*. 1 *How much do you cost?* 1 *Barbie Girl, Pamela Anderson!* 1 *OMG that's a man, she tricked me, science fiction-mental illness.* 1 *Suck me, it'll only take five minutes, open yr mouth wide, lemme imagine my dick touchin' yr tonsils.* 1 *Tranny – but real pretty – definitely fuckable.* 1 ass grab & run. 1 pretending to talk on his phone while hitting on me so no one around would see. 1 look to the left, a guy simulates jerking off, 1 look to the right, a guy fondles his crotch then stalks me for several blocks, following me all the way to the women's toilet stall of a bar, forcing me to push & push harder, clasping the door shut, then locking it immediately.

I think I understand why Aileen Wuornos finally exploded.

(I checked in the dictionary and I didn't find kamikaze listed as a synonym for skirting gender; however, when I started I did dream of a divine wind, and I did know that wearing a skirt made me happy. Then along came a battle with my body, shaving it till it bled, locking horns with a blue-toned beard shadow, smearing war camouflage, a layer of foundation over a base of red rouge; and the rest? The shoes, the nails, the work, the werk, for you, for me, for him, for what, for whom, enough? *ENOUGH!* Do you love it? *I love it!* I'm not quite sure who I'm talking to, but I sure do talk to myself a lot: Okay, I'll try taking hormones every day, fingers crossed they'll help decrease my rowing upstream... 28 degrees at 9:27 p.m.; the iceberg's melting, melting, further littering our filthy Seine. I'm trying to fit an ox and a doe-eyed newborn fawn into the same soul. Albino peacocks and Arctic drag queens are regents of my regime – a no-man's-land? Right now in reality I can go for a stroll with a straight man for over an hour without being bothered. But I did not come out as trans with the goal of constantly playing girl to a boy, so why is it being presented as my only option? Very boring very basic questions to which I respond and resist by doing *some* some of the time, refusing to do *all* all of the time. It is an inadequate compromise where *my dysphoria* meets *their expectations* meets *our lack of AN ENTIRELY DIFFERENT WORLD.* **WHAT THE FUCK DO YOU WANT FROM ME???**)

As I gaze at the Moulin Rouge, I neither feel like a badass chick nor an independent woman. I recognize a feeling called loneliness cozying up to my non-statued self on this birthday of chosen aloneness. If I were at home in Berlin, some dunce might've had the bright idea to hold a surprise party with 30 people, and... reader, I know that would have increased my lonely by 30! So for tonight I must be satisfied with the friendship of that tiny flower I see blooming in a garden plot. Red & pink, we've found each other again, birds of a feather, pooled into purple, oft eschewed by the clueless fashion world. My newfound flower friend raises her middle finger to the fashion rules. My middle finger follows in *toe*. I tell her I wish I could one day be buried beneath her, so she can feed on my nourishment. This may not be possible since I don't know her name and can't ask her for it. No. That's not true. One can always ask. Sadly, however, she is unable to answer in a language discernible to human ears. But wait – could it be? *Fuchsia?* Did she transmit it to me via a telepathic whisper? Yes. Fuchsia is her name. And I am Alvina. And we are now properly introduced. I stay beside her until the clock strikes 11:06 p.m.: the exact moment I was born, officially crossing the bridge from my 20s to my 30s, to a place where other meanings transform my being. Time means something completely different to Madame Fuchsia. Moreover, she uses her time differently. While I believe I must move around in order to find substance, she stands in one place and waits, for the sun, the rain, the creatures that pass. She learns just as much in this fashion. I was once a person reading a brochure about what to do when lost in the forest: Staying in the same spot is the best way to be found. So? So: Plants send out signals in order to evade predators and whisper hints to pollenating bees. I, in turn, whisper things to myself which attempt to prove that older is wiser: *What's good for your body is too often detrimental to your soul and vice versa.* It shall do as an 'alright' philosophical start to my 30s. Meanwhile: *Am I a woman trapped in the wrong body, or simply a soul that is trapped in a body? And wants out?*

(An eccentric elderly lady passes by, amethyst-dressed and with 10 pounds of makeup; we exchange smiles like one applies perfume to a handwritten letter or sniffs the pages of a cherished novel. And I know that Madame Fuchsia has taken on a human form, vanishing around the corner; ephemeral...)

The clock strikes midnight, and I would explain my feelings like this: *content*. Just that. And with no frills. I spent three years longing for 30, and the past few weeks fearing it like Dracula fears daylight and garlic. Penny Arcade says: 'In the 1970s I was in my 20s and who the hell wants to be in their 20s again? Only the most boring people look at their 20s as the high point of their life.' I say to myself: *Good riddance.* 20s: the time in life when we're most expected to focus on chasing hedonistic gratification, the doing side of empty nothingness, the utter bore of placing utmost emphasis on following one's own desires, with the self at the base and the myself at the centre of the universe. How tragic to do everything for an own sake, to pursue something *only* because it is what *you* want in life. I refuse to believe the story I've been told, that the only form of liberation possible is individual. Life's trivialities and inanities are annoying. I aim for deep experiences, not fun experiences – silence as utmost intensity, silence as the opposite of a bourgeois dinner party, silence as death's spiritual leader. 30: it'll feel different in 30 years, when I'm 60; different when I'm 60, then I'll be fine with being alone and intensely connected to the world, like mother, like Diamanda, like goddesses. But to feel that way, the 30-year trip there can't remain on the exact same trail. Still, I *must* stop thinking I need to do everything now and at once just 'cause society tries to fool us that life declines after 30. I shall grow very old just in case something manages to take form and call itself wisdom. As Ms. Arcade says, 'I'll survive relying on the kindness of *strange people*.' If I become the oldest person in the world, I shall have gone through an entire set of human lives in my lifetime. But, unless an unlikely technological advance comes along, I will still be one of the billions of people who must handle the act of dying. I try to remind myself of this at least once every 24 hours.

My birthday is finished, done, finito. I allow my footsteps to bring me back to my home-away-from-home. I won't relay what various male strangers tried to get me to do along the way. For now their roles have been relegated to those of extras.

11 —

Reader, at the moment of dying, will I wonder: *What was all that?* Studies indicate that brain activity continues for up to 10 minutes after death. Perhaps it takes a while for the soul to understand it is free to go...

    I just woke up to my last full day in Paris. I still haven't booked my tickets to leave. I am doing everything last-minute again. Hitchhiking would be an alternative if I harboured a death or rape wish. Since I've got other plans, the decision's narrowed down to train, plane or bus. Two are slow, but good for the environment; one is fast, but frightening. It is the first morning of my 30s, and I have not outgrown my paralyzing indecisiveness. It stubbornly remains on the fence whether the issue at hand is penne or spaghetti for dinner, or keep my venis or invert it into a vagina? I am challenging the 11 a.m. sun: *If you won't burn me to death, my eyes must find out which of us actually burns harder. Our staring contest would end with my blindness – free at last to love only with my deeper values...* I catch myself romanticizing a very difficult experience and decide to stare down a grey feral cat instead. It doesn't take long for her to notice that she's being watched from the window above. We have now been locked in this duel for 16 minutes and counting. I don't know if we're too stubborn for our own good or if we've simply become one another. Her-eyes-now-blue, my-eyes-now-green? No. *Our* eyes. At last, she peers down at her leg and begins licking it. *Phew*, that could have gone on forever, and the next day the apartment owner would have wondered what I was doing still lingering about. Speaking of which, where is he? Should I worry? Not yet. He probably just slept over at his lover's house.

Lover. *Lover.* Why did I just remind myself of that word which seems so afraid of the word *Me?* A thorn enters my side, a chip lands on my shoulder, yes, I accept that 95 percent of sparks aren't meant to become blazes, for otherwise the whole world would burn down many times over. However, 95 mustn't be 100. I know this world's not fair, and we, especially my *we*, rarely get what we deserve. But despite being pushed from uphill to upstream, a thing or two may still be in my own hands, yes, at least a handful of my dreams must be able to come true! I write-I write-I write in hopes of so many things, one of which is that in 10 years time a he who's not in his right mind will be *my reader* and propel a 3-page, overemotional email into my inbox, professing the profound connection between he & I that no Hollywood director could ever meat grind into a linear lie. But I am too serious, in fact dead serious, when I say I don't know if I can remain alone for another decade. I used to be certain surviving was a vital political statement, but now I'm starting to believe I should die in protest against this world that has the nerve to create such extreme hypocrisies... *Gas ovens. 23 Valiums. Stormy seas. Cliffhangers. Memories of drawn knives. Memories of drugged drinks.* If I am to keep my promise to grow old, intimacy can't take ages to cradle my body within its grip on reality. Maybe upon my return to Berlin, I should hand over a love letter to my mathematician-poet at the library? After all, I've got nothing to lose. I mean: I have almost no pride or dignity. Indeed, I've got nothing to lose. I can still keep my crying RoRo, my dancing Nijinsky, my sparkling Rafa. A storm is brewing indoors; it never provides a safe flight. Storm – what bits and pieces shall fall off this time? Ripe autumn apples (red) and large bits of steel (silver) come crashing against my skull. Is that what a life with me entails? Hysterical Spectacular? I don't know. I am the expert at aloneness! The space between my legs acts as a black hole, black widow, or Bermuda triangle. Men cum. Men go. Men never return. I am finished. Too much freedom keeps pushing you until you fall. It would take an amount of time closer to eternity than our years to spot the few millimetres of blue sky. A full bolt of lightning races through the clouds, eradicating all shadows and centring my electric senses at the mouth of the Catatumbo River in Venezuela with its 160 consecutive days of thunder.

Dearest mathematician with a name I've yet to learn,
*I am not a harbour for vanities. I know full well that you've hardly noticed me. Perhaps in a world where I'm constantly noticed, this is one cause behind the effect of my **I** noticing your **You**. I was thinking of not writing this letter, since… it makes me come across as obsessed, but, ahhh – to allow oneself space to dream is no synonym for obsession. Vitally, saying no to one's courage seldom has noble reasons and never magical outcomes. I am writing this not under the name 'fate' but in order to be true to that with no name, which ignites sparks even down dead-ended one-way alleys.*

Yes, I will begin my letter to him like this. I will put it down in words, and it will hurt a little less. I will send him a question mark that asks if he too knows what it is like to be in a room full of smiles and laughter, wondering: *What's going on, what am I doing here, and how can I leave as soon as possible without anyone noticing?* If he too has been forced to upgrade IMAGINATION into an unlocked caps lock by a strange sense of alienation, which connects to the secret sadnesses that reside outside? And-and-and, has his entire life also desired a changed world that is more than just exchanged places?

To flow endlessly, and never hold back. Or is life a house where we're not allowed to live? (don't stain the couch! don't raise the roof!)

I will embrace my mathematician by crafting compliments like intricate origami: *You with your deer eyes, mathematical brilliance, unique demeanour, quirky little habits*, NOOOO, hardly crafty origami, BRAINLESS BITCH TROG, more like basic paper planes thrown in every elementary school classroom since the invention of airplanes in 1890 – what a CLICHÉ-CLICHÉ! But oh my dearest deer, mathematical genius, there are times when even the cliché to end all clichés is the truth, and the truth does not force itself upon originality when it is simple. TOUCHÉ-TOUCHÉ! Ohh, useless! I am noticing that for every single word I write, a horrifyingly stupid hope grows inside me, irrational and unfounded: *That he will respond.* That I will learn his name or 100 more important things, not his eye colour (blue) or his hair colour (auburn brown), but things that bring us closer to the answer to the question which is always too big to begin with, even for just one single being: *Who are you?*

Dear Mathematician, do you remember the only time we had a conversation at the library? I was crying because I had read a particularly emotional stanza in Clarice's 'Near to the Wild Heart', and you asked me if I was alright. You treated me like a person. Just that. Not a scary monster or a sexy vixen. You cared enough to put your hand on my shoulder. I said I was fine, that the book was simply magnifying my spirit. I excused myself to go to the bathroom, and dreamt of a future where we licked each other's tears. When I returned you had left the building, nowhere to be found.

(True Love... It needs a leaving, a longing, and two fantasy worlds that get to work with no concern for what makes sense.)

Oh, My Dear Mathematician, I am your devoured doe risking strides beyond nonsense too far out on a tightrope with her umbrella opened wide. I know that a man's bold romantic gestures go crazy and desperate when crafted by a woman, but please be that rare man who grasps that expressing strong emotions is an invitation to open up, not a demand to solve my every problem. The most common response to discomfort is none at all, but like Kurt Cobain, John Lennon and Lou Reed, you're not mediocre, right? Upon receiving this bolt of static electricity, you'll simply stare into the horizon and state: *An emotionally intense, intelligent woman is stimulating, not intimidating.* In turn I will never question why you spend so much time with the hysterical insanity of rationality! I promise not to be jealous of the numbers in your equations. I won't view them as threats, rivals, or enemies. I understand: You are friends with each and every one of them. They mesmerize you. They help you find solutions, obscure, then illuminated. And I must allow you plenty of time alone with your friends. (*I get it, I get it to the core, writing, writing, my breathing words, your living numbers, they are bridges, bridges connecting our mountain minds to the divine!*)

Oh READER, I cannot see the world through my reader's eyes, but I know my letter is far too much, and much too long. As if I were determined to have him. As if I were determined to lose him. And yet, I withheld it all: the part where he enters my soul for hours before making love to me or even thinking of me for 5 minutes straight; the part where I envy his clothes, his croissant, his pet animals, the produce his hands pick up at the grocery store, and god forbid his girlfriend; the part where woods were chopped down only to die of hunger, where even a censored letter will end up in a prison called The Garbage Can where no one can hear it scream. The call of the maladjusted: a shriek of ostentation silenced in the depths of a wishing well. *Letter.* It is more than just a letter, it is an entry into the sweepstakes of proving oneself a worthy companion. My sentences console my celibacy. My neuroses confide in my words, cheering them on. The timing is finally perfect. The timing is finally perfect because I have allowed it to move slowly. If he responds with great zeal, it will be the biggest thrill my love life has felt in years. I can only hope my soul won't be too overwhelmed, fainting from the vertigo of an *I can't possibly manage this.* Foolish swooner! Sometimes one needs things to happen in reality, at least as a supplement to one's imaginary life. Yes. I have made a decision. It is a sin not to listen to a voice within that is scream-singing to you: *OPEN UP!* To love and not be loved in return is no sin. I will be afraid and brave! Everything hurts anyways, so I might as well try something. My exaggerations expand existence, my willingness to risk humiliation builds worlds, opening borders like a pink ribbon tied around a ticking time bomb – pomegranate. I will be afraid and brave! I am filled with doubt: I will never learn his name nor 100 more important things. I won't feel ashamed of confiding in strangers. I will give him the letter. I shall see if I can turn nothing into something. It is a gift that only dreamers can uphold. It is rare to see it sealed with a kiss.

12

When my life comes to a close, I shall have broken the world record for the number of mornings torn apart by detours into the late afternoon. At 4 p.m. I finally hit the streets for my last day in Paris. This time I have a well thought out strategy. I sing to myself, quietly at first and then louder, LOUDER, and LOUDER STILL: 'KAIGOMAI KAIGOMAI RIKSE KI ALLO LADI STI FOTIA, PNIGOMAI PNIGOMAI PETA ME SE THALASSA VATHIA AMAAAN AMAAAAAN!' I repeat this chorus for 30 minutes and at last, NO MAN has bothered me. Yes, in singing to myself I am making myself visibly plural. I am feeling less alone. My social life is filled with friends in high places: Athena, Aphrodite, Persephone. The solution to the incessant sexual harassment on the streets of Paris has been found: Sing blaringly in Greek. I don't know karate, but I do know Crazy. Crying is different. Creepers flock around exposed vulnerability like flies, providing yet another reason to regard the world with grave animosity. And my raucous singing: I suppose it really only results in a transition from 'sexy tranny' to 'crazy tranny', lowering me from the status of touchable freak to untouchable freak. *Aman aman!* But, *amen!* I've got a 10-euro note in my pocket. Someone else needs it more than me. I hand it to a homeless woman limping in rags, smelling of vodka. She tells me her life story – a brother who molested her, a mother who beat her, a battle with depression, a forced eviction, a car crash that dislocated her hip. She cries in my arms, and I kiss her hands, her cheeks. *Touchable freaks.* We nestle into ten instants called minutes, until our day decides it's time to *carry on*... I am experiencing what one calls A Positive Outlook On Life. Fleeting for sure, but I won't whine or moan; I just have to make sure I don't get any impulsive ideas, like allowing some random man to impregnate me, forcing the gift of life upon an innocent little critter. Yes. My direction may be more or less directionless, but I can still state with utmost uncertainty that it is another.

My dear readers,
Have you been brought to the brink of extinction by my tendency to continually follow up each question with a bigger one? Our trip together is about to end, and with it this story which is not a story. If I manage to stem the impulse to bonfire all my words, it will still take years&years and yet more years&tears to attain a legible form. Do any of us have such patience? By chance I pass by the Notre-Dame cathedral. I christen it another product of one famous architect and one thousand forgotten slaves. I look towards the Seine as 150 tour-boat passengers stand up and point their phones at the church towers in synchronized unison like a dance of flamingos or a performance choreographed by Pina Bausch. A young woman on dry land can't cross the square without repeatedly staring me up and down. *How very inconspicuous of you, you little-smidge-of-dribble-piss. Am I really more captivating than that monumental cathedral you may have travelled halfway 'round the world just to see?* She stops and points at me, giggling frenetically and encouraging her boyfriend to do the same. He ogles my legs for a split second before chuckling to play along. I know this game.

She starts to double over, she doesn't care about being discreet, she deems me unworthy of this discretion. (How will he ever tell the truth if she acts this way?) She is playing the role of a woman harassing me. It is a relatively rare occurrence that still plays out at regular intervals. Whenever it happens, Tori Amos's song 'Cornflake Girl' plays inside my head with an added verse that goes a little something like this: *Sweetie, you'd better stop rolling on the floor laughing your ass off cuz as soon as you turn your back your boyfriend's likely to beg to fuck or be fucked in the ass and I keep saying no cuz I hope you're less of an asshole than him, but little-miss-dribble-piss, you get love, and I just sex, so next time I might fuck to ruin that love for you, now how'd ya like that?*

Joie de vivre, are you there, somewhere, embedded within my overweight of despair? I have been laid to rest in a port of roses, wishing I didn't need to be dead to survive without thorns. Like Greta Garbo I don't feel interested in being a silly temptress who makes men salivate. No. Like Garbo I want to be *left* alone, which is different from wanting to *be* alone. I'm dreaming of waking up next to the same *he* I fell asleep with, then going for a six-hour solitary stroll to show my feelings to crows and sheets of paper until the cows moo: *Go home…* Oh reader, when I walk past a pond and see swans and ducks sharing a nest, I grasp things without knowing… they've read 'The Ugly Duckling' together, thus deepening their feelings of solidarity!!! One day I shall paint the lips of my favourite human bright pink, heralding a sacrosanct kiss with a serenade of favourite words. Now standing in front of the Notre-Dame cathedral, I bow down, a lone bush under the ecstasy of its lilac blossoms! Like Anne

Sexton I often find myself asking the question of suicides: *Why build?* I find part of the answer inside all the flower species that smell so pungently they stranglehold the rest of my senses into forgetting everything bad that ever happened for a minimum of 12 seconds – *lightness*, just minutes ago I was heavy as one without strength, and now, imagine, for that freshly hatched sentence I am as powerful as God.

Paris, I am preparing to say goodbye to you. One must bid farewell to places with the same sincerity one uses when saying goodbye to people. The amount of cheek kisses delivered does not constitute a hint. Still, I feel the need to leap over to the Montmartre Cemetery and return to Nijinsky's grave one final time to kiss his right cheek and add a last dash of pink to Petrushka. A couple comprised of two sad clowns is queer beyond homosexuality. Me&Nijinsky. And Claric-e: *Have we lost the knack of being humans? Are we good drivers, save for the detail that we don't pay attention to traffic? Why this world? And why this constant border between own world and outside world that stitches a mask to our face, tearing fresh wounds with red cascades each time it's yanked off?* The gates are open, and I become a visitor of all the dead dears in that parallel universe called Cemeteries. My only real home is the dungeon six feet below the tower of perpetual bad luck, so I'd better make myself (un)comfortable. The lack of expectations may be what saves my future. My first big love of the past, Shawn, was buried thousands of miles from here, at a funeral I've only seen photos of; for who would have wanted a crazy ex-girlfriend, who wasn't even his ex-girlfriend, just crazy, in attendance? I don't know how many people in this Montmartre graveyard committed suicide, but I do know that neither they nor Nijinsky were deficient or *complètement malade*, just too sensitive for life in the world as we know it: This world that continuously has me wishing to stab a knife through it or myself. *(There must be a place in heaven for the oversensitive – There must be a place in heaven for the oversensitive – There must be...)* My dear Vaslav, may your blood pelt down and flood the society that killed you. I can't recall seeing a single photo of you where you look happy, or wait, what about all the photos of you dancing on stage? That was not happiness. That was *ThePerfectFeeling*. And I know it by heart. Like the moment of vomiting, you feel your entire existence hurtling out of you. A magnified presence that the world has doomed *An Impossible Existence* while we deemed it *ordinary*, shrugging our shoulders then crying ourselves to sleep.

    I walk up a stairway and a hill, upwards towards the highest point of the cemetery, and I recite to myself: *Heights are plains to me!* On the horizon a large cloud hovers over Paris like it's giving birth to the entire city. Around me each individual grave resembles a mini-cathedral. Dalida's tomb crashes into my immediate field of vision, drawing me to a new vista for my endless magnetic connection to madness and suicide. I run up and hug her statue so hard my ribs nearly crack as one single blood drop plummets onto her shrine. Dear reader, once you've sharpened life to a point, finding a point to life transforms into a constant battle. 'So what,' say the little epiphanies treasured in blades of grass and patterns of irregular water currents in a river. So. What.

I claw at my own mind, and a black widow devours herself. The red hourglass transforms into a red beak, and a black swan flies over a broken rainbow. I have been known to smash champagne glasses with the mighty clench of my own fragile fist when I'm in this mood. If I go up to someone's table at a fancy restaurant and *just do it*, I shall be regarded as a monstrous aberration. If I instead find a way to hit the highest note never recorded by a non-existent species, even the windows shall shatter. *The People* won't know what hit them, and in the ensuing commotion I will see my chance to eat off their plates. And take it! Today I am less lonely and more hungry. But no one at this restaurant ordered a vegetarian meal. Typical. People who won't listen to a pig's squeals keep both me and the world starving... I travel back to reality, to the question of booking my transportation: one thing I hate about taking a bus in summer is seeing all the flying insects getting crushed by the windscreen! Still, the death ratio is much lower when 60 people travel by bus than when two travel by car. Still, I don't want to hurt anyone or anything. It is inevitable. It will end only with death, with insects taking their revenge by feasting on our bodies. Until then I can just do my best. I don't think I'll take the Environmental-Destroyer-Missile Airplane. If it crashes I shall most likely be cremated on the spot and no rat no worm no nothing will be granted the pleasure of chewing my meat down to the bone.

Thoughtfeelings, thoughtfeelings, reader, my overthinking, my overfeeling, it hurts, it hurts, oh how it hurts, and without it I would be what I long to become: a newborn jellyfish placidly listening to the world's songs and groans. *Living Water...* In Swedish the plural word for jellyfish is pronounced *man-eater*; however, while my flesh still throbs through human awareness,

I wish to ask myself: *What has this man done to deserve my sex?* If the answer is *Nothing*, he will be given exactly that, *Nothing*, no matter how handsome he is. Withholding means: I conserve my power. Another side of me desires to do what's forbidden: turning up the heat in a microwave oven, fucking the first guy that comes across my path in some murky alleyway or backroom with a fairly ugly carpet, transforming myself into a carbon copy of his projections and expectations until he cums and goes, leaving me alone and bewildered in the only place he wants me to exist. No, I refuse. They expect my availability to be *Whenever, Wherever*. And I'd rather sing Lauryn Hill's 'respect is just a minimum', but I may be better off enthralled by abuse than trapped in solitary confinement, to at least exist touched by more than just the lukewarm air of a penumbra!

I go silent. I gaze across the graveyard; I see hundreds of tombs and statues, but only three living human beings. I'm highly unlikely to become a trans girl interrupted. I lay me down, one ear to the ground, and one to the sky. I listen carefully – tree roots, skeletons. The earth oracle or my mind speaks. The lowest rank of the female & LGBT class, exiled to the status of cis women and gays in 1957, form a chorus, I join: Will a day come when we're no longer made to feel like sex workers whether or not we're working? How many living famous men have not been 'caught with a tranny', like we were some crime, and instead willingly admitted their attraction to us? *None.* Lou Reed and David Bowie? *Yes, but they're dead.* How many trans women do I know in long-term, open, loving relationships with men? *None.* Janet Mock? *Yes, but I don't know her...* A thought, a suggestion, or is it a petition – how much would it change the world and our reality? Die Mauer – with only a crack it can sprout a plant, but will it take more for Malina or Beethoven or them to hear? I see a full football team standing in front of the goal of their own freedom like they were defending some free kick in the 90th minute. Trans girls are the ball – kicked and chased, barred from revealing the vast secrets of our world concealed by patriarchy for centuries. The Parameter – Wailing Wall: Annihilate All Slogans! I issue my first ultimatum: Every man that's attracted to us comes out of the closet tomorrow at 3:33 in the afternoon; stadiums shall be crammed full, and the wall of machos who 'only like real pussy' will have so many holes, it shall undergo a metamorphosis into the true more beautiful form of a scattered archipelago! In the land still far from transformation, a trans woman unburdens: 'I fucked the two brothers who work at my corner store and they both said, "Don't tell my brother, he doesn't know I like trannies..."'

You know dating a trans girl is like opening a bag of chips in church, everyone stares with scorn but deep down they want some chips too... I know, I know, I've received 7 or 8 invitations to dinner dates and 9000 invitations for quick sex from men standing alone in the past 4 years, and when I say they must meet me for a drink in public first, I receive 10 nos for each yes.

Oh, can one feel apart and unhappy for too long to ever be together and happy? Perhaps this pain is sadness and loneliness. Perhaps it is something darker than that. 33 percent of us have tried to die by own hand. My theory is that lack of love kills more trans girls than punches, stares, stabs, dysphoria, rapes, gropes, guns and bullying put together. Picture yourself as a person trapped in a crack where you can easily fuck five guys a night, without recalling the last time you touched what's intimate. Even our murderers are the men who secretly screw us and deem it less shameful to openly shoot us. Martyrs of Freedom – Liberation's got no room here. Until they who are everywhere and nowhere come out there may be no way out.

The grass is a cushion, it savours my skin's satin caresses. I am still lying on the cemetery ground, still listening carefully. I hear all the so-called small things my eyes can't perceive in an earscape eons beyond chatting carcasses and traffic jams. The tectonic plates of Iceland return; they shift within me and the earth and everything and it all unlocks itself into place for a fleeting now-instant that is bound to leap into a wall – this time perhaps hard enough to make it shift, breach, fall, or break my own skull if brittle little fragile men refuse to move their asses as much as they fuck our asses.

> '*I would like to make a book to disturb people, like an open door leading them where they would never have gone of their own free will. Simply a door communicating with reality.*'
> — Antonin Artaud

13 —
Scream of Consciousness
– Cry of Love

Four years ago in Delhi, I mustered up the courage to leave the metro's mixed wagons and enter the ladies' compartment for the first time. Within minutes my mind quit racing about as my body memory recalled what it felt like to be tranquil in public, unfractured by men's ogling stares. The cadence of my breathing loosened, and my whole self folded into a serene peace and quiet. Soon enough I began to worry about the consequences of my five o'clock shadow, of the timbre of my speech. Since no woman questioned my presence, my fears stayed where they belonged – in the back of my head – as I relaxed where I belonged for my entire three-week stay.

Here in Paris, I allow myself 10 breaths while waiting 10 minutes for the metro to arrive at the station near le Cimetière de Montmartre. As I enter the wagon, two young men with British accents burst into giggles. They pretend to be laughing at some stupid photo they've seen on their smartphones. One of them shouts 'I'm gonna take a selfie,' while placing his phone at an angle that clearly focuses on me, missing all the seven remaining pimples on his pale forehead – reminders of recent adolescence. I sigh: *here goes another Sisyphusian situation...* Every time I hear strangers cracking up beside me on the sidewalk, or in the metro, or at the corner store, I think they're laughing at *me*, not some well-told joke or that funny TV show or a do-you-remember-that-time-when. Too often I'm unhappy to be proven right. And what do you know? As the train slows into my station and I head towards the exit, the boys raise the volume of their laughter by several decibels, yes, their laughter ERUPTS – heeheehee to HAHAHA. Didn't anybody teach them that it's rude to laugh at people? Answer: they don't see me as a person. When I get off and pass by the window, I see them hovering with their respective phones, recording videos of me. Earlier I compared this behaviour to the way famous people get treated. It was a joke. Seriously: The world upgrades the value of famous people and amputates mine. To be famous, Instafamous especially, is treated as if it were a very important job in itself. I find that idea extremely tedious. Yes, just as tedious as how being a trans girl seems to be a full-time job as well, but without appearance fees, influencer bonuses, or even a lifetime free pass on public transport for incurred damages.

    Tears and raised middle fingers are acts of defiance in equal measure, but these two boys are only going to see the latter, because if I start to cry now I may *never* be able to stop. I have two flashbacks: 1. The time a gang of 15 children followed me chanting 'Tranny! Tranny!' 2. The time a psychologist told me I was being paranoid when I said that people in the streets constantly stare at me. Okay, reader, I swear this time that this is *the last time* I'll tell you about these incidents. I will thereby be providing you a comfort I simply do not have. Unless you're like me, and if so, I hope we can hold each other as we break down so the flood won't sweep us away. How can we claim our own voice when it's almost impossible to speak through tears? No, leave it to the interpretation of well-meaning journalists, with their cleanly formulated and violently-lyingly-simplifyingly 4500-character newspaper interview versions. And reject this novel! Because it is too much! Because I am too much! *Call us back when you're ready to sit back, relax and be observed! We'll get you photographed applying lipstick in front of a mirror, we'll let you be the backdrop in an avant-garde gay man's story of 'the streets' that you own; we might even let you write a memoir IF you include a Coming-Out scene and have The Surgery!*

OH, PISS OFF, YOU SOUR-FACED TALKING DISH-CLOTHS, I WON'T LET YOU KEEP ME FROM DIGGING DEEPER!!! The cornerstone of the lesbian and gay struggle is openly loving who you choose while I'm supposed to settle for 'JUST EXISTING', and no books, no articles, no nothing's EVER written on the myriad of men from all walks of life who only want us on the down-low, from Drake bathing in bucks to your Uber driver dying within the gig economy. The box is heavy; opening it may threaten the straight square you used to build a never-not-shaky foundation...

(Do we incorporate all this into heterosexuality, 'queer' heterosexuality beyond binaries, or abolish heterosexuality altogether? Pretty straight in a sexual sense, the opposite of straight in its broader sense; will being with us publicly make all these he's lose some of

their precious masculinity, normality, maybe even become a slight bit LGBT? Finally, straight men made vulnerable – a key to defeat patriarchy. I'm certain it scares them, but after living through 8 rapes and 200 gropes it feels like consoling a baby that scraped his knee; and what can I say when my tongue's been tugged out by trauma: that the trouble with feral cats is we seldom live long if not adopted, that my child within merely survives for I can still soliloquize?

The white artsy 'feminist' softboys with their normal-life Natalie Portman girlfriends are hardly the most open, they talk to us but near-never caress us free from our intimacy-solitary grief. Rather it's drug dealers, the men who share our streets and have no comfort zone to leave. I've lost count of the amount of times I've heard 'girl, let's get high and fuck all night' from these far-from-always-violent machos. In 4 years in Berlin, I've seen just one man cuddle with a trans woman in broad daylight. He sold speed, weed and ecstasy. He softened the borders between women & men.

LISTEN UP, STRAIGHT SOFTBOYS, NEUROTIC NICE GUYS WHO DO NOTHING, I DON'T WANT SUPPORT FROM A 'GOOD ALLY', I WANT SUPPORT FROM A GREAT LOVER! *A charitable glance from above is no nestle on our level. If you began walking down the streets hand-in-hand with us, our lives would glide 5 times lighter, for you've got 10 times our power, yet here we are, suffering with 15 times your courage! I've heard you utter the PC phrase 'trans women are women', so how does that relate to **your** sexuality; will you start seeing us when our boobs grow, our skin glows, our scent pheromones fragrant female? OR is even a cunt not enough for you clean, comfortable, closed-minded, short-sighted,* white, Western, colonial-christian-binary 'progressives', so scared to stray from status-safe lives with wives, with kids, while the supposedly more conservative hetero machos seem to simply see long legs, pretty face, sexy booty and have no issues fucking OR raping us, behind closed doors, **always** behind closed doors, never misgendering us, yes dear they **really** see us as women and proceed to treat us as terribly as they wish they could get away with treating all women. It feels like hell where gropes roast us hot for a moment better than the room temperature you keep us in every morning of this life waking up alone in our beds, morose in our beds, alone in our beds, bestowing ALL your love-affection-protection-devotion upon the women who were born into what we must fight our entire lives for. (Again, this world's not fair, some give everything and get nothing, others give nothing and get everything, and that truth is larger than life, as status embraces status embraces famous older men falling for younger Instafamous models, as few men want women they deeply admire, and trans women could be to straight manlihood what Yoko Ono was to the Beatles – your drop-dead gorgeous tickets out of the sick and boring heteronormative world!)

– Aman aman, we're forced to perpetually prove we're not **too much** to men who constantly give us **too little**. So I am Catwoman, I am trans woman, both need 9 lives –

Hey open-minded men, you're the ones who gave me 1900 OkCupid likes in 3 days, with mainly white, middle-class boys fretting when detecting a word starting with T; now, if I could turn my soul inside out, surely you can ask yourselves some questions on what all this is about? Do you wonder how t-girls survive a life of endless trauma, ceaseless stress? Most block every feeling, but some like *me are anomalies among rarities, clinging to dead-end hopes, lying down solo beside a purple lily each time we want to die. I'm no longer convinced it's enough, I need YOU at times, my sad clown soulmate, but you never give me that tenderness-kiss, so perhaps it's high time I stuck my head in a gas oven leaving a beautiful corpse as the ultimate sex-toy gift, stiff like a Barbie doll for all the 600 million tranny chasers to store in their closets. MY REVENGE: A stink bomb that reveals* **The Whole Shebang!**

– Oy vey, I am a stubborn 120-pound antelope trying to carry a 2-ton hippo across the Nile so crocodiles won't dare to bite us as often –

Forgiveness, dear men of the bourgeois avant-garde, are we too Other for you, do you respect us too much to love us, do you dehumanize-dewomanize-desexualize the hypersexualized? Honesty – it's a near synonym for beauty. Truly, as we come in so many shapes and sizes, delusional bigotry's behind any hetero guy's generalizing: 'I'm not into trans girls.' Well hon, maybe you've already slept with one, and you had no clue, but if she told you, you'd identity crisis and flee to where it's easy or hit her with the hatred of your own vulnerability, wouldn't you? Yes, leave the world-expanding to us, we're practically perishing here, and I know I attracted you like a magnet. Hard metal's never invisible, yet you remain hiding inside a comfort zone where NOTHING EVER CHANGES!

My heart beats, it takes beatings, vulnerability means taking sensitivity to a volatile risk zone; sårbarhet, the ability to be hurt, an emotional vagina dentata scraping the sky to open a world not for consumption, your hand pulsating into mine, a river Main into a river Rhine into an ephemeral eternity of burning Whys, a fractured skeleton dancing on Mercury, not Venus nor Mars, right here, inside the extra-ordinary of that skipped heartbeat we all need to beat the normal life ❤❤❤

HYPOCRITES, HYPOCRITES, COWARDS, COWARDS, NOWHERE NEAR THE BRAVERY OF SISSIES! Lest we were put on this Earth solely to suffer, a day shall come when we escape this cesspit with or without you. I cry. I cry the deluge against your walls. For by the time you read these verses I may or may not have a vagina, I may or may not even be alive, but I dare say you'll never find a soul that tightly grips such depth, such warmth, such wetness, as mine, as mine.)

Stop.

Catch your breath.

Reflect.

Back to the streets of Paris: Reader, I think I just reclaimed my poise after the British teenagers' laughter on the metro. I cannot let these strangers hurt me the way friends & family & lovers can, and do. I am not a pre-death experience. I frolic into the Gare du Nord railway station. The intercom interrupts the swarm of the human beehive, calling my pink lips to leave Paris Right Now & At Once, not for home but for away... Just take the first train to the wild waves of Bretagne... Dance forever held over luminescent sand by the bad boy of ballet, who might transform into Devendra Banhart so I can sincerely ask him why he has five hermaphrodite tattoos – if we're just some idealized symbols to admire safe inside his shallow life with young Snow White-lookalikes, or 10,000-layered luscious womenhuman-forces-of-nature he would French kiss with zest – then uncover the answer in if he knows where to find the nest of the strand's black swan triad. Have the cygnets survived yet another day? 5 of the original 6 are left in the family. Did the sixth die of illness, a fox, or a bored and mean-spirited hate-crime-committing human being?

Listen. Stay. (They are verbs. They are more actions than any action.)

(Yab-Yum, can we become one with ambivalence, we both hurt & we both matter – or are our lives islands of bottled messages floating upon weeping orgies? Critical Compassion – (re)think, challenge, change, give new chances – I'm sorry, forgive me, please ❤)

Sitting still at the train station, silently observing the people moving their bodies to different destinations, I write. While trains travel across tracks like blood running through veins, I write, practicing the same craft as Sappho, as Kalonymus, as Mirabai. Exposed bones never hidden behind muscle, my hands amble over my exercise book as my sunshine spotlit pen steals the stage so surrounding commotions won't frighten the moment. I am unhinged, not broken, just open. In my Berlin den I will sleep alone in a bed 50 feet from a flock of mute swans, as home remains... restless. Most people's strategy for handling a world where dreams rarely come true is to begin dreaming smaller and then stop dreaming altogether. My strategy? To keep dreaming. Bigger than ever. Just that? No. My secret recipe is to combine these dreams with the realization that self-fulfilment is a less meaningful goal than sleeping. I won't live life to the fullest, I'll just *live*. And I won't achieve! But I will care. *Always.* And I shall let *everything* touch me! If we're going to have any leaders, let them all be people with hyper-empathy who know how to follow and would never dream of calling a person toxic. Then, at last, we'll reach a world where we don't need to choose between the lesser of two evils – and then some!!! I believe that everywhere in the world there are perfect and premeditated Scandinavian Design Madonnas and messy and real Rihannas and then Amys & Bülents & Fionas & Diamandas who expand each and every category. And me? I am a messy perfectionist, a severe inclination – think Sylvia Plath and Sarah Kane and millions of so-called 'nobodies', girls who drowned while trying to swim across the ocean and no one cared! I am trying not to die, but it saddens me so that the strongest, deepest, smartest women are still the ones who end up alone. Together, we know life's not easy and realize it's not all our fault. Meanwhile, I remain a feral cat on its own secret mission outside, scurrying off into the night with her eyes fixed on the full moon, climbing a meaningful tree to a place no one can see so she can sit and read Clarice Lispector in peace. If the world were to end, *this* is how I'd spend the final hour.

'And suddenly I feel that we shall soon part... I own up to my solitude that sometimes falls into ecstasy as before fireworks. I am alone and must live a certain intimate glory that in solitude can become pain. And the pain, silence... We will meet this afternoon. And I won't even talk to you about this that I'm writing and which

contains what I am and which I give to you as a present though you won't read it. You will never read what I'm writing. And when I've noted down my secret of being I shall throw it away as if into the sea. I'm writing you because you can't accept what I am. When I destroy my notes on the instants, will I return to my nothing from which I extracted an everything? As I think of what I already lived through it seems to me I was shedding my bodies along the paths...'

After those words, and nearly 200 pages, I may have finally gotten over my pathetic, basic-bitch 30-year crisis. *Good.* What does *good* mean? To understand that the destitute know more about how to live together than the well-to-do; to console without having anything comforting to say; to organize a race: *who can run 100 meters the slowest...* Reader, at last I may have found an inkling of an answer! I'm still at the Gare du Nord train station staring at its sky-high glass ceiling, heading nowhere, but leaving the exile imposed upon me by youth. I've been a cross between an 8-year-old and 80-year-old for as long as I can remember anyways, regularly emulating various animal sounds like some sort of lyrebird, and in 12 hours I shall return home to Berlin after all. *Home.* What is it? Stronger. No!!! *Deeper.* Let me enunciate the word: HOME. A place to surpass the limits of the possible world: a tiny room of my own where I can stay & read instead of going to a party. *Home.* I cannot describe my personality with the help of my belongings except for perhaps my shrine of dead flowers, worn-out books & volcanic stones, my nightstand sign stating *DON'T WASTE YOUR CRAZIES*, and my script draft stacks screaming *BURN ME! Home.* Each time I think of a practical task I must complete, my stress levels triple. Fix-the-lapdog-repair-the-toilet-seat-(HOW?)-fill-in-the-insurance-papers-call-the-plumber: PARALYSIS! I wish instead to arrange flowers by the colour of their scent and call that disorder: Freedom! *And love-lust?* An answer from The Mathematician does not provide The Answer, but a solution can solve one equation (1+1=3). There's nothing to celebrate in wanting everything. Sylvia Plath said it means you're dangerously close to wanting nothing. Yet, at the deepest end, wanting everything may simply mean to become everything and live larger than one's own life...

(Hemidemisemiquaver rest.)

I see a man dressed in grey petting a pigeon. They're sitting in an abandoned corner of the train station, 6 meters adrift from all other members of their species, where the wind whisks all things paper and plastic. They mirror one another in a form of symbiotic, up-close movement that looks like an intimate dance to the musical score played by my broken heartstrings. Why this calamity? I am touched by their presence. I am falling in love with them both. Since I lack the need to stay and talk to either pigeon or man for 3400 seconds, the love shall remain pure, with no expansion... Paris! I am holding hands with you as I make my catwalk through your avenues to sit at one final café and savour the charisma of your ambiance. Paris!! Please allow the fish in your Seine to swim slowly, to grow big, to stay healthy. *Morals.* How many can a story have? I have hundreds, and yet I'm no storyteller. Let me just unravel, and disconnect the dots, and never revert to 'that's *your* problem', as it's always *ours*, and nothing has nothing to do with me. *Life.* It is so slow, reader; we'd need millions of pages to tell that story properly, only to be told off for our refusal to feign the sameness of every rain shower, every rape, every heartbeat, every teardrop, every tree, every city light. *Life*. Alright, I am not a cool edgy subcultural star striking a pose on a stained red carpet like Kathy Acker or Jean Genet, nor am I a member of a six-girl-gang, chatting while clutching cappuccinos at a coffee shop after A Day Of Shopping & Strolling. I am the sensitivity of a skinned tomato; my eyes connected to hands that continuously chop onions, inevitably slicing knives into my fingertips with a painful regularity that leaves stains and scars and dismembered parts in its wake. *Why am I telling you all this?* Crying's got no cure, but that doesn't mean it needs one. I may be strong and beautiful, but you must let me be ugly and weak! To look like Marlene Dietrich and write like Virginia Woolf won't bring happiness to a person. Just ask Clarice. A feminine being's beauty frequently insults her mind, and a pretty trans girl is a species hunted for her fur by night. Me, I will not 'pass' as basic for the sake of having slightly fewer hunters, won't be a trophy he'll receive for succeeding at being average. I didn't come out to dress like a grey mouse, and I shall either survive or be destroyed, by myself or others. As I sit at this loud café in Paris, I use histrionics to curse its ineptitude as a centre for creating 'great literature', and realize (*Eureka!*) that Rafael Nadal looks like he is about to burst into tears each time he smiles!

My writing is unable to head in a fixed direction. It may help me climb out of some holes, but in insisting on utmost depths and crooked slants it digs just as many. Clarice's suspicion was that writing took her further and further away from *own life*, an attempt to be more than human, to evolve that definition past definition, yes, like the quest for truth: *Worth-less? Hurts-but-worth-it? Worth-more-none-the-less?* The Secret Morse Code of Freedom. *Worth-it!* To watch out for life in its most delicate layers, the details worth paying attention to; shifting opinions on life after death every day, yes, that's the way to treat the unknown! The riverlike-changing human not set in stone remembers vital stagnants: never learn to lie, learn the hard way by living the soft way, lack a poker face, let cheeks turn bright red and eyeballs dart about in search of an escape that always exposes them to every onlooker. CIRCLES, reader, CIRCLES PROVIDE A COMPLETELY DIFFERENT DEFINITION OF PROGRESS! At the café, teacups turn into wine glasses as dusk morphs into night. I have not kept track of time. I have forgotten the difference between hours and minutes. I better make sure to be on time for my... WHOOPS! I still haven't managed to book my trip back to Berlin! *Bitch, for once, a quick decision!* Okay! I will endure the 16-hour bus ride! The person sitting behind me will surely snore. The people sitting in front of me will certainly talk loudly in German. It'll render sleep impossible. It'll feel like torture. It'll be alright; I can still complain, and I will complain. I shall arrive in Berlin feeling tired and covered in dirt and oil: we must make sacrifices for doing the right thing. Luce Irigaray was thrown out of the university by Lacan and his (Twitter)followers for writing *Speculum of the Other Woman.* Now, at age 88, I've heard she does yoga early each morning and feels annoyed by nearly everybody – a unique combination! People like us are deemed too intense yet uneventful to ever last long even as The Other Woman. We always come close, so they consider it necessary to push us away. Later, at midnight, we convene in synergy with the sea that can't be viewed from the surface, crying till we laugh at the notion that a woman who belongs to no one is nothing. And yet... I swear I saw your reflection in my tears!

Now, back to booking my bus. The least expensive one leaves at 7 a.m. *Click-type-click, BOOKED!* I head back to my home-away-from-home in a flash. I pack all my bags. I go to bed at once. Being an environmentally friendly individual might help me sleep at night, but it's so difficult when living means insects getting crushed by windshields and underneath my feet!!! I outline another anti-suicide pact: I will watch out for insects and do as few things as possible that threaten to bring us to the brink of an apocalypse. I will also stop thinking for a second so I can fall asleep.

What the apartment owner gets up to is, however, out of my hands; he arrives at 3:30 a.m. with his lover again. My nerves are the high-strung nerves of the-day-before-an-early-morning-trip, so the key turning in the door is enough to jolt me awake. I pretend to be *ZzZzZzZz*, and *XXX*-activities commence three feet from my feet. They crank up the volume of their noises. If they fuck like the other night, I'll be in for a marathon session. I'm sure they could endure the entire three hours it takes to jog 42.195 kilometres, but please God, I beg of you, make the two of them run fast enough to reach the finish line before I must leave the bed for my bus! I don't wish for the occurrence of any embarrassing incidents: for example, me trying to sneak by without anyone noticing, only to trip and fall right on top of them as if I were making an extremely awkward and wholly inappropriate attempt at starting a threesome. And what if I were to make it out the door without being noticed?

They would wonder what kind of strange person disappears into thin air!

I dare to take quick peeks at the clock on my trusty dumbphone. 4 a.m. arrives and passes: Still they fuck. *4:48*: Same. *5:33*: Still no end in sight. I've set my alarm for 6, I must leave by 6:15. *5:43*: Something is shifting. They are shrieking louder. Breathing quicker. Gyrating faster. Are they in for the final sprint? The opening stanza of Beethoven's 5th Symphony plays inside my head: *Dun-Dun-Dun-Duuuun, Dun-Dun-Dun-Duuuuuun!* If they aren't finished by 6, I must be brave like the tiny flying fish I've seen jumping out of both rivers and oceans. And. And? What is this? *DONE? DONE! YES!!!* They are panting on the other side of the finish line! *5:55*. I dare to raise my head and look. They have already fallen fast asleep in each other's arms. What a relief for all three parties in this room!

I shut off my alarm so as not to wake the sleepyheads. I have 5 minutes left to spend in whichever way I choose: 5 minutes alone in my mind, free from exterior requirements to do-do-do. This means a full ownership of my own inner world – all 86 billion brain neurons... *Nothing* is freedom, for I can't stand everything and all at once! 4 more minutes... NOTHING IS MEANINGLESS! Sometimes a body, for whatever reason, is unable to keep breathing, so the heart stops beating, whereafter certain developmental genes stay active for days. Other times a political rally gathers 500,000 people, and I am thrilled I can attend it by myself, as solidarity provides space for solitary, and life grows larger than self; yes, *change* may be a collective process, but to be a collective mustn't kill off the empathy instilled in an intimate one-on-one conversation between individuals. *Active Empathy* is the deep meaning of *love*. Yes. **_Active_**

Empathy is love – non-detached compassion beyond the fixed borders of identity politics. There is a drum beating out a rhythm behind the algorithm. It is the only message that can save us. Are we still able to not just hear, but *listen?*

I believe you. It did happen.

The clock strikes 6. No. I was too busy thinking too much and missed my precise wake-up time. No harm done... For once! *6:01*. I go to the bathroom to brush my teeth. I am getting ready to go home. *Home*: It is not the other side of the rainbow. Then again, neither is *away*. I don't know if the exact definition of home will ever rest peacefully in me, but not knowing shouldn't cause us so much trouble... I take one final look in my bag: *Passport (Check!), Books (Check!), Lapdog (Check!), Charger, Wallet, Makeup (Check! Check! Check!)*. All the boxes on my list have been checked: *SUCCESS!* Still... Ravens have paranoid thoughts and so do I!

Crawl three laps underneath the bed in case your sense of touch picks up what memory couldn't see... Yes! Dear electric shaver, thank goddess, you're there and can carry on your everyday job of chopping down that alien-beard at birth till that day when the stingray-like *zap-zap-zaps* of 14 separate laser treatments will permanently stop something I hate... for once in my life...

6:15. The sunrise hasn't begun to ask anything of me, but it is time I left the building. I feel a slight pain: the pain of a departure, a pain that only the maximum amount of longing can erase. My homesickness is clouded by fear of the negative spirals and bad habits I may cultivate again once I enter my den, like a bacterial culture in a lab. *Unstoppable. Insufferable.* Nonetheless, staying is not on my palette. Meekly, gently, slowly, so as not to wake those that woke me, I close the door behind my body and breathe in another direction. The streets guide my breath as they begin their hustle&bustle. An old man is taking his Labrador out for a morning walk. The Labrador is adorable, and I want to speak to her in a voice which resembles that of the Three Witches in *Macbeth*, but instead I talk to her in Greek: *Skilos. Skilos Gorgona.* This means: *Dog. Dog Mermaid.* Why am I calling her that? I don't know. You ask too many questions, reader. I am a weird sister. There are seldom logical reasonings behind my strange associations. No swimming, no fins, no gills, no water, no scales, just a gut feeling pointing me down an unexpected road. And you, you are my reader, you've either followed me here or left me in the gutter kicking & screaming – there where failure provides my only source of self-worth. Reader, *ne me quitte pas mon chère, ne me quitte pas!* We've nearly made it all the way to the end and I can still feel your hand holding mine – a pulse beating into a pulse: an invincible mortality!

I wish it was just you and I, reader, but though I'm not lost, I appear to be found. Yes, ravens know when they're being stalked, and so do I. This is our Grand Finale, so the stakes are raised; unlike most men thus far, this *he* doesn't turn around as soon as I head into a café or down the escalator of some station. In fact, he follows me into my metro wagon. It's nearly empty. It's a Sunday, so no people are in a rush for rush hour. Four party kids get off at the next stop. They are chasing the next afterparty. Now it's just me & he, and a very old lady who is likely to be hard of hearing. The man sees his chance. And takes it.

Like a weasel, he's crawled into an underground burrow to get ahold of whatever baby animals he hopes might be lying in wait. Fuck, I'm stuck in a cylinder with no escape! He says: 'Excuse moi, mademoiselle.' I say: 'Je ne parle bien français.' He switches to English: 'THE LAST TIME I SAW A PAIR OF LEGS LIKE THAT I WAS IN A BIRD'S NEST!' A creative statement; it makes me laugh. I shouldn't have. He takes it as a signal to fire the next missile: 'I like that black swan tattoo above your tiny tits... I've got a tattoo too, you wanna see... It's right here.' He points to his crotch. His crotch of course, of course his crotch! I turn away. He wonders if I want to go back to his place. 'No, I do not, I want to go home.'

'Sure! I could go home with you, where d'you live?'
'I live in Berlin.'
'That's a bit far.'
'Yes. Yes it is. And this is my stop. I'm taking a bus back to Berlin right now. Adieu et au revoir.'

I exit through the rear door on the right-hand side of the train. He's not trailing behind me. The mobile cruising ground has closed, the broken record is paused. It is 6:48 and I have 12 minutes of breathing room left to spare. My soul makes a wish: to sprout that rare blossom of enlightened empathy that can only bloom underneath the smouldering spotlight of severest hate!

    I head up the stairs to the bus station, and all my blood seems to rush towards my head. I lose my steady footing. Handrails catch my clutch, preventing me from falling. Half of my body is weightless while ants are having a rave party inside the rest. I feel more & more alive, and I am not able to think or worry or stress. No pestering voice is persecuting me with the peril of a missed bus; my brain can't word together questions like *shall I faint or shall my body balance itself into equilibrium?* The latter triumphs and I walk forward toward the station. Seven minutes remain to complete a two-minute stroll. I begin singing a song to myself. I begin thinking a thought: *Who invented song?* A someone who understood that singing lyrics can bring us inside the emotional core of words...

Dear Paris, Dear Reader, in our final minutes together, I shall sacrifice beauty at the altar of a beautiful moment! I know I haven't provided you with one of those all-knowing linear narratives, by now we must all understand how dangerous they are, as life and history and love and hate and fights and makeup sex and pleasure and pain and chaotic inner monologues and wars and peace and whatever warpeace you'd call the top wondering why the bottom won't eat cake are not guided by one common leitmotif, and we mustn't fool each other into believing simplified lies about our worlds, our lives, our murders. Reader, I think I've loved you enough to not lay this textbody before you like you were my executioner. A non-linear wish: *I came into the world crying and screaming. I sincerely hope I won't leave it the same way.* My future resides inside the 36,000-sexed fungal internet network between trees in a forest. I am managing to survive because I carry the instincts of both pigeons and rats; though I'm not sure if I have wings or roots, I can run & hide, and I know how to lick my wounds. I have experienced so much pain that it can no longer cause me to suffer as terribly. I will not conceal my contempt for success stories; they serve themselves and no one else. Fame & fortune – a pair of irrelevants, like big testicles. Cool, composed, self-assured, professional – all characteristics we try to attain in order to better become machines. I don't possess these qualities, and I have quit trying. I am not a person who beams with the smiles of gratitude. What presents do I have to give? Very few. And I gift them to you with the tenacity of a cascading flood that crashes open a dam, tearing up the roots so our mouths can flow to their natural destinations. With soaking wet feet and great hesitance, I have decided to trust the world enough to confess all my deepest fears, though I'm well aware there's a global complot to take advantage of my weaknesses.

"But if you, down in the depths of hell, break the chain and bring me to your side – blessed is thy name."

The raw pus inside my freshly drawn hot-blood must tarnish this paper! Reader, I hope my jokes from the gallows have made you laugh out loud on a train as your hands turned to silk, gently holding the fluttering weight of *our* soul within *your* pulse. *Home* should never be the place where your whole heart is, but it is the place where you can safely close the toilet lid so no snakes will slither out to bite you in bed. And, in the event of a fire, if you're lucky, it's also a place where you know people care more about your well-being than about whether the furniture has been destroyed. That hasn't always been the case. Is it now? A few voices interrupt my thundering self-doubt; they grow louder, louder still, till they gain the upper hand, and I can at least manage to hear the word even if it is without a capital letter.

I board the bus. The man behind me is already sleeping. He's snoring. The couple in front are speaking loudly in German. It is alright. What awaits? Oh, just another day inside a body that pushes a soul with its endless 'needs'. Life, what's the matter with you? Several times a week you create new problems for me to overcome. Halt! Stop trying to chain me to misery! Impossible! Tragedy or paradise, Emotionally-High-Strung Bouncy-Ball Version of a Human, vaulting from wall to floor to ceiling, with tiny things that always come UP to bring you DOWN. And sometimes, yes, sometimes big things too, that cause you to completely alter direction... Now, dear reader, I shall go to a place so dark it scares away all fears. Death can't threaten me any longer, rape tried, *HA*, that pathetic crime; die alone – it's fine, it's fine, (?), yes, I've been equipped for worse things, yes, they may shoot my corpse, yes, dear death, a refrain to unveil invincibility: *'I'm burning, I'm burning, throw some more oil on the fire, I'm drowning, I'm drowning, cast me in the deepest sea!'* Brain-storm. De-press. Soul-stress. Sleep-less. God? God-less? Goddess? Far from perfect, but I made you **_FEEL_**: (CAPITAL-**Bold**-Underlined-*Italics*) Blasting through the border of any parenthesis or period: my heart laid bare in the middle of a heavily trafficked street, well aware that the risk of getting run over is far higher than the chance *That Someone* will brake, pick her up, embrace her. Then... A scream of love! Perhaps some hearts are so big they must constantly burst and break... The overflow within the overflow deluges our *we* wide open into a borderless *us*. Oh!! To know that one exists and therefore never be able to just exist? *To rest in longing* or *To rest and not long*? Oh!! Can I make it home?

This must leave the textbody and creep into the world
or it'll all have been in vain.

Acknowledgements, Afterwords and Afterworlds...

Since writing this book five and a half years ago, my life has changed dramatically. I now more or less pass as a cis woman, and it makes my daily life on the streets so much safer, though as soon as someone learns I'm trans I'm generally back to square one – othered. The category of trans hangs around my neck like a noose, because societal transphobia still largely tells passing girls to say nothing and swim or say something and sink. This must change. Being a trans woman is no negative disclaimer or marker of fakeness, but rather a signifier of a soulstrong woman who fully knows herself and dares to be real – a waterlily who had to grow through one extra element in order to bloom and see the sunshine.

With this book I hope to do a lot of things, and the lyrical, literary, poetic is most certainly at the forefront. I believe I've also managed to be brutally truthful instead of falsifying a storyline that fits into an over-simplified empowering portrait. And beyond the artistic and general existential, my political hope is to contribute to a world where straight trans women are given just as much long-term *affection* as ephemeral *attention*. The fact that straight cis men give us so much sexual attention and so little, and at best fleeting, intimate affection is one of the greatest travesties and hypocrisies of today's world, and it says so much about straight cis men's fragility and inability to be themselves, to be vulnerable, to deviate from the herd. Even men who are generally nice, caring guys, just don't care about us. Let this please change. If trans women are still going through this shit in 30 years, I swear I will cut the cis-generic world into pieces!

We are living in strange and alarming times, where bill after bill threatening trans rights is drafted and passed. Why this fear? How can trans women be portrayed as violent? As far as I know, no straight man has ever been killed by a trans girl for hiding her, even though this occurs on repeat in many of our lives, while straight men continue to kill us by the thousands – not because they hate us for being different, but because they fear their desire for us will make *them* different. Different? Piss and shit and lies, any reader of this book or view counter of trans porn will understand that there is no desire on this earth that is more mainstream. Indeed, if every trans woman globally one day collectively outed all the men who've sought us out, a full-blown revolution would occur by nightfall.

A few years back, my trans woman friend heard the following words from her neighbour: *You need to move because every time you walk by I get so horny, so if I see you again I need to either kill you or kill myself.* I'm sorry, but what the fuck is wrong with this world?

To my trans sisters, I don't want to forget any, but I'll include many: Kassandra, Selin, Camila, Isabella, Mathea, Sanni,

Nicole, Yagmur, Vikramaditya, Tiresia, Yuna, Anna, Danica, Juliet, Xenia, Ksenya, Kamalanetra, Dimitra, Natasha, Veronica, Saga, Amanita, Victoria... The list grows longer and stronger and I swear to fucking god I wouldn't be alive without you, and I cry as I write these lines, because all of us know this to be true...

To the trailblazers, some of whom I've had the privilege to meet: Jenny Hiloudaki, Cris Miro (yes, she dated Maradona), Paola Revenioti, Bülent Ersoy, Cristina Ortiz Rodriguez La Veneno, Paca La Pirana, Ms. Major, Anna Kouroupou, Coccinelle, Sylvia Rivera, Marsha P. Johnson, Roberta Close, Bambi, Sevval Killic and April Ashley. I don't care if you bitches were/are always politically correct or not, that's beyond the point, and any queer activist who looks down upon you for some perceived transgression should actually be bowing at your feet.

To my cis sisters, although, yes, my relationship to cis women is fraught... Too many of you constantly other us and question and doubt and frown upon men's desire for us – none of this is helping anyone. But some understand us more than others – Banafshe, I'm thinking of you. Lidija. You too. Nina, Louisa, Therese. To my trans brother Sam. To the icons, Björk, Pamela Anderson, Fiona Apple, Diamanda Galás and PJ Harvey; to the political thinkers I adore, Angela Davis and Luce Irigaray, to the writers, Clarice Lispector, Violette Leduc, Marina Tsvetaeva, Sylvia Plath, Anne Sexton, Arundhati Roy, Elfriede Jelinek, Ingeborg Bachmann, Penny Arcade, Svetlana Alexeivich, Jamaica Kincaid, Camila Sosa Villada and Unica Zürn.

To my editors and publishers, Emily Kiernan and Sarah Gzemski at Noemi Press, and Elte Rauch and Fannah Palmer at The New Menard Press. I don't always believe in myself, thus I need others who believe in me, or else I'd likely spend my days and nights just combing my hair with a fork. To David Uzochukwu for making my dream book cover come true – Pamela Anderson meets Björk, or me in a nutshell?

To my readers, whose comments helped me get this novel to a more finished state: Rob Doyle, Roisin Kiberd, Banafshe Hourmazdi, Leif Holmstrand, Theo Iliochenko and Janani Balasubramanian (I know I'm forgetting someone here and I hope I'm not).

To my mother – always – the one who didn't just create me in the physical sense.

To Vaslav Nijinsky.

To Yona.

To Jan, who made my crazies surface at 19, creating my need to start writing (always these male muses...).

To Serafeim and Sotiris for showing me your heart, your love, your body&soul, and sharing big dreams with me in 2019-20 and 2022-23 respectively, albeit in too-hidden and imperfect ways. My fellow good-looking loners, you didn't know how to handle falling in love with a trans woman for the first time, but you did help me understand that there's love out there for a girl like me. I forgive you, Serafeim, you always made me feel fully heard. I'm still trying to forgive you, Sotiris Patsalias, our love affair made me feel run over by a bus. Yoko Ono once said, 'A dream you dream alone is still a dream, but a dream you dream together is reality.' Singing duets like birds of paradise, then leaving me solo at the moment it came time to build, I thought I was the poet and you the engineer, so was it plain fear that forced you to make sure the dreams we dreamed together remained dreams? Was it more important to be normal than free and happy? I still don't understand, and the best and the worst thing about not understanding is that it is so much vaster than understanding, it opens the mind up to endlessness, like a continuous mathematics equation with no solution, there's no stopping it...

(The siren did the forbidden and lured the good future family fathers away from the correct, straight, narrow life path. An unforgettable moment, never part of your world? There are so few examples of relationships between two people like us ending well. I walk down the street and every other man smiles and flirts and comments on my beauty. To boot my IQ is sky-high. And yet, somehow, I'm an embarrassment to be with? How can society have the audacity to be so hypocritical? How fun is it to be forced to normalize a guy covering you in kisses only to block you the next day? The opposite of truth, trying to reverse the flow of a river. Can a society please finally arrive where people are themselves and stop lying? I can't breathe, and I can't apologize for not being a trophy received for being average!)

To the couples between straight cis men and trans women who've sprung up in the public eye since I wrote this book in 2018: Janet Mock and Angel Curiel, D. Smith and Dustin Michael, Kylian Mbappé and Ines Rau, Hunter Schafer and Dominic Fike. So many men wish they could be as brave as Angel, Dustin, Kylian and Dominic – we trans girls carry magic within us due to what we've lived through and the complex power dynamics and multitude of worlds we've seen, and some guys really see our knowledge and depths beyond our sexiness. May these couples inspire more men to love us out of the shadows and into the light. May white men ask themselves WHY all these men are men of colour, and what it is about white Northern European maleness that makes them so transphobic? While posing as the most progressive, white middle-class bourgeois 'leftist' men may very well be the most conservative in the world.

I hope in our future world, it'll be considered completely ordinary for a straight man to have had seven girlfriends in his life, one of whom was trans. When desire's on fire, let's not let narrow minds kill us at our most alive.

And last but not least, to Loving the World or Getting Killed Trying, even if it feels damn near impossible and far too painful sometimes, as one can understand from the content of this book... and the content of this life... However... at least it surefire gives life *content*. Yes, we've got the order all wrong, it's more vital to be kind to others than yourself, first give the world some love, then you can love yourself... Oh love... Love is both my occupation and preoccupation. Writing is just my missionary duty. Both have caused me unspeakable levels of pain. And unbearable amounts of pleasure...

And now... It's time for me to grow shy for a while, like I always do after an act of great boldness...

Notes and References

As this novel is a work of autofiction, which takes place in the real world, one can find several references to things that exist in reality. I don't intend to write a formal bibliography as this is not some PhD dissertation or verified scientific report. My collection of various references is more akin to Ariel in *The Little Mermaid*'s cave full of artefacts from the human world, which her curiosity brought her to, and with which she enjoys spending time as she gazes through the clearing towards the sunlight and the forbidden surface. So please judge me in this way and no other, and forgive me for any eventual imprecisenesses lost in the space between my mermaid brain and human logic: Ariel and I, found in transition...

First of all, we have the information on trans porn presented on page 11, which has been taken from Gamelink.com, an article in the International Business Times (https://web.archive.org/web/20200404014718/https://www.ibtimes.com/transgender-porn-best-seller-it-good-trans-people-2028219), and the Wikipedia page on transgender pornography (https://en.wikipedia.org/wiki/Transgender_pornography). Secondly, on page 12, we have a quote from Luce Irigaray obtained from her 1980 essay 'When Our Lips Speak Together'. On page 49, we have a quote from the 2017 film *I, Tonya*, and page 62, of course, features a paraphrase of the chorus from the Backstreet Boys' 1997 hit 'As Long As You Love Me'.

On the same page I use a quote from Clarice Lispector's only televised interview, from February 1977, and on page 69 I quote Fiona Apple's 2012 song 'Daredevil', followed by Martha Wainwright's 'Bloody Motherfucking Asshole' – both of these anthems of my life. On page 76, I quote the trans woman Nana Hatzi, and on page 79, I've used a quote from Marina Tsvetaeva's 1928 poem 'An Attempt at Jealousy'. Then, on page 92, I quote from Boris Pasternak's 1917 poem 'February', which also features in Regina Spektor's 2006 song 'Après Moi'. Next up: on page 94 and 95, I quote both the Wicked Witch of the West from the 1939 film *The Wizard of Oz*, and Regina Spektor's 2016 song 'Small Bills'. Page 101 features the first of several translated quotes from the classic Greek song 'Kaigomai Kaigomai', with lyrics by Nikos Gatsos and music by Stavros Xarhakos. This song features in the 1983 film *Rembetiko* starring Sotiria Leonardou, who also performs the song in its original version. On page 112 I quote Pasternak again, this time from his famous novel *Doctor Zhivago* (1957), and on page 113 I've included the famous quote by Holocaust survivor and writer Elie Wiesel. Page 118 features a line from the chorus of Michael Jackson's 1995 song 'They Don't Care About Us'. Page 119 contains a reference to CeeCee Jacobsen's viral TikTok-video on the differences between prejudice and preference, arguing that if you're attracted to a trans woman you indeed *prefer* her, and if you completely change your mind about that when learning she's trans, it's your *prejudice* that's speaking. On page 133 I quote Queen's song 'Bohemian Rhapsody', and on page 137 I quote Björk's song 'Pleasure Is All Mine', and then I begin to quote Ronaldo... Page 140 features a quote from the 2015 Ronaldo documentary, and on page 141 I quote a cryptic Instagram post he made in 2015 that went viral. Moving onwards and forwards to page 159 and another Greek film, *Oi Thalassies oi Hadres* (1967), which contains the song 'Crazy Girl', from which I quote. Uyuy, this list is getting tiring, let me take a paragraph break...

Paragraph Break

Okay reader, I'm back again, and better than ever, to page 168, where I paraphrase the iconic line from the film *Clueless*: 'Why should I listen to you anyway? You're a virgin who can't drive.' And 'Ne Me Quitte Pas' on the next page [169] is, of course, also a paraphrase from the 1959 song of the same name by Jacques Brel. On page 173, I quote Nijinsky from *The Diary of Vaslav Nijinsky: Unexpurgated Edition* (1999), and three pages later [176] I quote Nijinsky again: 'Now I will dance for you the war... the war that you did not prevent,' which he reportedly yelled at the audience before his final dance in public at the Suvretta Haus in St. Moritz in 1919. Then I move on to another one of my conversation partners in this novel – Violette Leduc, but the quotes here are not her own, they're rather taken from the 2013 biopic *Violette*, which introduced me to her astonishing work. Page 187 and 188 feature quotes from this film. The next thing I quote [page 191], critically, is the 'Queer Nation Manifesto' from 1990, which famously stated 'Every time we fuck we win', which I continue to stress is the height of tone deafness if one wishes to include straight trans women's experiences. On page 188 and 230 I reference the murders of trans women in an us/our-form, and I wish to point out something here that I couldn't in lyrical prose, but definitely would've in a non-fiction text: murders of trans women generally occur in the intersection between trans misogyny, racism and sex work. Most trans women getting murdered are sex-working trans women of colour, and I, as a white trans woman, who used to be, but is not currently, involved in sex work, am significantly less likely to face such extreme violence.

The Sylvia Plath reference on page 193 is a quote from *The Unabridged Journals of Sylvia Plath* (2000), which many times served as some sort of bible to me. Page 196 contains the term 'cis-jenny', which alludes to stand-up comedian Lux Venerea's joke about cisjennifers. The lyrics on page 199 are from Nicki Minaj's remix of Wyclef Jean's 2007 hit 'Sweetest Girl (Dollar Bill)'. Page 203 features a quote from Djuna Barnes' classic novel *Nightwood*, which in all honesty feels like drinking diamonds, like *The Little Mermaid*, which I do indeed paraphrase on page 205: the song 'Les Poissons' (1989) where Sebastian the Crab runs and hides from the French cook. And I continue referencing on the next pages: first from TLC's song 'Waterfalls' (1995), page 205, and then from Scarlett O'Hara's monologue in *Gone with the Wind* (1939), page 208. And then it's 'Ne Me Quitte Pas' again, but why am I bothering to state the obvious?! Time for one last paragraph break...

Vaslav Nijinsky has done a grand jeté from his page to mine, and I quote from diaries again on page 210, and since I'm repeating myself, let me say that the song 'Kaigomai Kaigomai' has excerpts quoted again on page 211, 222, 250, and 251. Page 214 contains a quote from Penny Arcade's performance *Longing Lasts Longer*, which I saw in New York in 2015. Anne

Sexton's 1966 poem 'Wanting to Die' includes the lines: 'But suicides have a special language / Like carpenters they want to know *which tools* / They never ask *why build.*' This, of course, is what I am referencing on page 225. Page 225 also features paraphrases of various questions Clarice Lispector posed herself, as well as the title to Benjamin Moser's 2009 biography about her, and on the next page [226] I give a nod to the song 'Je Suis Malade' (1973), written by Alice Dona and Serge Lama, and made famous by Dalida. For the statement on page 228 on famous men publicly dating trans women, I wish to make the addendum that since I wrote this novel in 2018, some well-known men have indeed begun to open up, which I expanded upon in the 'Acknowledgements, Afterwords and Afterworlds' section. Page 229 contains references to Ingeborg Bachmann's novel *Malina*, and on page 231, the final chapter begins with a quote by Antonin Artaud, published in the collection *Selected Writings* (1976), edited by Susan Sontag. On page 238 I paraphrase the title of Devendra Banhart's poetry collection *Weeping Gang Bliss Void Yab-Yum* (2019). And the long quote on pages 239–240... It is so important to me... It summarizes so many feelings I have had so many times in my life... and it comes from my favourite novel/not-novel of all time, Clarice Lispector's *Água Viva* (1973), which I have probably read more than 20 times. On page 241 I'm again conversing with Sylvia Plath's journals, and on page 243 I'm referencing some of Luce Irigaray's thoughts in her book on Nietzsche, titled *Marine Lover* (1980).

Last but not least: page 247 references 'Ne Me Quitte Pas' once more. And that, my dear reader, is... Part of My Wooooooorld!

About the Author

Alvina Chamberland is a Swedish-US American author of predominantly literary autofiction. In 2015, Bokförlaget ETC published her co-authored book *Allt som är Mitt: Våldtäkt, Stigmatisering och Upprättelse* (*All That Is Mine: Rape, Stigmatization and Reparation*), which received a grant from the Swedish Arts Council. In 2018, her novel *Utelåst – Uppväxtnostalgi för freaks* (*Locked Out – A Nostalgic Account of Growing Up for Freaks*), a parody of the coming-of-age genre, was published by Dockhaveri Förlag. She resides between Athens and Berlin and has no real hobbies, only intensity and serenity. *Love the World or Get Killed Trying* is her English-language debut.

About the Publisher

The New Menard Press is the British imprint of HetMoet Publishing, an indie press based on a historic sailing barge in Amsterdam, the Netherlands, and was founded by Elte Rauch in 2018. The Menard Press was founded by Anthony Rudolf in 1969.

Please get in touch at info@thenewmenardpress.com

Subscribe to our newsletter, visit:
www.thenewmenardpress.com

Follow us on:
- @thenew_menardpress
- TheNewMenardPress

Love the World or Get Killed Trying
Alvina Chamberland

This edition was first published in The United Kingdom in April 2024
by The New Menard Press

Copyright © 2024 Alvina Chamberland
Copyright © 2024 The New Menard Press
Cover photo © 2023 David Uzochukwu
Author photo © 2023 David Uzochukwu

Alvina Chamberland asserts the moral right to be identified as the author of this work in accordance with the Copyright, Designs and Patents Act 1988. A CIP catalogue record for this book is available from the British Library.

ISBN 9789083384139

First edition, April 2024
Reprinted, June 2024

Thank you for buying an authorized copy of this book and for complying with copyright laws by not reproducing, scanning or distributing any part of it in any form without permission of the publisher and author. The New Menard Press supports copyright. Copyright fuels creativity, encourages diverse voices, promotes freedom of speech and creates a vibrant culture. You are supporting indie writers and publishers and allowing them to continue to make books together.

Text editing by Emily Kiernan & Fannah Palmer, copy editing by Ilse van Oosten
Typeset in Lyon by Kai Bernau & Ilya Ruderman
Book design by Thijs Kestens, Armee de Verre Bookdesign, Ghent, Belgium
Printed and bound by Patria, The Netherlands
Distribution and Sales: Booksource, Glasgow (orders@booksource.net)
InPress Ltd Newcastle upon Thyme
www.inpressbooks.co.uk

www.thenewmenardpress.com